# the KILLING

# the KILLING
## UNCOMMON DENOMINATOR

Karen Dionne

AN ORIGINAL NOVEL BASED ON THE AMC SERIES
DEVELOPED BY VEENA SUD
THE KILLING IS BASED ON THE DANISH SERIES FORBRYDELSEN

TITAN BOOKS

The Killing: Uncommon Denominator
Print edition ISBN: 9781781169803
E-book edition ISBN: 9781781169810

Published by Titan Books
A division of Titan Publishing Group Ltd
144 Southwark St, London SE1 0UP

First edition: June 2014
10 9 8 7 6 5 4 3 2 1



A CIP catalogue record for this title is available from the British Library.

Printed and bound in the United States.

**TITAN**BOOKS.COM

"Three great forces rule the world: stupidity, fear and greed."

ALBERT EINSTEIN

For the fans.

# DAY ONE

SEATTLE: JANUARY 24, 4:30 P.M.

# 1

Neil Campbell knew how to play the odds. Most people didn't understand statistics the way Neil did. Because most people were stupid. They thought the more times you did something, or the longer you did it, the greater the probability became that you'd get the outcome you wanted. Play the lottery enough times, and sooner or later, you're bound to hit it big, right?

Not so. The truth was, each time Neil cooked up a batch of methamphetamine in his Rainier Valley Trailer Park kitchen, the chances of the whole mess blowing up in his face remained exactly the same. It didn't matter how many times he'd done it before, each batch was potentially as dangerous as the first. He didn't know the exact odds stacked against him, but he knew they were high. More than his chances of being caught in the crossfire of a drive-by, which were already considerably higher for him than for someone who didn't live in a deteriorating trailer park in a forgotten section of Seattle. Not as low as being struck by lightning. Definitely greater than his chances of winning the lottery.

Neil understood numbers. He'd been a computer programmer. And an actuary. And a cost estimator, and a day-trader, and an online poker player, and a bookie. Head Accountant for Jameson, Dunow, and Pierce had been his most recent iteration, which sounded a lot more impressive than his windowless cubicle had deserved, stuck in a strip mall shared with a hair salon, a sandwich shop, and three empty storefronts. After the King County grand jury had indicted the company six months previously on five felony counts of obtaining money by false pretenses, and another of forgery of a public record, the shopping mall got a fourth set of whitewashed windows and Neil got a new career. Lucky him. But he always landed on his feet. He knew how to press people's buttons, to find their weaknesses, to exploit them. He had no pity for drones, and meth heads were so easy. But it *was* a pity that providing them with their crank put him at risk.

A meth cooker could tip the odds in his favor, though: use only high quality ingredients, make sure his work area and equipment were cleaner than clean. Still, the risk remained. The important thing was not to get greedy. That's where dumb people messed up. Doubling the size of the batch. Buying cheap ingredients. Buying Sudafed too often from the same place, or buying it the same time you bought your batteries and camping fuel. That was a purchase guaranteed to increase your chances of landing on the wrong side of a set of prison bars. A place Neil vowed he'd never end up again.

He unwound the lithium foil from an Energizer battery four-pack and tore it into thumb-sized pieces, then shoved the pieces down the neck of a two-liter soda bottle, turning his head against the rotten egg smell as the lithium reacted with the anhydrous ammonia and the vent fan over the stove struggled to keep up. He topped off the bottle with Coleman lantern fuel, then screwed the lid tight.

Outside, a car horn honked. Once, twice, then full-on, non-stop. He waited. The honking continued. He left the bottle on the table and walked over to the window and pushed the mini blinds aside and waved. Hugo waved back. The honking stopped. Neil sent him a smile: *Good boy, yes, that's exactly what Daddy wanted you to do*, and Hugo flashed a cherubic *Daddy! Daddy! Look at me!* grin and leaned his full weight on the steering column again.

Neil let the blinds fall. It wouldn't be long before Hugo figured out how to unlock the car doors, and then what would he do? He couldn't cook with him in the house. Wouldn't. He wasn't some lowlife tweaker getting high in front of his kid. He cooked for the cash.

Hugo was the only other human being that Neil truly cared about. Hugo was his blood, his property. And Hugo was okay as long as he stayed in the car. Child Protective Services wouldn't see it that way, and if Hugo didn't stop announcing to anyone within a quarter mile that he'd shut him in there alone on a frigid January day, CPS was going to show up on his doorstep sooner rather than later. But he knew better than to put his son in danger. He understood the odds.

He sat back down. Shook the bottle once to speed up the reaction, then gave the lid a quarter-turn to vent the gases without letting too much oxygen in.

The bottle glowed red.

# 2

The explosion rattled windows and doors. In the house trailer across the street, Stephen Holder jumped off the sofa, grabbed his jacket, slid back the security chain, and banged out the front door.

Seconds later, Logic joined him. Live-action drama beat *Judge Judy* any day.

"Yo, fools—where's the fire?" Ridgeback yelled, then doubled over laughing when he caught up to them in the front yard and saw the burning trailer.

Logic—early twenties, drug skinny and wiry to Ridgeback's gorilla-hairy 285—snorted.

Up and down the street, Rainier Valley residents watched the spectacle in the gathering gloom. Flames poured from the trailer's windows and door. No one attempted a rescue. House trailers were notorious fire traps, decrepit house trailers even more so, decrepit house trailers with an out-of-control meth fire in the kitchen the absolute worst. If the cooker who lived there was inside, he wasn't coming out.

"Yo—lookit." Ridgeback jabbed a finger into Holder's arm and pointed toward a battered Escort in the trailer's driveway. Holder squinted. Inside the car, backlit against the flames, he saw movement. A little boy waving his stubby baby arms and crying.

"What you doin', fool?" Logic called as Holder sprinted across the street, dodging the crispy bits of house trailer that littered the yard and fluttered like fireworks from the sky. The air reeked of ammonia and burning plastic. Holder pulled his sweatshirt over his mouth and nose. He grabbed the driver's door handle, then jerked his hand back, the metal red-hot, pulled his jacket sleeve over his hand, and tried again.

*Locked.*

Another explosion from inside the trailer. Heat singed the back of Holder's neck, curled his hair. He pulled his hoodie over his head and rapped on the car window, smiled at the little squawler, mimed opening the door. But the boy couldn't. Or wouldn't.

He looked around. Found a fist-sized rock in a row of rounded beach stones lining a long-forgotten flowerbed, and smashed the backseat window. He scrambled in, reached between the front seats, and grabbed a handful of jacket. Dragged the boy into the back and scrambled out again before the heat ignited the fumes in the gas tank and the whole thing blew.

In the distance, sirens.

Holder tucked the howler under his arm and sprinted across the street.

Logic high-fived him as he ran up, and slapped him on the back.

"Yo, fool—look at you! You a *he*-ro!"

Holder's retort was lost in a wail of sirens as a fire truck and an EMS unit turned the corner. They drove to within a hundred feet of the burning trailer and stopped.

"What they doin'?" Ridgeback asked after several seconds had passed and nothing had happened. "How come they not gettin' out?"

"They 'fraid a gettin' high," Holder said.

Logic laughed. He and Holder bumped fists.

Holder could have told them that a contact high was the least of the firefighters' problems. That the phosphine gas fumes from a meth fire could overwhelm a firefighter in seconds. Permanently destroy their lungs. That the hydriodic acid formed during meth production can dissolve your skin just as quickly. That a meth fire was so toxic, nothing was going to be done to help the cook inside the trailer until the Hazmat guys arrived. Basic stuff. Firefighting 101. Stuff he learned his first year at the Academy.

Instead, he rocked on his heels and watched the flames lick up the siding and melt the tarpaper along the edge of the roof; just another fool hanging with his BFFs. Standing among the empty beer cans and rusty bicycles littering the lawn of a broken-down trailer, holding the wailing son of a cooker who just blew hisself up.

Ain't undercover grand.

"Le's go inside," Ridgeback said. "It's cold out here."

And dark. And rainy. And for Holder, potentially dangerous. When the cops rolled up, he was as likely to get picked up and questioned as his BFFs. Maybe even more so. Holder didn't just dress the part of a player, he *was* the part: boot-cut jeans, layered oversized hoodie, mustache, and a soul patch with a chin strap and a goatee. A skinny six-two, though his weight was due to genetics, not drug abuse. Cigarette tucked behind his ear. Scruffy light brown hair, dark lady-killer bedroom eyes, and a lazy drawl he'd perfected as a teenager that made him sound like he was permanently stoned. No one would mistake him for an officer with the King County Sheriff Department, even if he'd been wearing a suit and a tie—certainly not the two Seattle Police Department units that rolled up and parked in front of the trailer next to the one that was on fire. Seven years, vice and narcotics. Mostly undercover. Street level stuff. Buys and busts. Joaquin shooting Rahim. Blah, blah.

He nodded at the patrol cars and held out the kid toward Ridgeback. "Gotta go."

Ridgeback shoved his hands in his pockets. "Hells nah. You found him, you keep him. I ain't your lame-ass babysitter."

"I'm not askin' you to keep him, fool. Give him to the cops. You be the hero."

Ridgeback considered, straightened, held out his hands. The boy wrapped his arms more tightly around Holder's neck. Holder peeled him loose and handed him off. Started down the sidewalk, then stopped, looked back. Little man waitin' for his pops to come and get him—that was just sad.

He slouched off with his head down, hands shoved deep into his jacket pockets, a ratty-assed junkie looking for a place to score, as the Hazmat team arrived at last and the serious action began. He watched from the corner of his eye as the pumper started knocking back the fire and the EMS guys finally broke out a stretcher. Saw the uniformed officers—unis—get out of their car and trudge up the broken sidewalk to the neighboring trailer. He noted the open door, Tiffany's red Toyota in the driveway.

The lead officer stepped carefully over the rotting porch boards and did the cop knock with the flat of his hand against the side of the trailer, then announced himself and went in.

Moments later, he came back out. He bent his head and spoke into his shoulder radio.

"We got a 10-84."

"You want an ambulance with that?" the radio crackled back.

"Negative," the cop said.

Holder ambled faster. Turned the corner, and broke into a run.

10-84. *Coroner case.* A dead body.

# 3

Detective Sarah Linden—long red hair pulled back into a ponytail, navy police jacket buttoned over one of the high-necked Scandinavian sweaters she tended to favor—stood in the living room of the run-down trailer. She could hear muffled voices from outside; the firefighters were still working on the burnt wreckage next door. She bent over the body jammed between an overturned coffee table and a faded sofa. Male. Caucasian. Maybe six feet, 230 pounds. Early to mid-thirties. Blond hair. Socks, no shoes. Jeans and a black sweater. Stretched out on his side with one arm over his head and his fingers extended like he was reaching for something. Like a basketball player going for a jump shot, or an outfielder trying to snag a homerun ball. Small-caliber entrance wound in the center of his forehead. Eyes open with the slightly surprised look of the newly dead.

"You found him?" she asked the SPD uniform.

"Yes, Ma'am," the officer answered. "They were afraid the fire was going to spread, so they sent me over. The door was open." Defensive. Knowing the question would be asked, and not just by Sarah.

"Name?"

"Johnson. Sam."

He reeled off the rest of the pertinent information: unit number, incident number, badge number, his time of arrival, the steps he had taken to secure the scene. Under Sarah's unwavering gaze he backed out of the trailer, leaving her standing alone.

Sarah turned a slow circle looking for objects out of place. A pillow on the floor could have been thrown. A spilled ashtray might indicate a struggle. A torn magazine. A dangling curtain. Her eyes scanned every corner as she mentally filed the scene away, the body's sprawl, the tired furniture. A crime scene was compromised the moment somebody found the body. You only got one chance before the techs finished with it and the yellow tape came down.

"You ready?" One of the techs, standing in the doorway.

Sarah nodded and turned to leave. The techs moved in, taking photographs, bagging evidence, collecting samples. She stepped onto the front porch and shielded her eyes against the drizzle, then started for the crowd behind the police tape. The gawkers melted away at her approach like ice cream on a summer sidewalk. In a place like this, a detective was better at breaking up a crowd than a riot squad.

She walked up to the only person who stood her ground. Mid-forties. Jet-black hair. Light blue Inuit-style embroidered anorak. Skin like tanned leather.

"You the manager?" she asked. Only someone who had a stake in the outcome would stick around.

The woman nodded.

"Name?"

"Caroline Fraser."

"Who owns the trailer?"

"Tiffany. Tiffany Crane. They say there's a dead man inside. Is it the boyfriend?"

"Do you know where Ms. Crane is now?"

The woman shook her head. "She pays her lot rent on time, I don't ask where she goes."

"Does she always pay on time?"

"Yes. No. Well, except for last month. After the boyfriend moved in."

"Does anyone else live in the house? Kids? His? Hers?"

"No one. Listen, can I go now? I gotta call the owners. Tell 'em what happened before they see it on the news."

Sarah held out her card. "If you think of anything else—"

"Yeah, yeah, I know. Give you a call." The woman shoved the card in her coat pocket without looking at it and hurried off.

Sarah turned around and squinted against the failing light to study the Crane trailer. Emergency lights strobed as the firemen at the trailer next door mopped up. The radio said it was a meth explosion. A man had been badly burned. The incidents could be related. Or not.

She took out her phone. "Rick? It's Sarah. I'm sorry. I'm going to have to cancel our dinner plans… I know. I'll make it up to you, I promise."

She made another call.

"Regi? Sarah. I have to work late tonight… I know, I already called him… Yeah, another time. Listen, can you keep Jack overnight? I can pick him up for school in the morning… Thanks. I owe you." She returned the phone to her pocket. "Did you run the plates?" she asked the uni, nodding toward a faded red Corolla in the trailer's driveway.

"The car belongs to the trailer's owner. Tiffany Crane."

"Do we have an I.D. on the vic?"

"Lance Marsee. M-A-R-S-E-E. Age thirty-two according to the driver's license in his wallet. No priors."

"Can I see the wallet?"

The uni handed over an evidence bag, not yet sealed. Sarah fished out a man's leather wallet, good quality. Better than most trailer residents would own. She flipped it open, scanning the usual array of credit cards and small bills. She fished out a dog-eared business card in Lance Marsee's name, which declared him to be an employee of Stratoco. The company name was unfamiliar to her, and the card itself looked like it had been in the wallet for quite some time. Perhaps Marsee didn't have many opportunities to hand them out. At the back of the wallet was a photograph, carefully folded. The recently deceased stood with his arm around a blonde woman's shoulders. They looked like a couple. Was the woman Tiffany Crane? It was an outdoor shot; Puget Sound or possibly Lake Washington. Pine trees and a strip of silver-gray water in the background.

Sarah waved the business card and the photograph at the uni. "Mind if I keep these for a while?" The uni shrugged. Not his job to argue with a detective.

Sarah fished inside her jacket for her cigarettes and leaned against the Toyota. Tiffany's car. Was she dead like her boyfriend? Missing? Abducted? Had she gone into hiding because she witnessed what happened? Or was she simply off doing her regular Tiffany thing, oblivious to the fact that her life was about to forever and irrevocably change?

She looked at the photo again. Something about the couple's expressions—so into each other, so obviously happy—threatened to crawl under her skin and take root. She pushed it away. Every crime had a ripple effect. Every life lost was a potential heartbreaker. Her job was to find out what happened, so their tragedy wouldn't be a complete waste. Bad things happened when you let yourself get too close to a case. It wasn't easy finding the right balance. Some detectives never did. They drank too much, started using, lost their marriages and families—sometimes all of the above. Rick was always pressing her about why she became a homicide detective in the first place, but that was a question for another day. At any rate, Sarah hadn't met a cop yet who wasn't lugging around a few suitcases' worth of baggage.

She took a final drag, then tossed the cigarette and crushed it under her foot. The light was failing, and she had a lot of ground to cover. Including finding the girlfriend.

# 4

5:00 P.M.

"Girlfriend?" one of the recent transfers to Homicide asked, nodding toward the photograph in Detective John Goddard's open wallet.

Goddard shook his head. He pulled two ones for the vending machine and flipped the wallet shut. The picture of Claire—long dark hair, white skin, wide face, wider smile, sharp cheekbones, kohl eyeliner—*his sister*—hidden from the uni's prying eyes once again. Goddard didn't take issue with the man's assumption. What with his blond hair and blue eyes, no one had ever mistaken him and Claire for full brother and sister. But genetics did strange things sometimes. Likewise he didn't hold the uni's curiosity against him. The kid was, after all, a cop. Even if he was as green as a Seattle spring.

Goddard could have told the uni that he was six years married with two kids. Or that he carried Claire's picture in place of a family photo as a reminder of the one he couldn't save—even though the whole cop-with-the-troubled-kid-sister scenario was so clichéd it would have been laughable if it didn't apply to him. But home life stayed at home. Goddard tried to keep things that way. Neat. Orderly. Compartmentalized. But he didn't always manage it.

"Goddard. We got a body at the shipyard. You're up." Detective Lieutenant Michael Oakes stepped into the hallway just far enough to deliver his pronouncement, then retreated back into his office like a turtle pulling into its shell. Oakes was in countdown mode until his retirement, and it showed; not only in his perfunctory, get-it-done-and-I-don't-care-how-you-do-it manner, but in his appearance as well: early sixties, thinning light brown hair worn long enough on top to be dangerously close to a comb over, stocky build threatening the seams of his serviceable dark gray suit, shaggy brows, and jowls that wouldn't have looked out of place on a basset hound. Then again, Oakes had always considered niceties and preambles a waste of time.

He poked out his head again and aimed his finger at the uni. "And take Louis with you."

"First name, or last?" Goddard asked the uni once he was certain his commander-in-chief was done playing Jack-in-the-box.

"Uh, last name, sir. And it's Joe. Joe Louis. Like the boxer."

"Okay then, Louis. Grab your coat and let's go."

The Port of Seattle was a great place to stash a body. Cruise ships, cargo ships, the North Pacific fishing fleet, the Seattle-Tacoma Airport, four public marinas and conference facilities surrounded by a ring of parks around Elliot Bay combined to make it the eighth busiest seaport in the United States. Over two million shipping containers passed through the port every year, making it inevitable, Goddard supposed, that occasionally, a body would be found inside one.

Or in this case, between. He and Louis navigated the rain-soaked maze of shipping containers like drowning moths heading for the lights the techs had set up until they found the two containers in question. The body between them was covered with a tarp. Not that a tarp was going to make much difference. An outdoor crime scene was always dodgy. Add in the fact that it was six o'clock and full dark after a day of steady rain, and they'd be lucky to find any trace. Real life wasn't like television. Goddard had once spent two hours on the witness stand trying to explain to a group of cop show-indoctrinated jurors why absolutely no physical evidence had been recovered from a particular crime scene. The defense got an acquittal on that one, in large part, Goddard was certain, because the jurors were convinced they were looking at a case of shoddy police work rather than the realities of the job. The CSI effect was definitely alive and well in the city of Seattle.

"What have we got?" he asked.

One of the techs lifted back the tarp. "Male. White guy. Two hundred, maybe six-two. Looks to be somewhere in his mid-thirties. Gunshot to the back of the head."

Goddard mentally added "blond," "affluent" (the Burberry raincoat), and "barefoot" to the description. "We know who he is?"

"Not yet. No wallet."

"Who found him?"

"One of the checkers, a couple of hours ago. Though it looks like a homeless guy got to him first."

Which explained the lack of a wallet and the missing socks and shoes. No witnesses, no I.D., most likely no trace. Goddard's solve rate was already below department average; this case was going to send his stats into the toilet. He shone his flashlight between the containers and over the body, looking for something—*anything*—then pocketed the light and carefully climbed the rain-slicked, welded-steel rungs of one of the containers to the top. Walked to the edge and shone the light down, trying to imagine the scene as it had played out below. Who the players were, who was standing where, what happened, how it happened, why. There were basically only two possibilities. Either the man was shot where he was found, or he was shot somewhere else and his body brought in and dumped. Goddard favored the first option. If the man was killed elsewhere, bringing his body to the shipyard and stashing it between the containers was a lot of effort to go through to hide a body that would inevitably be discovered. Unless the killer or killers were counting on the elements to remove the evidence first, in which case it wasn't such a bad idea after all. Still, killing the man in the shipyard made more sense. Bring the guy out at gunpoint and end it with a quick bang to the head. That's how Goddard would've done it. Occam's razor, *lex parsimoniae.* The simplest explanation was most often the correct one, in police work as well as in science.

He pulled up his shirttail to wipe the rain from his glasses, then put them back on and trailed the flashlight from the body to the end of the container, following the path the killer or killers would have taken to get in and out. His light picked out something in the mud. Plastic-looking. Shiny.

"Down there," he called to Louis, keeping the light trained on his find. "Go around the other end and see what we got."

"It's an I.D." Louis waved over the tech to take a photograph, then pulled on a glove and picked up what looked to Goddard like a corporate identification card dangling from a broken lanyard. He aimed his flashlight. "Yep. It's our vic."

And *that* was how good police work was done. Goddard *was* a good detective, despite his current miserable solve rate, even a great detective, the kind of cop who was able to blend equal parts science and imagination to get results.

Most of his colleagues thought emotions only clouded the truth. But for Goddard, it was important not only to think a case through, but to *feel* it. To become his victims as far as he was able; to crawl inside their head and experience their final moments so he could give them a voice and they could tell what happened. Yeah, his method carried a greater emotional toll. But for Goddard, there was no other way. The day you stopped seeing your vics as individuals from whom the ultimate had been taken was the day you needed to start looking for another job.

# 5

According to his I.D. tag, the dead guy worked at GenMod Labs, a name that was instantly recognizable to any Seattle resident over the age of thirty as the city's oldest and largest biotech firm. The dead guy also really was a "guy"—Dr. Guy Marsee, a fact that Louis seemed to find a great deal funnier than it deserved. Goddard put Louis's reaction down to new-guy nerves.

Department of Motor Vehicles records showed Marsee lived in one of the new downtown high rises—the penthouse, Louis and Goddard discovered after their search warrant got them past the doorman and the building manager pressed the elevator button for the top floor. Apparently Seattle's biotech industry wasn't in as much financial trouble as the papers wanted people to believe.

The building's manager confirmed that Marsee lived alone. She used her passkey to unlock the apartment at their request and stepped back.

"Did Guy do something wrong?" she asked after they'd cleared the apartment and signaled that she could come in. Her use of the victim's first name was telling. Goddard would've bet a month's wages the question wasn't asked out of idle curiosity, but Louis was so inexperienced, the wager would hardly have been fair. Mid-thirties, trendy haircut, short skirt, high heels, tight jacket, plenty of cleavage—everything about her appearance said this was a woman looking to make a permanent move to the top floor.

"How well do you know Mr. Marsee?" he asked. "Do" and not "did." He hoped Louis picked up on his use of the present tense. This stage of the investigation was about gathering information rather than giving it. Everyone was a suspect, including overly ambitious potentially gold-digging building managers.

She flushed. "Not well. I mean, no better than I do the rest of the tenants. Not enough to help with your investigation. Sorry."

*Bingo.* Shakespeare nailed it: *The lady doth protest too much.*

She leaned forward. "Seriously, what did he do? What *are* you investigating?"

Goddard didn't think it wise to tell her that the guy whose apartment she was eying up was on a slab. Best to keep her guessing, and keep her talking. "I'm afraid we're not at liberty to divulge that information at the moment."

"How long has Mr. Marsee lived here?" Louis asked, moving the conversation along.

"I don't know exactly—I'd have to look it up. Maybe three years? And it's 'Dr. Marsee.' He's a scientist, though, not a medical doctor."

"Does Dr. Marsee get many visitors?"

"Not that I know of. His brother drops by once in a while, but that's about all. You really should ask the doorman. I just manage the building. I don't keep track of who goes in and out. I do know that Guy—Dr. Marsee—is hardly ever here. He spends most of his time at work."

"At GenMod Labs."

"That's right."

Goddard left Louis to practice his interview technique and walked to the middle of the room. Building superintendents could be a great source of dirt, but if this one had any, she wasn't dishing. He clasped his hands behind his back and took in every detail, analyzing and categorizing. You could learn a lot about a person from the way they lived. In this case, the warm cherry wood floors, black Italian marble fireplace, white sheepskin throw rugs and white leather pit seating practically screamed that this was a man with absolutely no imagination. The decor was as predictable as a classic spread in *Architectural Digest*. Even the art objects on the open shelves that divided the room into living and office space were exactly what you'd expect to see in a magazine photo: Egyptian bronze gazelle, Islamic tinned-copper bowl, an intricately carved wooden bust of a Polynesian woman in the style of Gauguin. All eminently passable knockoffs—indiscernible to the average person from the real deal. But when it came to art objects, Goddard was far above average thanks to a degree in fine art from the Rhode Island School of Design and six years working art fraud in L.A. To Goddard, the inconsistencies were so obvious, the artwork may as well have been plastered with "Made in China" stickers.

He picked up what looked like an eighteenth-century Qing porcelain vase and turned it over to confirm that it too was a fake.

"Should you be touching that?" the building manager asked.

Goddard played dumb cop and put the vase down without comment, then headed for the master bedroom, the manager following on his heels as self-appointed museum guard. Clearly, she had no idea that the art items in Marsee's apartment were worthless. Marsee might have thought his counterfeits were genuine as well, but Goddard didn't think so. His gut said that everything about the apartment was an act; carefully contrived to convey the impression that Marsee was worth more than he actually was. If that was the case, judging by the building manager's awestruck reaction as she escorted him past the "valuables," it was working.

Inside the bedroom, more wannabe over-the-top luxury: white carpet so dense it was like walking on a cloud. Caramel-colored bedding that Goddard was willing to bet came, not from Neiman Marcus, but from Pottery Barn. Recessed lighting. More bogus-art-filled bookshelves surrounding the upholstered headboard of what was easily the biggest bed that Goddard had ever seen. Twenty feet of floor-to-ceiling windows. No window treatments, but this high up, none were needed. Anyone looking in would have to be sitting in an airplane.

He opened the double doors to a walk-in closet. Shoes lined up like they were waiting for the starting gun at a marathon. Hangers so evenly spaced he could have measured the variation between them with a micrometer. Whatever else he had going on, Marsee had some serious obsessive-compulsive issues.

Goddard chewed on his thumbnail as he studied the contents. What struck him more than the scarily precise order was the complete absence of personal objects. Most people kept all sorts of junk in their closets; sports equipment, shoeboxes crammed with old photos and mementos, whatever else they didn't know what to do with. But aside from the shoes and the clothing, this one was empty.

On a hunch, he retraced his steps and checked all of the wastebaskets, first in the bedroom, then the office area, then the kitchen. Just as he'd guessed, they were spotless, empty. Like they'd been wiped clean. Or like they'd never been used. The manager said Marsee had lived here three years, but the apartment was as cold and impersonal as a hotel.

There wasn't even any mail on the hallway table.

He checked the fridge. Two bottles of Stella, a stick of butter (not margarine), a half-dozen eggs, an open package of low-salt bacon, and a wilted bunch of carrots and a green pepper desiccating in the vegetable drawer. Enough food to sustain someone who dropped by just often enough to make it look as though he lived here. Like the whole apartment was a setup. A very expensive front. For what, Goddard couldn't begin to guess.

Or maybe the guy just preferred eating out.

"Who lives downstairs?" he asked. Nothing he'd seen so far indicated that this was the murder scene, but if the apartment was the abduction site, and the abduction had been preceded by a struggle, the person in the apartment below might have heard something.

"Esther Cobert," the building manager said.

Louis gave a low whistle. "Seriously?"

"Seriously."

"I'm supposed to know who that is?" Goddard asked.

The manager and Louis exchanged the kind of *can you believe this guy?* looks that teenagers usually reserved for their clueless parents. "Only if you're into the indie music scene," Louis, who clearly was, answered.

"Well then, let's go talk to her."

The manager shook her head. "She's on tour. Europe, and after that, Dubai. She won't be back for months."

"Is anyone staying in the apartment while she's gone?"

"No one. Not even the dogs. She always takes them with her."

Another dead end. Goddard pursed his lips. He'd thought—hoped—naively, perhaps, but hoped all the same—that once they had an I.D. for their victim, the murder would be relatively easily solved. Lord knew he needed an easy case.

He walked to the windows and clasped his hands behind his back while he admired the million-dollar view. The rain had stopped. The city spread out below, watercolor reflections shining back from glossy pavement. To the right, the Space Needle. To the left, Mayor Adams's waterfront project and the Port of Seattle.

He turned around. "Okay, we're done here. Louis, grab Marsee's computer and let's get back to the station." Maybe the techs could find out why an art lover living on top of the world ended up in a Seattle shipyard. If Goddard was lucky.

# 6

An hour of knocking on doors in the rain and the dark and the cold while the techs finished processing the scene and the M.E. took care of the body, and Sarah had nothing. Nobody wanted to talk to the cops. Of course, even if she'd found someone willing to open their door to her, they only would have lied anyway. Everybody lied. The guilty lied to protect themselves. The innocent lied to protect the guilty. The rest lied because they could. Because it was human nature. Because the police wanted—needed—their help. Because in this kind of neighborhood, kids were taught from the time they were old enough to breathe that you never, ever offered information voluntarily to a cop.

Still, she had to go through the motions. She slid behind the wheel of her silver Ford Focus and blew on her hands to warm them, then reached inside her jacket for a cigarette. Took a last look at the crime scene, the burned trailer beside it, the lone remaining patrol car, the KIRO news van, the cameraman, the TV reporter broadcasting from beneath the requisite oversized black umbrella. Let her thoughts go where they wanted as she closed her eyes and leaned against the headrest and took a long drag, reviewing impressions, sounds, smells, mentally shuffling the information. So many pieces, with no idea yet which ones were important or how they fit. The beginning of a new case was always both exciting and depressing. Intellectually, she relished the challenge of a fresh puzzle. But the downside of being a homicide detective was that each new mystery began with someone's death.

Right now, the first thing she needed to do—the most important thing she *could* do—was let the details soak into her mind and into her pores until they became as much a part of her as her own memories. There were so many ways you could go at the start of an investigation, and until the evidence pointed solidly toward one of them, all of the directions were valid. That's why you had to choose your path carefully. Going down a wrong road wasted time. And when a case involved a missing person—if Tiffany Crane was indeed missing—time was one thing you didn't have.

The victim: Lance Marsee. Living in his girlfriend's trailer in a bottom-of-the-pond trailer park that attracted the lowest common denominator. The dregs nobody wanted. Drug dealers. Prostitutes. Thieves. Sex offenders who couldn't find anywhere else to live.

The girlfriend: Tiffany Crane. Owner of a broken-down trailer in said trailer park and a beater in the driveway. Lot rent paid on time until her boyfriend Lance moved in. Missing, though whether it was by choice or against her will was impossible at this point to say. Presumed innocent until Sarah found out otherwise.

The crime: Single gunshot to the head. Close range; less than six inches, the M.E. was likely to rule judging by the stippling and the fouling that Sarah had noted on the victim's forehead. Cold. Brutal. Efficient. Committed with what motive and by whom remained to be seen.

She stubbed out her cigarette. Flipped on the wipers and

put the car into gear. Twenty minutes later she hung a right into the precinct lot and parked, hunching her shoulders against the wind and the rain as she hurried inside. She peeled off her jacket and draped it over the wooden coat rack in a corner of her office, then pulled the elastic from her ponytail and shook out her hair. Outside the arched windows across the hallway it was fully dark. Except for the spatter of rain against the glass, the station was quiet, the lights dimmed for the night shift.

She refastened her ponytail, then snapped on her desk light and checked her watch. Almost seven. She'd give it till ten. With Jack squared away at Regi's for the night, in theory, Sarah could work as late as she liked. But she'd been making a concerted effort over the past couple of years to pace herself. It was part of the deal she'd made with her lieutenant. That as far as she was able, she'd get home at a reasonable hour. Get enough sleep. Not forget to eat. Besides, there was only so much she could do until the girlfriend turned up.

She booted up her computer. IAFIS confirmed what the uni had told her at the crime scene: Marsee did not have a criminal record. Tiffany, however, had been arrested twice; once for shoplifting when she was nineteen and a second time one year earlier for possession of a stolen object—a Cartier watch she had allegedly lifted from a customer at the Black Bear Casino where she worked as a waitress. She claimed that the watch's owner—a Desmond Whittaker—had given it to her as a gift—a seemingly unlikely story at first, in view of the owner's report that it had been stolen. But after the watch had been recovered and the victim had refused to press charges—most likely because he didn't want his wife to find out that he was involved with a cocktail waitress—Tiffany's side of the he-said, she-said became more credible. If she had been guilty of anything, it was naivety for accepting the watch in the first place. For believing a casino high-roller would ever leave his wife for a cocktail waitress.

At any rate, two minor arrests did not a murderess make. While the missing Tiffany was definitely on the suspect list, in theory, anyone at the park could have been responsible for Marsee's death. Running the location brought up dozens of reports, most centered on the park's rampant drug trade, methamphetamine apparently being the drug of choice. Judging by the dates of the incident reports, as soon as one meth lab was put out of business, a half-dozen more sprang up to take its place. Sarah felt sorry for the guys working narcotics.

There was one place she could check for Tiffany right now: the Black Bear Casino—if she still worked there after the theft charge. Best not to spook the woman; she probably didn't have much love for the police after her run-ins. She looked up the number for the casino and dialed.

"Black Bear Casino, how may I direct your call?" It was a man's voice, oozing customer service.

"Is Tiffany Crane working tonight?"

There was a pause. "I'm afraid Miss Crane is no longer employed here. What is this regarding?"

"I'll call her at home. Thank you." Sarah put down the phone. No need to warn the casino's owners that the police were interested in Native American business affairs. So Tiffany was unemployed. No wonder she was late paying rent.

She pulled out the business card and photograph she had taken from Lance Marsee's wallet, and laid them on her desk. She did an internet search for the company name on the card; Stratoco turned out to be one of the major players in Seattle's aerospace industry, with a glossy highly maintained website. She picked up her phone and dialed the contact number, slightly surprised when the call was answered immediately. The space industry clearly worked as late as she did. Two minutes later she put the phone down. Guy Marsee *had* worked at Stratoco until September, but had left the company, for reasons the woman on the other end had not been willing to discuss. No wonder the single business card had been so dog-eared. It was just a reminder. She would have to go ask her questions in person, both at the casino and Stratoco, but that was a job for tomorrow.

She drummed her fingers on the desk. She needed to see the more personal sides of their lives, or at least what they were willing to share with the world. She picked up her office phone and dialed a number.

"Officer Khan, can you come to my office?"

A moment later a tall uni, barely out of his teens, or so it seemed to Sarah, stuck his head around her office door.

"You wanted me, Detective?"

"Do you have a Facebook account, Khan?"

The young officer grinned. "Doesn't everyone?"

"No."

Khan's smile wavered. "Did you need me to show you how to sign up?"

"No, I just need access to the site. Please log into your account on my computer." Khan looked uncomfortable, and Sarah resisted the urge to roll her eyes. "I won't be looking at your profile, Officer, just other people's."

Two minutes later she was looking at Lance Marsee's profile page. People put a ridiculous amount of personal information on the Web. Even when people set their Facebook page to "private," a great deal of information slipped through—posts they made on other people's pages; things their friends and relatives said on their own pages about them. Sarah had taken a class last year from a twenty-something who knew more about Facebook data mining than Mark Zuckerberg. When you wanted a quick and dirty overview of someone, social networking sites were hard to beat.

As it turned out, Lance Marsee hadn't ticked the right "privacy boxes". Marsee's educational listing was impressive: a bachelor of science in mathematics, a master of science in astrophysics, and a Ph.D. in the same, all in just under five years, and all from MIT. His personal profile was more Spartan. There were no children listed and a quick sweep of his photo albums revealed no likely candidates. The only family member linked to the account was a Guy Marsee, a brother, whose own profile page showed him to also be resident in Seattle.

Sarah switched her attention to Tiffany Crane's online profile. No children listed, educated no further than sophomore year, but her romantic history was colorful. Relationship status updates, coupled with wall posts from supportive female friends, revealed that Tiffany was separated from husband #2, who was now in prison for an undisclosed but serious crime. Sarah switched to the SPD database; Edward 'Eddie' Crane was doing a ten-year stretch for assault and armed robbery. That was one potential jealous ex out of the suspect pool.

She browsed through Tiffany's online photo album, and confirmed that she was indeed the woman in the picture with Lance. Judging by the recent photos of an end-of-summer picnic, she'd socialized with her coworkers at the Black Bear Casino; they might have some insights to share. Sarah also spotted the shot of Lance and Tiffany together, a hard copy of which stared at her across her desk. It was one of many photographs of the two together.

Sarah put down her pen. From the outside, Lance and Tiffany seemed to be from different planets. Their pairing sounded like the opening line of a bad joke: "A waitress and an astrophysicist walk into a bar..." What was a girl like Tiffany doing with a guy whose bread and butter was the physical properties of heavenly bodies?

She picked up the photograph and held it under the desk light. Still no clue as to where it was taken, but now that she knew more about his background, Lance looked every inch the stereotypical nerd. Pudgy body and slumping shoulders from too many hours hunched in front of a computer, oversized head to accommodate his super-sized brain (or maybe it was just his receding hairline), shirt buttoned all the way up to his double chin. Then there was Tiffany: casino waitress, multiple ear piercings, ragged haircut that was supposed to look trendy but that to Sarah looked like Tiffany had cut it herself, cropped T-shirt that revealed a rhinestone bellybutton stud and a butterfly tattoo. Pretty enough in an average-to-rundown way. But to Lance the Science Nerd, she must have seemed as exotic as a jungle bird.

"Hey, Linden."

Detective John Goddard stood in the open doorway with a file folder in one hand and a Styrofoam cup in the other. She gestured him in. Sarah tended to keep to herself as much as possible—she worked better alone—but when it came to the other detectives, Goddard was all right, even if his current solve rate was less than stellar. Six feet of solid muscle and sandy hair, average-looking in every way, the original Mr. Nice Guy. Goddard tended to talk baseball more than she cared to listen, but baseball season was months away. Anyway, one bad habit was hardly a deal breaker.

He sat down in the extra chair and handed the folder across the desk. "Looks like we're going to be working together. I picked up a case a couple of hours ago. Man found between a pair of shipping containers at the Port of Seattle. Same last name as your vic."

"Guy Marsee is dead? I just flagged him as my vic's only living relative."

"Well, now he's a dead relative. Crazy, isn't it? Two brothers found dead in the same city on the same day. As soon as we made the connection, Oakes sent me down to talk to you."

Sarah opened the file on Guy Marsee and flicked through it. Apart from the preliminary police reports, there were some recent bank statements, electricity bills, and other mundane paperwork, presumably taken from the man's apartment. Nothing that leapt out at her. "Any leads? Cause of death?"

"Nothing yet. Gunshot to the back of the head. No witnesses, and the M.E. estimates the body was outside for at least five hours, so probably no trace. The techs are taking apart Marsee's computer as we speak, but his apartment was as sterile as a clean room. I doubt there'll be anything we can use on it."

"My guy was found in a house trailer in Rainier Valley. Single small-caliber shot to the forehead. My best lead is his live-in girlfriend, except that nobody knows where she is. It's too soon to run a trace on her cellphone, and she's not been active on social networking for several hours. Of course it wouldn't be that easy." Sarah handed over her own thin file and her notes on the couple's recent work history and online presence.

Goddard thumbed through the pages and passed them back. "It's never easy, is it?"

Sarah didn't answer. She didn't need to. They both knew that real police work was nothing like the way it was depicted on television, where detectives solved a new case every week, and that in less than an hour. In real life, cases often took years to resolve, police labs had to make do with hand-me-down equipment, sometimes purchased by the officers themselves. Officers frequently bought their own fingerprinting tools as well; binoculars, evidence-collection materials—even weapons. As for DNA analysis, good luck getting your results back in under a week. Assuming the sample you collected was large enough to run in the first place, and it wasn't degraded.

"How do you want to work this?" Goddard asked.

"I'm going to the casino where my guy's girlfriend worked first thing tomorrow morning, see if I can track her down. We've got a BOLO on her, but so far, we're not getting anything. Then I'm going out to Stratoco to talk to my victim's ex-coworkers."

"My guy worked at GenMod Labs. I'm going to head over there as soon as their doors open. I'll let you know what I find out."

"Sounds like a plan." Sarah checked her watch. Seven-thirty. She stood up and stretched, then crossed the room for her jacket.

"Going home?"

"I'm going to the hospital. There was a meth fire this afternoon at the trailer next to my crime scene. They found my vic when they were clearing the area. The men were neighbors. I figure the burn victim might know something."

"I'll ride along with you. It's a stretch, but he might have something on my Marsee brother, too. How badly was he burned?"

"I wasn't close, but it seemed pretty bad."

"Then we'll have to hurry."

Sarah nodded. In retrospect she should have gone to the hospital earlier, but she knew from grim experience how much time detectives stood in waiting rooms, trying to convince doctors to allow them access to critical patients. They cared about the person, not about what information they could yield.

Sarah shook the rainwater off her jacket and put it back on. No doubt Rick would accuse them both of burying their emotions if he'd heard Goddard's remark, but it was the reality of the job. People did stupid things. They got hurt.

Blew themselves up. Some of them didn't make it. Cops dealt with the fallout and cleaned up their messes so that regular people didn't have to.

She turned off the desk light and followed Goddard out the door. Welcome to homicide, where the clock never stops.

# 7

The silence in the burn unit at Harborview Medical Center was painful. There wasn't any other way to describe it. Tiny sounds: the hum from the overhead fluorescents, beeps from the medical equipment, whispered conversations from the nurses' station—Holder's own footsteps as he squeaked across the linoleum—loomed larger and more ominous than they should have against the crushing stillness. Holder had never been inside a burn unit, didn't want to be here now, did his best to avoid hospitals altogether whenever possible, for that matter, so he couldn't say exactly what he'd expected. Doctors running around carrying clipboards yelling "Stat!" Nurses calling frantically to orderlies for assistance. Patients wrapped up like screaming mummies. This place was more like a nursing home—or a morgue.

Or maybe he just watched too much bad television. Whatever. He certainly hadn't anticipated a silence so deep the elevator he stepped out of could have been the portal to another planet. He supposed the clinical atmosphere was meant to be reassuring. "You're in good hands at Harborview." All he knew was that lying in a bed in one of the sterile glass pods he passed on his way to the nurses' station was the last place on Earth he'd want to be.

He leaned an elbow on the high counter and flashed his badge with his left hand. The nurse was cute. Short, with baggy blue scrubs turned up at the ankle. Filipina or Latina or some kinda "a"—dark eyes, curly brown hair, skin the color of whipped latte. He kept his right hand hidden below the counter. That hand was a mess, wrapped in gauze and with a giant pink blister covering the palm. His reward for playing Boy Scout and snagging Campbell's little boy. Not that Holder would've minded some loving nursing attention, especially from a nurse as cute as this one, but that wasn't why he was here.

"You got a man, Neil Campbell, burned in a meth fire. Woulda come in a couplea hours ago." He arched an eyebrow and winked. *You and me, babe—we're the authority figures here; we're in this together.*

She consulted her chart. "That would be room 1011. But don't go in. Not like that." She pointed to a sign on the wall behind her:

**VISITOR GUIDELINES**

- **Visitors are limited to immediate family members or those designated by the family.**
- **Visitors are required to wear a gown, cap, mask and gloves while visiting.**
- **Visitors are required to wash their hands with disinfectant soap prior to entering and after leaving the patient's room.**
- **Plants, flowers, and plush toys are not permitted in the burn unit.**
- **A quiet atmosphere should be maintained at all times to promote rest and healing.**

Holder nodded and touched his finger to his forehead to show he got it and drifted off. Found room 1011 past a dogleg in the hallway and stood outside the plate glass window looking in. The man on the bed in the middle of the room was so buried in gauze it was impossible to tell where the bandages ended and the sheets began. A jagged green line on the monitor next to the bed showed he was hanging in there.

Holder closed his eyes and leaned his forehead against the glass. He wished more than anything that he'd busted Campbell sooner. If he had, Campbell would only be looking at jail time instead of a life sentence. Now he'd never hold a job again; never get his kid back. If he even made it. Holder knew a guy who was cooking in the back seat of his buddy's pickup when his bottle blew. Two years and a million skin grafts later, his face, chest, and forearms still looked like raw hamburger. Holder understood the temptation: Spend $65 at Walmart and walk out with everything you needed to make $2,000 worth of crank. Easy money. Except when it wasn't.

The thing about shaking and baking—the street name for the do-it-yourself process of making methamphetamine that had taken over from more standard meth labs in recent years—was that it was just too easy. Where the old-style meth labs called for hundreds of pseudoephedrine pills that had to be cooked over an open fire, with shake and bake, a cooker could turn out a few ounces of methamphetamine with a handful of cold pills and some chemicals from the hardware store shaken together inside a soda bottle. Anybody who could make a batch of cookies could whip up a batch of meth. And if you didn't have a buddy who was willing to teach you, you could find out everything you needed to know about how to do it online.

What the shakers and bakers tended to forget was that easy didn't mean safe. Do it right, and yeah, you could produce several grams of high-quality meth in less than an hour. But if you shook the bottle too vigorously, let too much oxygen in, loosened the cap too quickly—let a single drop of sweat come in contact with the lithium strips—you ended up holding an explosive fireball of corrosive chemicals in your hands. At least with the old meth labs, when a fire broke out, the cookers had a chance to run away. As far as Holder was concerned, anybody crazy enough to shake and bake should first make a standing reservation for their own sterile room at the nearest burn center.

"Family?"

He spun around. The man standing slightly to the left and behind him fairly reeked of cop, which explained why he'd been able to catch Holder by surprise. Buzz cut, compact build, rumpled hundred-dollar suit, feet spread and arms crossed like he was about to launch an interrogation. An in-your-face, by-the-book cop who couldn't have pretended to be anything other than what he was if his firstborn's life depended on it.

"A friend." Calling himself Campbell's friend was a stretch, but Holder couldn't exactly tell this cop that the reason he was gawking outside the man's window was because the burned man was one of Logic's cookers and Holder was one of Logic's runners.

"I'm sorry," the cop said, sounding like he actually meant it.

"So'm I." Truly sincere.

"I was hoping I could talk to him. Any idea what happened?"

Holder arched an eyebrow. Did this cop really think Holder was stupid enough to confess to knowing about the dude's meth lab? Maybe he should just cut the guy a break and tell him he'd been planning to use Campbell as the star witness in the case he was building against Logic and be done with it. Logic had at least a half dozen cookers in the trailer park that Holder had managed to sniff out, but aside from Campbell, they were all users, and therefore about as valuable to him in a courtroom as a cockroach. Campbell was different. He was smart—maybe the smartest person Holder had ever known. Articulate. The kind of person who'd make a great witness. And he wasn't cooking because he needed the dope, but because he needed the money. He seemed to care about his kid, keeping him out of harm's way. Holder was sure that he would've been able to turn him; he'd just been waiting for the right moment to reveal his true identity, explain the benefits of being a professional snitch. It figured that of all the cookers in the park who could've blown themselves up, Campbell would be the one to draw the short straw.

"Nah. Him and me don't talk much. We're not like, close or nuthin'."

"Did he have any other friends in the trailer park? Maybe his neighbor?"

*Oh snap.* Dude didn't care about Holder's snitch at all. Man was Homicide, tryin' to nail the body the cops found in Tiffany's trailer.

"I never been to his place. Wouldn't know." The lie was easy enough to disprove if this guy was as good as his body language wanted Holder to believe, but by that time, Holder would be long gone. He couldn't get involved. Not without blowing his cover. Anyway, he'd only been working the park a few months. Other than the fact that the trailer belonged to Tiffany, and that, according to the park gossip, the guy who'd moved in a month ago was the latest in a long string of loser boyfriends, he didn't have anything to offer. This cop could get that info elsewhere.

The cop gave Holder The Look—the one Holder used himself in the interrogation room—*I'm hearing you, buddy, but I'm not buying a word you're saying.* Holder threw back a look of his own: *Don' know why you don' believe me, man; I swear I'm bein' straight wit' you.* Played it cool, stood his ground.

The cop stared back, backed down. Holder took the cigarette from behind his ear. "Lissen, man. I gotta go have me a smoke."

The cop smiled, all Good Cop friendly now—*Yeah, I hear you, buddy; no smoking rules are a bitch*—and held out a card. "Sure. But if you think of anything that could help your *friend*, let me know."

Holder pocketed the card and slouched off down the hall. Dude was sharper than he looked.

He paused at the nurses' station. The charge nurse was checking a clipboard against a tray of meds. He laid on his best smile, pulled out his own card, tapped it on the counter to get her attention and pushed it toward her. "Call me when Number 1011 wakes up?"

She pushed the card back. "That's not going to happen for a while. At least a couple of weeks."

"Why's that?"

"When somebody's burned as badly as Mr. Campbell, we keep them under for as long as we can. It's just better for everybody that way. People tend to go a little crazy when they're awake, fighting us and screaming like they think they're still on fire. It's not pretty."

Holder couldn't imagine this five-foot bit of nothing wrestling an out-of-control burn patient the size of Campbell. He could, however, imagine her doing a very different kind of wrestling under far more pleasant circumstances. He gave her a sly smile that let her see a hint of what he was thinking and pushed the card toward her again. "Keep it. You never know. You might think of a reason to call." He winked.

She laughed and picked up the card.

Holder stuck the cigarette between his lips and sauntered off toward the elevators. Kept his back to the nurses' station while he pressed the call button and grinned. Oh yes, he did indeed have the touch, slayin' the ladies with his ill lady skillz.

"Sorry I took so long," Sarah said as she joined Goddard outside Campbell's hospital room. "I couldn't find a parking space." She nodded toward the window. "You talk to him yet?"

Goddard shook his head. "No, and according to the nurse, it isn't going to happen for a while. They're keeping him under. Too badly burned. She said she'll call when he wakes up, but that might not be for days—maybe weeks."

"It was a long shot, anyway." Sarah listened to the random beeps and hisses of the equipment keeping Campbell alive, then reached inside her jacket for her cigarettes. She caught herself and quickly shoved both hands into her pockets. Smoking in a hospital corridor? Really? Even though it was only a reflexive gesture and not a conscious act, the fact that she'd gone for her cigarettes at all was bad enough. She was going to have to give serious thought to cutting back. Maybe even quitting. She'd done it before—lots of times. She smiled thinly at the well-worn joke.

"There was a guy hanging around when I got here," Goddard said. "Tweaker type. A real loser. Tall, brown eyes, light brown hair, jeans and a hoodie. Did you see him on your way up?"

"No. He must've gone down in the other elevator."

"He made me as a cop right away. No telling why he was really here. His right hand was bandaged. Maybe from the meth fire. Want me to follow up?"

"Let it go. Not our case." Sarah's hand went again to her inside jacket pocket. Goddard clocked the gesture and reached into his own and pulled out a Nicachew and handed it to her. Sarah unwrapped it gratefully and popped it in her mouth. "I didn't realize you were a smoker."

"Was. Wife's expecting again. I promised I'd quit before the baby's born. It's going to be a boy this time."

"Boys are great."

"You have a son, don't you? John? Jim? How old is he?"

"Jack's twelve. A friend is keeping him for me overnight. Though I'm sure I'll hear about it from him in the morning."

Goddard shook his head in sympathy. "I hear you. My oldest is fourteen. If you think it's bad now, just wait a few years."

Sarah pressed her lips together to keep from answering back. It wasn't the fact that Goddard had somehow managed to corner her into making small talk that irritated her so much as it was his assumption that all teenagers were trouble, including hers. He didn't know Jack. Didn't even know his name. Goddard was a smart man. Didn't he realize that when parents presumed their teenage offspring would inevitably give them trouble the prophecy became self-fulfilling? She and Jack had a great relationship. Always had. Just because he was about to turn thirteen didn't mean that was going to change.

"Okay. We're done here." She started toward the elevators. Goddard took the hint and fell silent as he followed.

# 8

"Daddy! Daddy! Daddy's home!" Goddard's nine-year-old squealed from inside the house as he stomped up the front steps and crossed the wooden porch of his modest Pinehurst bungalow. He waited with his hand on the knob. On the other side of the door, the patter of footsteps stopped. The knob jiggled beneath his hand.

"Arianna—help me," Sophie called to her older sister. "It's stuck!"

Goddard smiled. They played the same game every evening: He announced his arrival with exaggerated footsteps, Sophie ran to greet him, he drew out the moment by preventing her from opening the door. He couldn't remember how the game got started. A silly routine that was quickly becoming more absurd as his girls got older, but one he looked forward to playing nonetheless. A few lighthearted moments at the end of what was often a very long and very trying day.

"Arianna! Help me!" Sophie called again.

He waited until a second, more sedate set of footsteps told him his teenage daughter was also on the other side of the door, then let go of the knob. The door swung open.

"Daddy!" Sophie cried when she saw him. "You tricked me!" She pointed an accusing finger. "You were holding the door."

Goddard pretended to be crushed by her accusation, just as Sophie pretended to be angry with him, then snatched her up and swung her over his head. She giggled and wrapped her arms and legs around him like a monkey as he leaned down to kiss his older daughter on the forehead. Arianna rolled her eyes. She didn't kiss back, but she submitted to his kiss, and from his hormonal fourteen-year-old, that was all he could expect.

Sophie snuggled against his neck. "I missed you!"

"And I missed you. But why aren't you in bed?" The same thing he said every night. Only this time, it really was past her bedtime. He was glad Kath had let Sophie wait up.

"Oh, Daddy." Sophie placed both hands on his cheeks and gave him a big, wet, little-girl kiss. She wriggled loose. "Don't forget to tuck me in!" she called as she ran off down the hall.

Arianna followed at a more leisurely pace, thumbs flying as she typed out a text message on her cellphone.

"Did you finish your homework?" Goddard called after her.

"Almost," she mumbled back.

Which meant she hadn't yet started. Why Kath didn't keep a closer rein on Arianna, Goddard didn't know. If Kath had been the breadwinner, and he the artist who got to stay home and paint in his studio every day, Arianna wouldn't be spending all of her after-school hours in her room texting her friends.

He kicked off his shoes and hung his wet jacket on a hook beside the closet—he knew better than to hang it inside—and followed the clatter of pots and pans to the kitchen.

"How was work today?" Kath asked as he came up

behind her and put his arms around her burgeoning belly and kissed the back of her neck. Six weeks until the baby was due. His son. Kath was having a harder time with this pregnancy than the other two. Nothing serious, just a lot of extra tiredness and swelling feet and the doctor monitoring Kath's blood pressure and the baby's heart rate more closely as the big day drew near. Technically, her pregnancy was considered high risk because of her age. The doctor had even written "elderly primagravida," translation: "geriatric pregnancy," on Kath's chart. The image the term conjured up of a gray-haired, elderly lady giving birth had made them both laugh. Apparently there was a big difference between having a baby when you were twenty-one and when you were pushing forty.

"Work was fine," he answered, as he always did. He didn't like lying to her, but what choice did he have? He couldn't very well tell her that he'd just come from the hospital room of a man who'd burned himself beyond recognition. Or that the man wasn't likely to live. Or that no sooner had he I.D.ed the body of a well-to-do art lover who was shot execution-style in the head, than he found out the man's only brother had been brutally murdered on the same day.

During the early years of their marriage, he'd tried answering the question honestly. But he'd quickly learned it was better for both of them if he divided his life into segments. Work stayed at work, home life played out at home, and never the twain shall meet. Besides, no one other than another cop really wanted to know what a homicide detective did all day. Especially not a homicide detective's wife. It turned out Kath was a sensitive soul, an artist who augmented his meager cop's salary by selling her watercolor paintings to tourists. Pretty scenes, all bright sunlight and dancing water and perfect pine trees. As if the world really was a nice place.

She smiled. "I'm glad. Supper's almost ready."

He grabbed a beer from the fridge and sat down at his usual place at the table. Took a long slug as Kath hummed happily to herself and bustled around the kitchen.

"I got a new commission today," she said as she put a heaping plateful of meatloaf and mashed potatoes in front of him and sat down with a glass of ice water to keep him company.

Goddard eyed the food and mentally divided the portion in half. Kath was a great cook—too good, really—but now that he'd reached a certain age, he needed to start watching what he ate. He'd been cutting back for almost two months. Lost close to six pounds. As far as he could tell, Kath hadn't noticed.

"A Mrs. Armstrong wants me to paint an entire series," she went on. "Two views of the Sound from her front lawn for each season, each depicting the water in a different mood. That's eight paintings!" Kath beamed.

"But that will take—well, at least a year. Maybe longer."

"I know. Isn't it wonderful? Now I won't have to worry so much about selling my other paintings."

The art world was a tough place to make money, without a doubt. Tourists' tastes were fickle. Some summers, Kath sold more than a dozen paintings. Other years, one or none. And whenever the economy took a nosedive, non-essential purchases like watercolor paintings were the first to go.

"She wants me to stay at her house as much as I can while I work," Kath continued, "and she's even going to set up a room for me as a studio. I went out to her home to meet with her today, and John—you should see it! The gatehouse is bigger than our own, and the main house is built entirely out of limestone—it looks like an English castle, with balconies and leaded glass windows all covered in ivy. The ceilings in the living room are low, with all this gorgeous exposed plaster and beam work, and the fireplace hearth must be at least twelve feet long. I could see into the dining room from where we were sitting, and I counted twenty chairs at the table. Imagine having a sit-down dinner party at your own house for twenty people!"

"What about the girls?"

"That's the best part. Mrs. Armstrong says I can bring the girls with me whenever I need to. The house has an indoor swimming pool they can use, and a billiards table—even an arcade with a pinball machine. Won't they have fun?"

"And the baby?"

"Well, there's the rub." She patted her belly. "No way to know if your son is going to be a quiet baby or a demanding one. But if I have to, I can make sketches at the house and take photos and come back here to paint while the baby is napping."

*And what about me?* Goddard wanted to say. Kath was glowing like a kid at a birthday party. So wrapped up in her own world, there was no room for his. He wished he could talk to her as enthusiastically about his current case. He wanted to share his concerns over his miserable solve rate, confess his constant worry that if his stats didn't improve, he'd spend the remaining years until his retirement behind a desk.

Instead, he smiled and nodded as she prattled on. Feigning interest in what she was saying while keeping his thoughts and opinions to himself. The same tightrope he walked every night.

No wonder so many cop marriages broke up.

# 9

Holder picked at the duct tape on the sofa in Logic's mom's living room as the conversation around him ebbed and flowed. Logic the Dope Dealer bragging about his new big-screen plasma TV. Ridgeback the Dope Dealer's Henchman going on and on about all the money he'd made that week moving product. A couple of guys Holder didn't know the names of laughing and jiving about something he couldn't have cared less about. The image of Campbell in his hospital bed stuck in his head, just as the hospital smell lingered in his nose and on his clothes.

He couldn't stop thinking about Campbell's boy either, disappeared forever into the bottomless pit otherwise known as the foster care system. He hoped somebody was watching out for the little dude on the first day of the rest of his sorry-ass life. It was tough without a moms or a pops in the picture. His sister was raising two kids by herself. Doing a good job of it, too. She'd raised Holder as well. Kids could turn out okay as long as they had somebody who cared about them.

"Bitch made me go once." Logic's voice penetrated Holder's fog. "Buncha raggedy assed tweakers slayin' the donuts."

It took Holder longer than it should have to figure out that Logic was talking about N.A., Narcotics Anonymous. And that the "bitch" he was referring to was his mother Jackie, an overweight woman who was sucking down oxygen for her emphysema in the next room. Jackie knew all about the drug business her son ran out of her living room. Most of the time she didn't care. But every once in a while she went all normal mother on him and tried to get him to quit.

"I ain't gonna live like that, you feel me?" Logic said. "I want the good life." He plucked a plastic bag from the tin stash box on the coffee table to make his point, packed a meth pipe, and held his lighter under the glass. Took a hit, held it in, blew it out, and offered the pipe to Holder.

Holder shook his head and passed the pipe to the tweaker sitting beside him.

"What's the matter? My ice not good enough for you?" Logic asked.

"I ain't no bag whore." Holder patted his stomach. "My body is my temple." It must have been the fiftieth time they'd had this conversation. It was getting dangerous.

Logic laughed. "Then why you suckin' on that cigarette?" He grabbed the meth pipe for another hit, then sank back in his nasty brown vinyl La-Z-Boy crusty with food scraps, dribbles of sour beer and other trace that Holder didn't want to think too hard about. Logic stared dreamily at the ceiling. Sniffed, wiped his nose, giggled.

Holder relaxed as the meth buzz took Logic to his happy place. The real question wasn't why an apparent health nut like Holder smoked cigarettes; it was how long he would be able to stay under this time without being forced to choose between taking a hit of meth or blowing his cover. It wouldn't be the end of his career if Logic and Company made him for a cop. Holder would just move on to another sorry trailer park and another batch of crank heads. There wasn't exactly a shortage of drug rings in the city waiting for him to bust. And it wasn't like he was undercover with the Mafia. Nobody was going to put a bullet in his head or chop off his fingers if he was found out.

Still, he badly wanted to see Logic and his pals locked up. A lot of the cops at County thought narco was a waste of time. That as soon as you busted one operation, another came along to take its place, so why even bother? But you had to stick your finger in the dike, even if the water was spilling over the top. If you didn't, then the bad guys had already won. Maybe Holder was too naive and idealistic for undercover work. But at least this way, he got to be the good guy for a while, lock a few of 'em up, keep the others lookin' over their shoulders, maybe scare some little pissant out of starting down the wrong road. And it wasn't like he was planning to stay in undercover forever. His lieutenant had hinted that there were big things in Holder's future if he stuck it out.

"Tiff's the one who oughta go," Ridgeback said. Still talking about N.A. "That bitch has some serious addiction. She burned through all her dude's cheese in what—three weeks? Prob'ly killed 'im, too."

Tiff—Tiffany—the tiny tattooed blonde who mostly hung out with a dark-haired tweaker called Claire. Tiffany owned the trailer across the street. The trailer where the cops found her boyfriend's body. The cops were no doubt looking at her as a possible suspect, though if Holder hadn't been undercover, he could've told them they were barking up the wrong tree. Tiffany and her new boyfriend seemed really close. No way would she have killed him. Though she might've been able to tell them who did. Anyway, he didn't need to break cover to offer his help. The cops working the case would be talking to Tiffany soon enough.

"You talkin' 'bout that bitty thing with the butterfly tattoo on her belly?" Holder laughed. "Man, she didn't kill nobody. You gotta have *balls* for that." He made his point by grabbing his crotch.

Ridgeback burst out laughing. Holder leaned across the coffee table to dap fists with him and grinned. There was a reason his lieutenant had tapped him for undercover straight out of the Academy. Aside from the fact that he and the tweakers happened to stand on opposite sides of the law, Holder really wasn't all that different from the junkies.

# 10

Sarah aimed her flashlight at the crumbling sidewalk leading to Tiffany's trailer and made her way carefully toward the front door. The last thing she needed was to fall or to twist an ankle while she was out here alone in the dark. Rainier Valley wasn't exactly the kind of place where, if you called out for help, somebody came running. Especially if you happened to be a cop.

A putrid, burned-plastic smell hung heavy in the damp night air. No telling how long the trailer next door was going to remain as it was, half destroyed and abandoned. The latest instance of blight in a neighborhood that already had more than its share. Earlier that afternoon, the cops had nailed a piece of plywood over the blow-out front door. The plywood was already gone.

Sarah pitied the people who had to live here. If Rainier Valley was like most trailer parks, the average age of its residents was close to fifty. Most of them would have moved in decades ago as college kids or young marrieds, thinking that a temporary stay in a trailer park was a smart way to get started and save money. Not realizing that once they bought in they'd be stuck forever, since a house trailer's value only went down. Sarah used to think the people who lived in trailer parks did so by choice, because they didn't aspire to anything better and lacked ambition. After she understood their situation better, she realized that most of them were hardworking, decent people who would have moved to a safer, cleaner place in a heartbeat if they could. But it cost thousands of dollars to relocate a trailer—assuming you could find a place to move it to—money the people at Rainier Valley didn't have or they wouldn't be living here in the first place. Chicken and egg. Catch 22.

No lights in Tiffany's trailer. Sarah climbed the sagging steps and knocked on the front door. The porch reeked of cat urine and mold. She waited. Knocked and waited again. Tiffany's continuing absence was beginning to worry her. It had been five hours since Lance's body was discovered, longer than that since she'd posted anything on Facebook. More than enough time for something bad to have happened to her. Not every cop read the BOLO alerts or paid much attention to them when they did, especially when the missing person was an adult. It wasn't that they didn't care, they just had a lot to do.

On the other hand, it was a big city. There were plenty of places for Tiffany to hide if she didn't want to be found.

Sarah knocked a third time for good measure, then turned and studied the trash-filled front yard. She herself had lived in a trailer park almost as bad as this one once. The social workers at Child Protective Services were normally careful about the foster parents they approved and the conditions in the homes they monitored. But every once in a while, somebody slipped through the cracks. People who had no business taking care of one kid ended up with several, not because they loved children, but because they loved the big bucks the state was willing to pay for taking care of them. There was good money in foster care if you played it right. Which meant that sometimes, kids like Sarah ended up in dumps like this. The really bad ones, you read about on the news. Foster kids placed with child molesters, or sold as sex slaves to a porn ring. Left outside coatless in the winter. Caged. Impregnated. Neglected. Beaten. Starved. For every case that made the news, there were dozens—hundreds—of kids who were barely hanging in there, doing whatever they had to do in order to survive a way of life that most people wouldn't wish on a dog. Sarah's way of coping had been to run. The longest she'd ever stayed in one place was two years. A lifetime when you caught a bad one.

She started down the sidewalk. Laughter drifted from the trailer across the street. Sarah had talked to the woman who lived there when she was canvassing the neighborhood that afternoon. Overweight, unkempt, on the high end of forty, barefoot and wearing a stained nightgown that looked like she lived in it 24/7. Bloodshot eyes and a breathing tube shoved roughly in her nose. The woman claimed she didn't know anything about her neighbors, but Sarah had seen the meth paraphernalia behind her among the dirty dishes on the coffee table. Oh yeah. Meth user on one side of the street, meth cooker on the other, but the neighbors didn't know each other. Right. And two plus two didn't equal four.

A stray cat skulked across her path as she made her way to the car. Thin. Black. Little more than a shadow. Another burst of raucous laughter came from the meth party across the street. In another trailer, a man and a woman were shouting. Somewhere down the street, a baby was crying.

Sarah steered her Focus around a plastic Big Wheel tricycle marooned in a pothole bigger than a child's swimming pool and headed for home. Just another day in the life of Rainier Valley.

# DAY TWO

JANUARY 25, 7:30 A.M.

# 11

Jack picked at the buckle on the backpack clutched in his lap and slumped lower in the passenger seat. His long, dark hair hid all of his face except for the pout on his lips. Sarah gripped the steering wheel tighter and turned her attention back to the road.

"Asking again isn't going to change anything," she said with a level of calm she didn't feel. Seven-thirty was far too early in the morning to butt heads. "The answer is still 'no.'"

"But *why* can't I stay with Regi? Regi's going to take the boat out today. She said I could come."

Regi had grown from being Sarah's social worker into a good friend—Sarah's only friend, when you came down to it—but putting the idea in Jack's head that he could skip school to go out with her on her boat was completely out of line. It wasn't like Regi to undermine Sarah's authority so openly. Sarah supposed it was payback for asking Regi to keep Jack overnight again. A not-so-subtle message that Sarah was working too hard. Again.

"You have school today, Jack. You know that."

"You never let me do *anything*." He sighed deeply and stared out the window.

Sarah bit back a sigh of her own. Never mind that she'd let Jack go along when Regi took the boat down the California coastline during Christmas vacation just a few weeks ago; the real problem was that all of the significant adults in Jack's life were women. He desperately needed a male role model. Someone he could look up to and confide in. A friend. By rights, it should have been Rick, but for some reason, she had avoided the inevitable introductions. Probably because both of the men in her life wanted to be the only man in her life.

They rode the rest of the way to Jack's middle school in silence. Sarah pulled into the drop-off queue with five minutes to spare and reached over to ruffle her son's hair.

Jack pushed her hand away. "God, Mom. Cut it out. People might see." He clambered out of the car without looking at her and made sure to slam the door.

She lowered the passenger window. "Have a good day!" Jack turned and glared.

Sarah watched her son trudge into the building. She thought about what Goddard said yesterday. That everything would change. But the spat didn't mean anything. Jack had never been a morning person. Regi had probably let him stay up too late playing computer games. Sarah pushed the thoughts aside and turned the car toward Rainier Valley.

The park looked worse than ever in the morning light. Trash bags torn apart by dogs, spilling dirty diapers across the sidewalks. Wires dangling from rusty electrical boxes. Missing roofs. Broken windows. She recalled an incident report, the recording of which had been passed round the station:

*"I'm sitting here watching TV,"* the complainant had said, *"just minding my own business, and somebody knocks on my door. It's the guy down the street. He says he wants to sell me his TV. I told him I had a TV. He goes away, then comes back ten minutes later. Wants to sell me his Blu-ray player. I tell*

*him I got a DVD player and that's just as good. Ten minutes later he comes back again and says, 'Look I gotta get me some dope, gotta get some crank—I'll sell you my girl for $40.'"*

One of dozens. She pulled over and parked in front of Tiffany Crane's trailer. Walked up the broken sidewalk and knocked on the door. She didn't really expect an answer, and she didn't get one. But she had to try. She cupped her hands against the window and peered into the living room. Everything looked the same as it had when she first saw the crime scene: dingy lace curtains, dark gray carpet she suspected had originally been blue, cheap pine end tables, orange plaid sofa. If Tiffany had spent the night in the trailer—if she was inside right now and refusing to come to the door—there was no way for Sarah to tell.

She turned around and studied the empty street, looking at each trailer in turn as if by staring hard enough, she could see inside to discern their secrets. Sarah had always been a deeply intuitive person—a skill she'd honed over the long years spent in foster care. If someone was about to crack you across the cheek or the behind, it helped if you were able to sense it. She'd broken a case more than once by listening to her instincts.

The thing was, *somebody* had killed Lance. Someone he trusted, since there were no signs of forced entry or a struggle. In theory, almost anyone who knew Lance could be responsible for his death. But considering that most violent crimes in the home were committed by a family member, right now, Sarah's instinct was to concentrate on the missing girlfriend. With two arrests and a husband serving hard time, it wasn't difficult to imagine Tiffany ending up on the wrong side of the law. The idea of her deliberately shooting her boyfriend in the forehead at close range was a stretch, but these things happened every day. They might have argued, or the shooting could have been an accident. Right now it was too early to rule anything out. Still, there was the matter of Guy Marsee, dead the same day. It seemed too much of a coincidence for the deaths not to be related, but why would Tiffany gun down her boyfriend's brother?

She considered the unlikely couple. Judging by the photograph Lance carried in his wallet, everything had been coming up wedding bells until Lance lost his job last September. Probably lost his house or condo or wherever he was staying not long after, and that's why he moved in with his girlfriend. Maybe after a few weeks of hanging around the trailer park with no work and nothing to do, he got depressed and started using. Maybe Tiffany got tired of supporting them both while her hard-earned waitressing money went up in smoke, they argued, things went south. Or possibly Lance started using first, and that's why he lost his job. Sarah would know more after she talked to Lance's coworkers. And got the autopsy report. And found his girlfriend.

She flipped her jacket hood over her head as the morning mist turned to rain. Her phone rang. She hurried back to the car and slid into the driver's seat, flipping the phone open as she did so. "Linden."

"Where are you?" It was Lieutenant Oakes.

"I'm just finishing up at the trailer park. Anything on the girlfriend or the BOLO?"

"Not yet."

"Then I'm heading over to the Black Bear Casino. See if I can get a lead on her. After that, I'm going to Stratoco to talk to Lance Marsee's coworkers."

"Go to Stratoco first. Talk to human resources. There's a guy named Hatchett called, says he's got something on your Marsee."

"Got it."

Sarah shut her phone. She brought up the address on the car's GPS and put the Focus into gear. The corporate headquarters of the biggest name in the private aerospace industry was an hour's drive away on the south side of the city. A location that made sense, when you thought about it. A company that built space rockets needed a lot of room. But it was a long way to go to talk to people Lance hadn't worked with in months, which was why Sarah had wanted to track down Tiffany first.

But a lead was a lead, and if her lieutenant wanted her to talk to someone at Stratoco who claimed to have a hot tip, she wouldn't mind going for a drive in the country.

# 12

Sarah drove with her window open whenever the rain let up enough to allow it, alternately savoring the cool ocean breeze and the damp, pine-scented air. One of the things she liked best about living in Seattle was that you were never far from water or a forest. The original Douglas fir and ponderosa pine from the old logging days were long gone, but the secondary forests that had replaced them were still impressive. A lot of people thought Washington State was too wet and dreary for them to ever want to live here. But what did they expect from a temperate rain forest? Sarah couldn't imagine living anyplace that didn't include an abundance of trees. Just one of the many reasons she would never take Jack to see his father in Chicago. Probably the least important one, considering that Greg had left them both when Jack was three and she hadn't seen or heard from him since, but still. That Greg had chosen to live in Chicago was definitely a factor.

People who knew that Sarah was raising her son by herself liked to tell her that one day, Jack would want to get to know his father. And when he did, it would be her responsibility to make it happen. Implying, or sometimes saying outright that if she wanted to be a good mother to her son, she'd have to let them meet. Even Regi dropped a hint from time to time as if it were an eventuality that Sarah would one day have to face. Regi may have been the closest Sarah had to a mother during her teenage years, but that didn't give her the right to get involved. Sarah was Jack's mother. She knew what was best for her son. If Jack wanted to get in touch with his father (or in the unlikely event that his father wanted to reach out to him), Sarah would throw herself in front of a bus before she let it happen. She smiled wryly at the thought. And people thought a mother bear was protective.

The GPS announced she was nearing her destination at last, directing her onto a winding, wooded two-lane that emerged from the trees a half-mile later into an expanse of manicured lawn worthy of a duke's estate. The crown jewel in the middle: a striking, six-story, modern-architecture building with a curved, mirrored blue glass façade and "STRATOCO" strung across the top in extravagant, 20-foot-high letters. As if anyone who managed to find this place wouldn't know what it was.

She parked in one of the visitor slots and went inside to find the human resources manager, Hatchett. While the receptionist rang his office, Sarah wandered the lobby. Photos of company officials posing with NASA scientists and politicians including two U.S. presidents filled a brag wall. A Plexiglas display case featuring a diorama of a future Mars outpost dominated one end of the room: red rocks and gravel dotted with slender silver pods arranged like spokes on a wagon wheel surrounded by tiny space-suited figures. According to the research she'd done late the night before, Stratoco's flights were limited to low earth orbit at present, but their ultimate goal was to develop the technology and the processes that would allow people to live on other planets.

An ambitious, expensive undertaking that, if they pulled it off, would be the first time humans left Earth's orbit since 1972. Other companies were working on similar projects, such as sending a married couple to Mars and back on a 501-day round trip using a unique orbit opportunity that came around once every fifteen years that would allow them to carry a minimal amount of fuel. But Stratoco was miles ahead of their competition—mainly because they'd won the contract after the government decided to outsource the space station resupply missions to the private sector so NASA could focus on more exploratory projects. According to Stratoco's website, each non-manned space flight cost the government a cool $56 million. To Sarah, the whole idea of strapping yourself into a small metal can and leaving Earth's orbit was more than a little insane, despite the popularizing of space travel in recent years through real-time Space-Earth social networking and guitar-playing astronauts. As far as she was concerned, life on Earth presented enough challenges.

"Officer Linden?" A ponytailed man in his late forties dressed in jeans and a blue and white galaxy-swirl T-shirt that read "Respect My Space" crossed the lobby and stuck out his hand. "I'm Peter Hatchett."

"*Detective* Linden," she corrected. "My lieutenant said you have something for me?"

"I do. Thanks for coming down. I know it's a long drive. Terrible what happened to Lance, just terrible."

"How well did you know him?"

"Well enough. But we don't have to discuss this here. We can go to my office."

He led her to a bank of elevators, then down a long hallway lined with framed Hubble telescope photographs. Most people didn't realize that the spectacular images of nebulas and galaxies had been color-enhanced to bring out specific details, he explained as they passed between them. Not unlike what she did as a detective, Sarah thought. Singling out the important details to draw a clear picture while tuning out the rest. The trick was figuring out which was which.

He showed her into a cramped office on the back side of the building and waved her toward the guest chair. She glanced out the window, secretly hoping to see space rockets. Instead, she was treated to a view of the employee parking lot.

"Can I take your coat?"

"I'm fine."

"Water? Coffee?"

"Nothing, thanks."

Hatchett sat down at his desk. He drained his water bottle, then fingered the objects on his desk in turn: stapler, pencil holder, rubber band ball, pen, stapler again. Sarah leaned back and folded her hands in her lap. She saw it happen all the time. Somebody decided to play Good Samaritan and called in a tip, then got all tongue tied when a real live detective actually showed up. In her experience, the best way to deal with the situation was simply to wait. People couldn't stand silence. Eventually they'd break and start talking to fill the vacuum.

Hatchett was no exception. He cleared his throat after several uncomfortable-for-him seconds. "Well then, I suppose we should get started."

"What can you tell me about Lance's employment history?" she prompted. An easy question to establish a baseline for the interview and to get the conversational ball rolling before he could start rearranging his desk again.

Hatchett's shoulders visibly relaxed. "Lance worked for Stratoco for thirteen years. He came to us straight out of MIT. Lance was a brilliant man, truly brilliant. The kind of genius who comes along perhaps once in a decade. I'm not exaggerating. He could have landed anywhere after he finished grad school, so we were delighted when he came to work for us. He started in aerospace engineering, then moved to production supervisor, and finally was working as a build engineer for high temperature composites when he was terminated last September."

So Lance hadn't left the company voluntarily. "Can you tell me why he was let go?"

Hatchett pursed his lips.

"Mr. Hatchett, this is a murder investigation. I need you to be forthcoming with me."

"Murder? I thought— Oh, wow. I didn't know. When I heard that he was found dead in that god-forsaken trailer park, I assumed it was from some other reason. Appendicitis. A heart attack. Whatever people normally die from. The news didn't say anything about him being murdered."

Which was true, all thanks to Oakes. Sarah had noted the omission when she saw the report last night on the eleven o'clock news. A meth fire in a trailer park was practically guaranteed a few minutes of airtime, even on a busy news day. All the more so when someone had been badly hurt. Add a murder at the trailer next door, and the double tragedy would have bumped the story to lead without question. Sarah didn't know how Oakes had managed to keep that particularly salacious detail off the air, but she was glad of it. Interviews were all about information. Giving. Getting. Withholding. Even when the interviewees were volunteers. In this instance, Hatchett's astonishment at the news of Lance's murder seemed sincere.

"So you knew Lance was living at Rainier Valley."

"Of course. He had to keep his address current with us in order to get his checks."

"His checks? I don't understand. Wouldn't his unemployment checks come from the government?"

"I'm not talking about his unemployment. I'm talking

about the severance package he received because of his early termination. You have to understand, Lance worked for Stratoco for a long time. His contract was solid. So when we decided we had to let him go, breaking the contract involved a fairly substantial payout. Eight hundred thousand dollars was the amount we eventually settled on. Half the money was put in trust, and the other half was dispersed in four equal payments over the first four months. A hundred thousand dollars a month."

"A hun—" Sarah had to struggle to keep her expression neutral. "Why was half the settlement put in trust? Why not give him the full payout and be done with it?" Zeroing in on the aberrant detail. Trying to develop the full picture.

Hatchett frowned and looked away.

"Mr. Hatchett—"

"Because Lance had a gambling problem," he said in a rush, as if he was relieved to reveal the true reason for his call at last. Or maybe he was only having second thoughts about the whole Good Samaritan thing and just wanted to get the interview over and done with. "He was also a pathological liar who was caught faking test results. That's the reason he was fired. We believe one of our competitors paid him to falsify his research, though we were never able to prove it. As I'm sure you can imagine, Stratoco didn't want to offer him a severance package at all under the circumstances. But Lance knew too much about our proprietary processes, and he used that against us. The termination agreement stipulated that Lance could never work in the space industry again. But Lance wouldn't sign it without a substantial amount of money in exchange. It was—messy."

Messy and intriguing. "Whose idea was it to put the money in trust?" Coming back again to the one detail that didn't fit. No gambler in his right mind would voluntarily tie up his own cash.

"It was his brother's idea. Guy Marsee hired a lawyer to set up the trust, with himself as beneficiary and executor. Maybe he got Lance to admit he had a gambling problem, I don't know. I certainly hoped so at the time. Lance needed help. The fact that he ended up living in that awful trailer park proves it."

"So you think the trust was set up to protect Lance from himself?"

"I did then, yes."

"And now? Do you still think the trust was set up for Lance's good?"

Hatchett frowned again and shook his head. "Now, I'm not sure. The thing is, over the past three or four weeks I've been getting phone calls from Lance's brother. The last one was just the day before yesterday. Guy wanted to know how much money was in the account. If Lance had accessed it. How *he* could access it. I thought maybe Lance had run through the money he'd been given, and Guy was worried that he was somehow tapping into the balance. I told him that as far as I knew, the account was solid, but that he really should talk to his lawyer, since his lawyer could answer his questions better than I could. Then after I heard that Lance was dead, I remembered Guy asking all those questions, and it just seemed—strange. I'm not making an accusation," he hurried to add, "but four hundred thousand dollars is a lot of money. Especially when you're the beneficiary." He shrugged. "It just seemed like something the police ought to know."

And there it was. The ultimate motive. The root of all evil. Money.

"You did the right thing," Sarah assured him, though Hatchett apparently didn't think so. He looked utterly miserable as he wiped away the invisible specks of dust on his desk, as if he deeply regretted having gotten involved and couldn't wait for Sarah to leave. Contrary to popular opinion, confession wasn't always good for the soul.

She took out her card, laid it on the desk, and pushed it toward him. "Thanks for reaching out. If you think of anything else you feel might be helpful, please don't hesitate to call."

# 13

Sarah left Hatchett drowning his misery in his water bottle and retraced her steps to the lobby. The conversation had been enlightening. Certainly worth the long drive. While Hatchett's fratricide theory was likely off the mark, given that the brothers had both died in the same window of time, the idea that Lance had been a gambler with ready access to hundreds of thousands of dollars opened up a number of investigative possibilities.

Assuming Hatchett was telling the truth. Sarah was always suspicious when someone offered so much information so freely. No one did anything without a motive. Helping the police with their investigation without asking for anything in return was usually fairly far down the list. Talking to Lance's coworkers could verify Hatchett's information. It could also catch him out.

She crossed the lobby and showed her badge to the receptionist. "I'd like to talk to a few of Lance Marsee's coworkers before I leave. The people who were closest to him. Can you tell me who they might be?"

The receptionist looked from the shield, to Sarah, and back to the shield again. Sarah didn't fault her for her reluctance. Anyone who thought a receptionist's job was a simple matter of greeting people and answering the phones didn't appreciate the delicate balance they had to walk between giving visitors like Sarah what they wanted and protecting the interests of the company and its employees. Make the right call in an uncertain or otherwise challenging situation, and you were on track to make Employee of the Month. Make the wrong call, and the next piece of paper somebody put on your desk was likely to be pink. Indispensable *and* expendable.

She offered her most disarming smile and put the badge back in her pocket. "I know everyone's busy. It won't take much time. Just a few questions."

"Okay," the woman said after another long hesitation during which she weighed the pros and cons. "In that case, I suppose Roger would be the best person for you to talk to."

"Roger—?"

"Roger Fairmont. He and Lance were working in the same department last September when Lance was let go. Let me see if he's available."

So the circumstances surrounding Marsee's dismissal were public knowledge. Interesting, though not altogether surprising. Work places were gossip mills. Bad news always traveled faster and farther than good. Sarah made a mental note to interview the receptionist as well.

The young woman spoke briefly into the phone, then hung up and turned to Sarah. "Okay, Roger's on his way down. You can wait for him over there." Indicating a leather seating area on the opposite side of the room.

Sarah shed her jacket and laid it on a chair, then selected another for herself with a view of the elevator and sat down. The table next to her was strewn with glossy magazines she supposed someone in the aerospace industry would consider light reading: *Aerospace Engineering*, *Aviation*

*Week*, *Aerospace America*, *Scientific American*. She left the magazines untouched.

Five minutes later, the elevator doors opened and a slender man with a neat crew-cut emerged. He looked to be in his late twenties or early thirties, and was wearing a dark blue polo shirt emblazoned with the Stratoco logo. He saw Sarah and headed in her direction with his hand outstretched.

She stood to greet him but he waved her back down and sat beside her. "Jennifer tells me you have a few questions about Lance. If you don't mind, we can talk here in the lobby. My office is a little cramped."

A descriptor that Sarah took to mean "messy." Not that it mattered to her where the interview was conducted. All she cared about was that she got her answers.

"How well did you know Lance?" she asked, again starting the interview with a simple baseline question. "I'm trying to get a sense of who he was. His likes and dislikes, his personality."

"Actually, I really didn't know him very well at all, to be honest. We worked in the same department for, I don't know—maybe two years? But Lance was like a lot of the guys who work here. Kind of a loner. Hard to get to know. He'd come in early and stay late. Did his job and went home. We're quite out of the way here, no places to go for a bite or a drink after work. I guess we might have hung out more if there *was* someplace close by. But in my opinion, he was one of those people who preferred to be left alone."

Sarah had noted the lack of restaurants and other amenities in the vicinity. The country setting was lovely, but it wasn't exactly conducive to after work bonding.

"Did Lance have any enemies? Anyone you can think of who might have wanted to hurt him?"

"Enemies? Well, sure. After his research came under scrutiny, we all hated him. You have to understand that to a scientist, falsifying test results is like, the ultimate sin. Everyone in the department was under suspicion until the powers that be decided that Lance had been acting alone. If he hadn't been fired, we might have lynched him ourselves. Figuratively speaking," the young man hastened to add, as if he suddenly remembered that he was talking not to a coworker, but to a cop.

Sarah nodded to show she understood that he hadn't just uttered a death threat. "So people felt threatened by Lance's actions," she said encouragingly.

"We did. Not only did Lance put our jobs at risk, his actions threatened the company's reputation. Worst-case scenario, Stratoco stock would have collapsed, and they'd have let us all go. Imagine trying to get another job in the industry with the stink of scandal on you. Even if you hadn't done anything wrong, everyone would assume you were guilty by association. Believe me, we were all more than happy when Lance was fired and the company dealt with the fallout so discreetly. But really—all of that happened months ago. We're over it. I can't imagine anyone wanting to hurt Lance now. Not after all this time."

The idea that any of the scientists at Stratoco would have killed Lance over the falsified research incident was a stretch. Still, it was one that had to be considered and then, if the consideration warranted further investigation, checked out.

"Let's talk for a minute about those faked test results," she said. "Everyone tells me that Lance was a brilliant scientist. Falsifying his research seems out of character. Why do you think he did it?"

Fairmont shrugged. "Why does anybody do anything? Stupidity? Fear? Greed? If I had to guess, I'd say that Lance's motivation was money. Rumor had it he was being paid off by a competitor, and Lance always needed money."

"Why was that?" Knowing the answer according to

Hatchett, but going for verification.

"Lance was into gambling—big time. I'm not talking slots or lottery tickets. He was hardcore. Blackjack, mostly. People saw him at the Black Bear Casino all the time, and there are plenty of others within driving distance." Fairmont looked rueful. "Most people here enjoy the occasional bet, myself included, but Lance was on another level. Most of the time he seemed to do pretty well. His intellect was so far above average, it can't have been hard for him to count cards, beat the house."

"But he didn't always win."

"No, he didn't. Nobody does."

"And is that where he met Tiffany? At the Black Bear?"

"Who?"

"His girlfriend, Tiffany Crane. The woman he was living with when he was killed. She works there."

"Gosh, if Lance had a girlfriend, he never said anything about her. Maybe he hooked up with her after he left Stratoco? He never dated much that I was aware of, and he was kind of geeky, but some girls go for that now." Fairmont shifted uncomfortably on his chair. "Listen, are we almost done? Jennifer said this would only take a few minutes. I'm in the middle of a pretty important trial."

"Just one more question. I assume Lance had a personal laptop in addition to the computer he used at work. Do you happen to know what kind it was?" It was hard to imagine a techie like Lance living without one, but no laptop or personal computer had been found in Tiffany's trailer. Either he'd pawned it to fund his gambling habit, or someone had taken it.

"Not a laptop. Lance used a tablet, the Surface Pro. Intel Core i5 processor, 4 gigs of RAM, 123 gigabyte hard drive. Lance always loved his tech toys."

"Expensive?"

"Not really. You can pick one up on Amazon for less than a thousand dollars."

A thousand-dollar tablet computer wasn't exactly a bargain at Sarah's pay grade. Aerospace engineers definitely moved in a different world. She made a mental note to check the pawnshops in the vicinity of the trailer park, and let Fairmont get back to work.

The next two interviews were clones of the first. The receptionist—even with her finger on the pulse of office gossip—wasn't able to shed additional light on who might have killed Lance Marsee, or why. Everyone knew that he had been fired, no one had kept in touch with him after he left the company, no one knew he had a girlfriend, though his gambling seemed to be common knowledge. No one but Hatchett seemed to know about Lance's enormous severance package, but Sarah wouldn't have expected otherwise. Any good human resources manager would have kept the knowledge of the payoff to himself. At any rate, she didn't need confirmation from Lance's coworkers; the details regarding the trust's existence and the payout schedule could be verified easily enough by talking to Marsee's lawyer.

She checked her watch. Half past ten. Plenty of time to drive up to the casino before lunch. She headed for the parking lot.

The moment she was outside, she reached inside her jacket pocket and tapped out a cigarette. Her hands trembled as she lit up. The way a few key pieces of information gave direction to an investigation never failed to get her adrenaline pumping. She shuffled these mentally into order. First fact: Lance had been a gambler who'd burned through $400,000 in cash. Second, his brother Guy was the beneficiary of $400,000 more if anything happened to Lance.

Third, only a handful of people—Hatchett, the lawyer, and possibly Tiffany—knew.

She slid into the driver's seat, took out her phone, and called Goddard. The call went to voicemail. She waited for the beeps. "It's Sarah. I'm finished at Stratoco so I'm heading to the Black Bear. Meet me at the station when you're done. I've got something on both our vics you need to know."

She took another drag on her cigarette and put the car into gear. So many possibilities, so much to explore. She had the next hour to mull everything over and select the most likely. For now, one thing seemed certain.

Someone thought $400,000 was worth killing for.

# 14

Goddard locked his fingers behind his neck, leaned back in his chair, rolled his shoulders, and stretched. He checked his watch. A few minutes after ten. It felt more like noon. He and Louis had been stuck in a cramped, windowless room at GenMod Labs for close to two hours. Whoever decided to set up their interview room with nothing but two molded plastic chairs and a Formica-topped table clearly watched too much television. Louis had been forced to perch on the edge of the table all morning just so the interviewees could take a seat.

Goddard would have preferred talking to Guy Marsee's coworkers in their offices. People opened up a lot more freely when they were on their own turf. But without a search warrant or a court order, he supposed he should be glad that GenMod had agreed to arrange for the interviews at all. Even if his aching back and shoulders disagreed.

"How many more?"

Louis consulted their list. "Six."

"Good lord. Let's do one more, and then I need a break."

The worst part about the morning was that for all their efforts, they'd learned next to nothing about their victim. Guy

Marsee had been a misfit and a loner. On those two points, everyone agreed. They all knew *who* he was, which was the reason for the overlong interview list. But nobody knew him well enough to offer insights into his personal life. All they *could* offer was that he sometimes shared a table at the Starbucks across the street with an employee named Rutz.

As to why Marsee had been shot dead in a shipyard, they hadn't a clue. And he *had* died in the shipyard; as Goddard suspected, the man had been killed where he was found. The SPD techs had just confirmed the fact, having located a fresh bullet hole in one of the containers.

"How you holding up?" Goddard asked.

"Fine, sir." Louis shifted on the table, scratched his nose, touched the back of his ear. Three distinct physical tells that he was lying. At least Goddard wasn't the only one who was suffering.

He thought about his conversation last night with Kath. He was sorry now that he hadn't been more enthusiastic about her new art commission. She probably thought his lukewarm reaction was because he was envious, but why should he be? He was doing what he wanted to do, too. No one had put a gun to his head after he finished art school and told him he had to become a cop. But he was worried. It was hard to put a finger on what was wrong with their relationship other than the fact that instead of growing closer over the passing years as everyone said they would, their lives seemed to be drawing farther apart. Other than the children, they had fewer and fewer things in common. As Kath became more and more wrapped up in her painting and the children with each passing day, it was getting harder to think of himself as part of a couple.

His thoughts were interrupted by a knock on the door, and a tall, extremely fat man in his late fifties with a shock of white Einstein hair limped in. He was wearing what

Goddard had come to think of as the GenMod uniform, despite his age: black Converse high tops, blue jeans, and a white lab coat with a row of writing instruments corraled in a pocket protector.

He consulted his list. "Dr. Nelson Rutz?" The man nodded. Goddard stuck out his hand. "I'm Detective John Goddard. This is my associate, Officer Louis. Please, take a seat."

"Is this going to take long?" The plastic chair creaked ominously as Rutz sat down. Goddard held his breath. The man had to weigh at least 350 pounds. And he smelled of cigarettes.

"Only a few minutes." Unless by some miracle Rutz actually had something useful to say, that is. Goddard nodded to Louis. He and Louis had been trading off the lead role all morning in order to relieve the boredom, and so Louis could sharpen his interview skills. This time it was Louis's turn.

"What you do at GenMod?" Louis asked with his pen poised over his notepad.

"I'm a data analyst. Same as Marsee."

"And what exactly does a data analyst do?"

Rutz looked at Louis as if he thought the officer sitting on the table in front of him was the village idiot. Goddard could imagine what he was thinking: *analyze data, of course.*

"*Simply* put," Rutz said pointedly, "a data analyst takes the raw data generated by an experiment or a study and analyzes it, or transforms it into a useable form. Sometimes we suggest conclusions or recommend a course of action, other times we merely present the data in ways that it can be easily understood. Data analysis requires both an eye for detail and the ability to see the big picture. As you might imagine, it's not a skill set that everyone has. It also helps to have a photographic memory, which both Marsee and I possess."

"How long did you work with Marsee?"

"Since I started at GenMod. Seven years."

"So you and he were friends?"

"I suppose he would have said so."

"But you wouldn't."

Rutz frowned, then dragged both of his hands through his hair and massaged his scalp. If the gesture was habitual, it certainly explained the Einstein doppelgänger look. Especially after Rutz made no attempt to smooth his hair back down.

"Listen, I know Guy is dead," he said. "I'd prefer not to say anything bad about him. But you have to understand. Nobody was friends with Guy. You couldn't be. Guy had the social skills of an amoeba. The sum total of our 'friendship' consisted of sharing a cup of coffee when we happened to run into each other at the Starbucks across the street."

"So you never got together outside of work? Maybe went out for drinks? Hung out at his apartment?"

"Of course not. I told you we weren't friends. I don't even know where he lives." Rutz shot Louis a disgusted look and pushed back from the table. "Are we finished here? I really need to get back to my work." Directing the question not to Louis, but to Goddard.

Louis glanced at the detective. Goddard nodded. Louis stood up and held out his card. "Thanks for coming in, Dr. Rutz. If you think of anything else—"

He broke off. Rutz was gone.

The Starbucks in the strip mall across the street was probably the last place in the city that Goddard would have chosen to get a cup of coffee. Unlike ninety-nine percent of the nation's population under the age of sixty, Goddard didn't like Starbucks. He didn't care that the chain that had essentially created the specialty coffee shop movement had gotten its start right here in Seattle. Or that the Starbucks brand had become so entrenched in people's minds and habits that millions wouldn't think of going anywhere else whenever they hankered for a cup. He just didn't understand the allure. Sure, the coffee was drinkable, but you could get a decent cup of coffee at a lot of other places. The prices were ridiculous, and the drink names irritated him. Caffè Marocchino. Caffè Americano. Frappuccino. If he wanted to learn a foreign language, he'd pick something easier, like Latin or Urdu or ancient Greek. He could never remember if a large was a "grande," a "venti," or a "trenta." More to the point, why should he have to? But if this was where Marsee had gone for coffee, Goddard could put up with the hassle long enough to check it out.

The waitress behind the counter—correction: the "barista" behind the counter—looked about as old as Goddard's teenage daughter. Arianna would probably enjoy working in a place like this, though God forbid she should ever turn up for work in a short skirt and pink tights, with tattoos up and down her arms, and Pippi Longstocking hair. Louis seemed to like the barista, though. Goddard could tell from the way he flashed his badge (as if the uniform wasn't clue enough) and leaned in closer than he needed to as he handed the picture they'd copied off Marsee's GenMod photo I.D. across the counter. He wondered if Louis was married. Probably not. He wasn't wearing a ring, but a lot of cops didn't. He thought about advising him not to. But he didn't want to be That Guy; the one who, simply because he had a few more years on the planet, went around telling everyone else what to do. Anyway, some things, you had to find out for yourself.

"Yeah, he comes in here all the time," the barista said in answer to Louis's question. "He always sits over there." Leaning farther over the counter than necessary as she pointed out Marsee's favorite table so Louis could see straight down her shirt.

Louis had the grace to blush. He averted his eyes. "Do you ever talk to him?" he asked. "I mean, other than taking his order?"

"Sometimes. We get a lot of regulars. I try to talk to all of them a little. Chat them up. It's good for tips, you know? Guy is different, though. He's like those Aspies. He won't look at me when he orders, and he always wants the same thing. The only reason I *know* his name is because we need it for the order. Otherwise I don't think he'd have ever told me."

*Asperger's syndrome.* Brilliant intellect, socially inept. If the barista was right in her armchair diagnosis, it would certainly explain what Goddard had observed in Marsee's apartment: every object precisely what was needed for the purpose for which it was intended, everything in its place, no messy, human detritus in evidence. Funny that no one he'd talked to at GenMod had thought to mention a similar suspicion. He supposed they were so afraid of crossing the boundary of political correctness and ending up in lawsuit territory, they figured it was best just to keep their mouths shut.

"Does anyone ever join him?" he asked. "Does he have any friends?"

"Sometimes this big guy with crazy white hair sits down with him. But I don't think they're friends. They both wear those GenMod coats. I figure they just work together."

"Can you tell us anything else?" Louis asked.

"Like what?"

"Oh, I don't know... Does Guy seem different lately? Happy? Depressed?" Not the line of inquiry Goddard would have pursued, but at least Louis remembered to keep his questions in the present tense.

"You know, now that you mention it, there was something odd. Last week, Guy was sitting at his table looking out the window like he always does, only this time, he was smiling. I thought maybe he saw somebody he knew outside, but no one was there. I watched him for a while, and he just kept smiling, but he wasn't smiling *at* anything, you know? Like he had a secret. Like when you've bought a present for somebody, and you know they're going to totally freak when they open it because it's the absolute perfect present for them? Like that. I remember thinking I was glad he had something that made him happy." She shrugged. "I know that doesn't seem like much, but Guy hardly ever smiled. For him, that was a big deal."

The shop door jangled. A blast of cold air swept the room as a group of GenMod employees piled in and queued up behind them, laughing and chattering.

"Listen, are you gonna order something?" The barista pointed to the lineup. "I don't want to get in trouble with my manager."

"Just coffee." Goddard left Louis to work out the details of his order and made a beeline for Marsee's favorite table before the lunch crowd took over. He sat down in the chair facing the window and tried to imagine himself as Guy Marsee: *I have Asperger's and I'm thinking about something that makes me happy.* It wasn't much, all right, but it was more than they'd gotten all morning at GenMod. Which said more about the waste of time the morning had been than that they'd finally gotten a lead. What was the saying? Cop work was one percent inspiration and ninety-nine percent perspiration? Or was that what Thomas Edison said about genius? No matter, if the saying fit.

He knew only too well that the one percent counted. No amount of perspiration seemed to shift his less-than-stellar solve rate. It was hard not to feel as though the Universe were conspiring against him. Not every murder could be solved in the public's understanding of the word. From a departmental standpoint, a case was considered cleared as long as someone at some point got locked up, whether for a week or a lifetime. It didn't matter if the charges were dropped at arraignment, or if the grand jury didn't indict, or if the prosecutor dismissed the case; as long as someone was charged, the murder was listed on the detective's record as solved. But Goddard's three most recent cases didn't even have that. He hoped the techs were getting somewhere with Guy Marsee's computer. He needed a break.

Louis joined him at last carrying two steaming cups. "You didn't say what you wanted, so I got you a Cinnamon Dolce Latte with extra cream and sugar. Hope that's okay. You look like a guy who has a sweet tooth."

*Ouch.* Goddard winced inwardly and sucked in his gut. He reached into his pocket and took out his phone, ostensibly to check his messages, but in reality to avoid the sugar bomb Louis had chosen for him. He listened to Sarah's voicemail and grinned. Maybe this was the break he needed.

"Linden's got something on our vic," he said, and stood up. "She wants us to meet her at the station. Grab your cup, and let's go."

Goddard left his on the table.

# 15

The moment she drove off the ferry and followed the sign to the Black Bear Casino, Sarah was acutely aware that she was now on Indian land. The Kulamish tribe operated several casinos on the islands in Puget Sound, although Sarah had never visited one. She'd heard other officers talk about boys' nights out at the Lucky Feather, the Wapi Eagle, the Silver Hawk, but gambling had never appealed to her.

The tribe welcomed outsiders—as long as they came to spend money. The rise of Indian gaming casinos had turned the tables on the status quo. The minuscule pockets of land the Indians had been shunted onto—"Native Americans," if you wanted to be politically correct, which not even the native peoples Sarah knew worried about overmuch in their everyday conversation—had become goldmines after the 1988 Indian Gaming Regulatory Act granted them the right to operate casinos on reservation lands. White men may have commandeered the country's natural resources, but now, in ever-increasing numbers, they were happily giving it back in the form of hard cash.

Mist from the Sound rolled through the trees as she drove down a graveled road to the casino, amplifying the crunch of her car tires and permeating the air with a chill that went straight to her bones. Even with the heat on high, Sarah shivered.

The mist gradually lifted and the casino building came into view—a massive modern structure in faux-log cabin style, surrounded by an expansive parking lot. This early in the morning, the lot was half empty. Sarah parked the car, flipped her jacket hood over her head against the rain, and crossed the lot to enter the casino through the large double glass doors. She took the stairs instead of the escalator to the upper level and paused to get her bearings.

It was almost noon, and the casino action was light. A few dozen diehards sat mesmerized in front of slot machines, but most of the chairs were empty. The machines' flashing lights, electronic music, and recorded voices enticing gamblers to play a show without an audience. No doubt the majority of the clientele from the night before were sleeping it off in their hotel rooms. A blackjack table in the middle of the room—the same table where Lance had been a regular if Roger Fairmont's information was correct—was also empty.

"Can I help you?" A Native American man in a charcoal suit, barrel-chested, with meaty hands and close-cropped hair, stepped into Sarah's path—subtly and effectively stopping her from moving further into the casino. She didn't need to read his job title on his nametag to know he was a security guard. Given the quality of his suit, probably high up in the ranks. Sarah supposed that to her Kulamish counterpart, the fact that she was law enforcement was just as obvious.

She smiled warmly and extended her hand. "I'm Detective Sarah Linden. Seattle Police Department. I'm investigating a homicide. I'd like to speak with one of your employees." She had decided on the drive over not to let the casino know that she was aware of Tiffany's ex-employee status. It would be enlightening to see how they spun it. She pulled her badge, knowing it had no power on this side of the water, but hoping that a mutual respect for the law by those who were charged with upholding it would yield results.

The man didn't respond. He also didn't take Sarah's hand, keeping his hands pointedly by his sides.

"I understand that Tiffany Crane works here as a waitress," Sarah went on in the same pleasant tone, as if they were having a normal conversation rather than what was beginning to feel like the start of a confrontation. "Yesterday, her boyfriend was found murdered. We're trying to locate her."

"You think she did it?"

"We just want to talk to her."

"This is Indian land. You don't have authority here."

"I'm aware of that... Mr. Franks." Sarah read the man's name off the gold plastic tag pinned over his jacket pocket. "I was hoping for your cooperation."

Sarah could have argued that Tiffany wasn't a member of the Kulamish tribe, and therefore didn't need the tribe's protection—she wasn't even Native American, for that matter—but she doubted it would make any difference. Either the man would say yes, or he would say no—even though there was no valid reason to refuse Sarah's request other than sheer contrariness.

To Sarah's surprise, however, the man seemed to relent. He nodded curtly and spoke into a walkie-talkie, then led Sarah through the casino's cavernous main room and down a narrow hallway. He stopped in front of a door that read, "Megan Crowd, Casino Manager."

"Come," a voice said in answer to the security guard's knock. The guard opened the door and stepped to the side so that Sarah was forced to enter first, then stepped into the small room behind her and closed the door. Boxing her in.

Sarah felt the hairs on the back of her neck prickle. There was no reason to believe that she was going to come to any harm. So why had her instincts skyrocketed to high alert?

Behind her desk, Ms. Crowd was all business, wearing a white, open-collared shirt under a dark leather jacket, with her black hair cropped short. The only concessions to her gender were a dash of lipstick, and an ornate pair of turquoise earrings.

She stood up and extended her hand. "Megan Crowd. And you are?"

"Detective Sarah Linden. Seattle Police." Going through the motions even though she had clearly heard the guard relate both Sarah's name, and her purpose via the walkie-talkie.

"You've already met my head of security, Charles Franks," the manager went on. "Please. Sit down. What can I do for you, Detective?"

"I understand that Tiffany Crane works here as a waitress," Sarah began as she sat down in the extra chair. "I'd like to talk to her."

"*Worked* here," Ms. Crowd corrected. "We had to let her go about a month ago."

So Tiffany had been fired. "May I ask why?"

"You may. However, I'm sure you'll understand that I'm not at liberty to reveal the details. What I can tell you is that coupled with a previous incident, her latest infraction made her continued employment with us out of the question."

"You're referring to the incident with the Cartier watch," Sarah said. "I've read the report. Frankly, I'm surprised you kept her on at the time."

"Tiffany was one of our more popular waitresses. The men in particular liked her. Besides, everyone deserves a second chance. Just not a third or a fourth."

Sarah could understand why the men who visited the casino would have been attracted to Tiffany, with her blond hair, elfin frame, and her tough-yet-vulnerable punk rocker look. Some would see hooking up with her as a walk on the wild side. Others would be drawn to her because they saw in her their wayward daughters. Affirmative action in reverse.

"So you're saying the incident with the watch's owner, Desmond Whittaker, wasn't an isolated case?" Sarah asked. "That Tiffany made a habit of getting in tight with the high-rollers?" Thinking of Lance and his hundreds of thousands. Their Odd Couple pairing wasn't looking so peculiar after all.

"I'm not saying anything of the sort."

Of course she wasn't. And yet she was. Sarah understood the game the manager was playing, dropping pieces of information into the conversation without admitting that's what she was doing. It wasn't hard to imagine the scenario: Tiffany taking note of the gamblers who seemed to be particularly lonely, targeting them, flattering them, getting close to them in the hope that some of the cash they were throwing around so carelessly would fall in her direction. Sarah couldn't fault her. Taking advantage of lonely men for financial gain wasn't a crime. Tiffany was only doing what she thought she had to in order to survive. In Tiffany's place, Sarah might well have done the same.

"What about friends? Is there someone Tiffany was close to who I can talk to?"

"No one," Ms. Crowd said.

Sarah seriously doubted that was true. If Tiffany had been as popular as the woman claimed, surely she would have had at least one girlfriend in whom she confided. But Sarah let it go. If the manager had decided to stonewall her, there was nothing she could do to compel her to talk. Besides, there were other ways of getting the answers she wanted that were far easier than sitting in this woman's office like a puppy begging for table scraps.

Sarah stood up. "Thanks for your time," she said

pleasantly, as Ms. Crowd and her security chief took the cue and got to their feet as well. "You've been very helpful."

A statement all three of them knew wasn't true.

As she was escorted back to the gaming floor, Franks at her elbow, Sarah heard the click of a phone receiver being lifted. After a moment the manager spoke.

"Chief Jackson please… yes, I'll hold."

She wasn't going to get anything else out of the Kulamish tribe. But not everyone who worked at the casino was Indian, Tiffany was proof of that. She turned to Franks.

"Where's the nearest restroom?"

The big man nodded in the direction of a large neon sign with a picture of a squaw, her feathered skirt picked out in bright yellow. Sarah smiled her thanks, and left him standing in the middle of the gaming floor, hands clasped in the usual "security" stance. Once inside the restroom she counted off three minutes, then looked out. Franks was back at his post by the entrance. She glanced round the floor, until she spotted a waitress collecting discarded glasses and paper mugs, her light brown hair swept up into a ponytail. Sarah walked over to her.

"Excuse me ma'am, I'm Detective Sarah Linden. I'd like to ask you a couple of questions about Tiffany Crane."

The waitress looked up from her tray, startled. "What about her?"

Sarah tried to smile placatingly. "Were you two friendly?"

The woman shook her head. "I'd only been working here a couple of weeks when she got sacked. I never really spoke to her." She lowered her voice, looking past Sarah as if worried that she was being watched. Sarah resisted the urge to turn her head, to check whether Franks was coming over. She'd better make this quick.

"Do you know who she *was* friendly with?"

The waitress shrugged her shoulders. "I saw her hanging

out with Jaycee a few times, like they had plans after work, getting changed together, that kind of thing. But Jaycee's not on today."

No matter. "And do you know Jaycee's last name?"

"Timberwolf. Jaycee Timberwolf."

# 16

According to her employment records, Black Bear Casino employee Jaycee Timberwolf was a twenty-six-year-old Native American, unmarried, and currently living with her mother and two sisters. The Timberwolf home was in the right-hand side of a wood-frame duplex in one of the older, established neighborhoods in Seattle. Sarah sat in her car, scanning the street. Compact houses set back from the sidewalk. Maples in the front yards grown so large they dwarfed the houses they had been planted to shelter; there would be dense green foliage in the spring and summer that turned every shade of red, orange, and yellow in the fall; now bare winter branches reached toward a gunmetal sky like blackened fingers.

Sarah locked the car and walked between a border of empty flowerbeds and up the wooden steps to the front porch. As near as she'd been able to determine by comparing Jaycee's and Tiffany's Facebook postings with their IRS filings, it appeared that the women had worked together at the Black Bear Casino for just under two years. And they weren't just Facebook friends; judging by the many photographs both women had posted in which they appeared together, they had clearly socialized in the real world.

The thump of a heavy bass beat could be heard from within the house. Sarah knocked on the front door. The thumping stopped. A few moments later, Jaycee herself came to the door wearing a fringed pink T-shirt that stopped six inches above her low-rise jeans, revealing a butterfly tattoo on her stomach identical to the one Sarah remembered Tiffany sporting in the photograph of her and Lance. The women were clearly close to have gotten matching artwork.

Sarah flashed her badge and stated her business, taking care to keep her voice low and gentle. No need to spook the girl. Would Jaycee mind answering a few questions about her friend? Jaycee nodded. "I'll be right back!" she called over her shoulder, then stepped coatless onto the front porch and closed the door behind her.

"Would you like to talk in my car?" Sarah asked as Jaycee rubbed her bare arms and shivered. It wasn't snowing, but it felt like it should be.

"Sure." Jaycee trailed Sarah down the sidewalk and slid into the front passenger seat. Sarah got in the driver's side. She turned the engine on and the heater to "high," then as the car interior grew warm again, she unbuttoned her coat.

"Got a smoke?" Jaycee nodded toward the overflowing ashtray.

Sarah reached into her jacket pocket, held out the pack to Jaycee, and took another for herself. "What can you tell me about Tiffany and her boyfriend?"

Jaycee took a drag, blew it out. "Oh, man—I swear, if he told her to jump off a cliff, she'd do it. She'd do anything he asked her to. I told her he was bad news, that he was going to bring her down, get her in trouble again. Looks like I was right." She waved her hand to take in the fact that she was sitting outside her house in a cop car answering questions about her friend.

"What sort of trouble did you think she'd get into?"

"Same as before. With the fancy watch she got given by the old guy from the casino. Whittaker I think he was called. Only that wrinkly lying bastard really did give her that watch. Tiffany wasn't a thief."

"Did he give her other things?"

"Like what?"

"I don't know. Jewelry. Money. Clothes."

"Well, sure. That was the point. He took her to his country house, too. Man, that place was *rich*! A mansion on the other side of Magnolia Bridge with all kinds of fancy things in it. She took a bunch of us out there for weekend parties even after he threw her over. An 'up yours' for the watch charge. Whittaker wasn't smart enough to take the spare key off her, and word is he's been out of the country for a while." Sarah made a mental note to check on Mr. Whittaker's whereabouts.

Jaycee shook her head. "He gave her some nice things, while it lasted. But she never kept any of them. That was part of the deal. She always turned everything over to her real boyfriend."

"I'm not sure I understand. The watch's owner—Desmond Whittaker—wasn't her boyfriend?"

Jaycee laughed. "That old dude? Please. He was like, seventy. Tiffany let him think she was in love, but she was just using him. You know, to get stuff. He was just a dupe in a line of dupes. He was nothing."

"Does this 'real' boyfriend have a name?" Sarah asked.

Jaycee laughed again. "Only a dumb one. He called himself 'Archimedes'. Like he was a genius or something. Never knew his real name. The guy was basically a crook. I didn't care to know."

She cracked open her window, stuck her cigarette outside the gap, and tapped off the ash. "'Medes always gave her a percentage. For her help, you know. Because he couldn't have done it without her." Looking at Sarah and raising her eyebrows to say that she too should be compensated for her assistance.

Sarah pulled a twenty from her wallet and gave it to the girl. She probably could have gotten away with a ten, but she wasn't yet ready to end the conversation.

"So let me get this straight," she said. "Tiffany's boyfriend 'Archimedes' paid her a share of the take she got from coming on to high rollers like Whittaker at the casino."

"It's not illegal, you know. And the casino knew what she was doing. It happens a lot. The casino doesn't care, as long as the gamblers are happy. It's not, like, prostitution, you know," she hastened to add. "Most of the time, sex isn't part of the deal. But yeah, that's what a lot of the girls do. And Tiffany's good at it. All the men liked her because she was different." She made her point by flipping her long, black hair over her shoulder.

"Including Lance Marsee? The man who lives with Tiffany in her trailer." Was this "Archimedes" actually Marsee? Had he been hanging out at the casino to keep an eye on his girl working the clientele?

Jaycee laughed. "You bet he did. He was the mark after Whittaker. Tiffany let him get close, let him buy her things, the usual. He came to a couple of the parties at the country house. Then the cash ran out." Jaycee's expression suddenly became serious. "We all thought she'd cut him loose. But she didn't. Hell, she let him move in with her. Like she wasn't playing the game anymore, like she'd really fallen for him. We told her it was a dumb thing to do. The guy's lost all his money gambling, and sold everything else, so what's the point in letting him stay? All he does is lie around all day and eat her food. And then she got fired because of it. Even the casino people don't want their girls going that far. I sure wouldn't have traded everything I had for him."

"I presume the 'real' boyfriend, Archimedes, didn't like that Tiffany brought Lance home to live with her."

"'Medes was pissed. She wasn't supposed to fall for a mark, you know. To be honest, I don't know exactly what the setup was with Lance. I know *he* thought she was his girlfriend... But after Lance moved in, Tiff didn't talk about 'Medes anymore. And it wasn't like she'd moved on, didn't care about him. More that she was afraid of him. Afraid of what he might do."

"Afraid of what he might do to her?"

"Her, him, both of them. That dude is *not* the kind of person you want to mess with." She shrugged, rolled down the window, and tossed the cigarette onto the frozen grass. Casually, as if dangerous boyfriends were a fact of life.

Jaycee opened the car door and swung a leg out, but Sarah placed a restraining hand on the woman's arm. "One last question," she said. "Do you know where Tiffany might be now? It's important that we find her."

"I don't have a clue. After she got fired, we really didn't talk much anymore." Her voice trailed off, and she blushed.

Sarah could fill in the rest. Jaycee was ashamed because she didn't stay in touch, didn't want to risk her own job by continuing to hang out with Tiffany after the casino let her go. There were friends, Sarah reflected as she watched the girl squirm, and then there were *friends*.

"Okay, thanks," Sarah said. "You've been a big help. If you think of anything else, give me a call." She handed the woman her card.

Jaycee took it, clearly relieved that Sarah hadn't pressed further. She shoved the card in her jeans pocket and ran back inside the house.

## 17

Holder turned off the water and stepped out of the shower. His eyes stung as he groped blindly for a towel. It was almost noon. He was just now dragging himself out of bed after a late night with the Trailer Park Tweakers, but that was okay. The crowd he was hanging with wouldn't recognize a sunrise if he painted them a picture of one and hung it on their wall.

He toweled off his face and chest and roughed up his hair. Slicked in just the right amount of gel to make it look like he didn't use any. Wrapped the towel around his waist and leaned over the sink to brush his teeth. Just because he was pretending to be a homeless guy living out of his car didn't mean he had to smell like one. Besides, homeless people had resources. A person could take a shower at shelter, or at a park that had a beach with changing rooms, or at a gym. The idea of a homeless person having a gym membership probably sounded ridiculous to some people, but not everyone was on the streets because they didn't have any money. For twenty bucks a month, you could get a gym membership with a locker where you could store your valuables, plus you got to work out, keep in shape. Only the loonies living in boxes didn't take a shower. But they could have if they wanted to.

He walked barefoot into his apartment's small kitchen and sat down at the table. The first aid supplies were still laid out from the night before. He unwound the wet gauze from around his hand and examined his palm. The skin was intact, so that was good, though it was white and wrinkly from the shower. Tender as hell and gonna hurt even worse when the dead skin peeled away, but Holder didn't regret what he'd done for a second. Imagine what would've happened to Campbell's little man if he hadn't come along.

Neil Campbell. Dude was in a bad way, for sure. All Holder had to do was flex his right hand to understand why they were keeping him under. Full body burns were no joke. Campbell was going to have a bad time of it from here on out, but he hoped for the little guy's sake that he made it. Wasn't his fault his pops was a cooker. And a loser pops was still better than no pops at all. Especially when your moms was completely out of the picture. Holder remembered asking Campbell about it; you had to get close to your potential informers, find their push buttons. According to Campbell, he'd got custody after the mother left. At least she'd stuck around long enough to sign the boy over. Done it properly. Some moms dropped their kids at school and never came back. Still, she could have found a nicer guy to have a kid with. Campbell wasn't a nice guy, except to his kid.

He flexed his hand again and pulled out a strip of gauze. Anchored one end with his elbow on the table and started wrapping. Held the gauze taut with his teeth while he cut off a piece of tape and wrapped the tape around his hand. The burn was going to leave a fair-sized scar, but it wouldn't be the only identifying mark on Holder's body. Some his dad had given him when he was a kid. Some he'd earned on the job. Some he'd added by choice: the word "SERENITY" tattooed across his chest in large Gothic letters, and the cross on the back of his neck. If Holder ever ended up on a slab in the morgue, the M.E. wouldn't need fingerprints to put a name to his body.

He left the first aid supplies on the table and went into his bedroom to get dressed. Jeans and a T-shirt, topped off with two thick hoodies. His trademark look. Part style, partly because of the weather. Holder could have added body armor beneath the layers since it was winter and nobody would have noticed, but he preferred to work clean. It wasn't that he was reckless, or that he enjoyed living on the edge. It was just that you could play your role better if you were authentic all the way down to your skivvies. No badge, no vest, no gun. Just your own quick wits and a devotion to the greater good.

He went back to the kitchen. Drowned a bowl of high-fiber cereal with skim milk and opened his laptop. Logged onto the King County Sheriff Department website and scanned yesterday's activity. Undercover didn't mean out of touch. It was important to keep up with what was going on. Maybe somebody he was getting close to got arrested. Maybe somebody he needed to steer clear of got out.

His phone rang. Not the burner he carried with him when he was hanging with the tweakers, but the cop phone he left at his apartment. He picked it up. "Holder."

"Gil here." Gil Sloane, Holder's contact officer and supervisor at County, a twenty-year narco with a shaved head and a scrappy fighter's build who rarely smiled. A no-nonsense cop who didn't pull punches, the kind of cop who always had your back. The kind that Holder aspired to be.

"Heard you saw some action yesterday."

"Yeah. Cooker set hisself on fire. My snitch. At least I hoped he was going to be."

"Heard you saved his kid."

"I did, for reals."

"I wish you hadn't. I'm not saying you should have let

him turn to toast, but you should have let somebody else take care of it. You could have blown your cover."

"I hear you."

"You'd better. You check the BOLOs?"

"I'm lookin' at 'em now."

"One's in your area. SPD asked us to keep an eye out."

Holder picked up on the subtext. *Lame-ass SPD making us do their job again.* The tension between the two departments wasn't territorial. More a matter of too few cops with too much to do.

"I'll check it out."

He hung up and scrolled through the reports until he found the one for Rainier Valley. He had a good idea of what it was he was going to find, and his hunch was correct: the cops were looking for Tiffany in connection with her boyfriend's murder. He memorized the details, even though he knew most of them already, and shut down his laptop. Maybe he'd go on a scavenger hunt this afternoon. He didn't have anything better to do, and he had a couple ideas where she might be. Wouldn't hurt to get in good with the SPD. You never knew. He might decide to give homicide a try one day.

"Yo, fools. Wassup?" Holder shut the door of his dark blue late-model sedan with his foot and swaggered over to where Logic and Company were clustered beneath an overpass, stomping their feet and clapping their arms with their hands to stay warm. It couldn't have been more than 40 degrees outside. Holder had heard the weather dudes predicting snow. The gang had a fire going in a barrel. Somebody had painted the symbol for radioactive waste on the side as a joke. At least, Holder hoped it was hand-painted.

"Logic's moms throw y'all out?" he drawled as he sauntered

up and held his hands over the barrel. "I don' blame her. Bunch o' skanky assed tweakers wearin' out the furniture."

"His mom's on one of her things." Ridgeback sniffed and wiped the snot from his nose with the back of his hand. "Cops come 'round yesterday, freaked her out. Logic told her they wasn't lookin' for dope, or you know where he'd be by now, but you know how she is."

Holder did indeed know how Jackie was. He'd already gone by the trailer. "If the cops were there yesterday, how come she's still swingin' her tomahawk today?"

"She says they came back again last night," Logic said. "She saw 'em 'cross the street, sittin' an' watchin' the house. She thinks they's some big bust goin' down. Made me take all my stuff and clear out."

"So what—you gonna make this your new permanent address?" Holder swept his arm to take in the piles of trash blown against a chain link fence, the crumbling bridge supports, the cement pillars covered with graffiti. "Oh yeah. Put a couch over there, set up your TV in front of it, table 'n chairs over here, hang a picture an' call it home. Y'already gots the fridge."

Ridgeback snorted.

Logic glared. "Yo, fool—you think livin' in your wheels is better?"

"Least they take me where I wanna go. An' my wheels is warm. Move over, big guy." Holder nudged Ridgeback to the side so he could move in closer to the barrel. "My balls is 'bout to fall off."

"Better'n bein' dead. Cops found Tiff's new man with a bullet in his head." Logic pointed his index finger like a gun and held it against Holder's forehead and grinned.

"For reals? Man, that's cold. Does Tiff know?" Play it safe by playing dumb. But how did Logic know that Lance had been shot in the forehead? Holder had only found that out when he read the BOLO report. Was it a wild guess? Or something more?

Logic shrugged. "Don't know, don't care."

"Logic, baby!" a woman's voice called out. "There you are!"

Holder followed the sound to the top of the hillside. Two figures were working their way down the embankment, wearing long, puffy down coats with their hats pulled low and scarfs wound around their necks. It took him a few seconds to realize who they were. Claire and Tiffany, half froze and looking like they'd been walking the streets all night looking for dope, or sex, or both. He almost laughed out loud. Police runnin' all over the city looking to find Ms. Tiff, an' she comes strolling up to him.

Claire sidled up to Logic and slid her arm through his, giving him her most innocent, wide-faced smile. Claire was pretty. Dark hair, dark eyes, mostly clear skin. She hadn't been using that long. Give her a few years, and she'd be as skanky as any tweaker with her cheeks eaten away and her teeth rotted. If she made it that far.

"Hey, baby." She leaned her head on his shoulder. "Heard you got some stuff." Her eyes were unfocused, hungry.

"Depends on what you got." Logic pinched her bottom.

She squealed and slapped his hand away. Rubbed her rear. Moved back in.

"Whatever you want, baby. You know I'm yours."

"How 'bout a smoke?" Tiffany asked Holder. Beneath her hood, her nose was red and her lips were blue. There was a cut over her left eyebrow that hadn't been there the last time Holder had seen her.

He gave her the cigarette he kept behind his ear and held out his lighter. She cupped her hand over his and bent down to shield the flame. Her hands were shaking, the backs raw from scratching. Must not've scored in a while.

She took a drag, straightened, let it out. Closed her eyes as the nicotine flooded her system and moved in closer to the burn barrel. Relaxed. Easy. Like all was right with the world. Like there was no place on Earth she'd rather be.

"Yo, Tiff." Ridgeback looked down sadly from his great gorilla height and reached over and patted her hand. "Sorry 'bout what happened yesterday."

"Sorry 'bout what, big guy?" She looked up at him and batted her eyes. Hoping to score.

"I gotta take a piss," Holder said abruptly. He hurried away from the group and ducked behind a pillar. Made like he was doing what he had to do while he listened and waited for what he knew was coming next. When Tiffany began screaming, he pulled out his phone.

# 18

"So that's Tiffany Crane."

Sarah stood outside the one-way glass with Lieutenant Oakes and studied the woman in the interview room. Tiffany was small; she looked like a little girl, hunched in one of the metal chairs with her arms wrapped around her stomach, alternately crying and rocking and moaning. Her jeans were muddy, and the dirty red sweater hanging off the ends of her fingers was so stretched out and baggy it looked like she'd been wearing it since Christmas.

Her grief over Lance Marsee's death seemed real, despite Jaycee's claim that Tiffany had only befriended Marsee for his money. Perhaps that was how their relationship started. But the fact that Tiffany had let Lance move in after he'd gambled away all his money seemed to indicate that her feelings for him had gone beyond avarice. Sarah hoped Tiffany would be able to pull it together enough to answer her questions. She couldn't wait to get started. Whether Tiffany was a gold-digging cocktail waitress or had been genuinely in love with the dead man, no one knew more about Lance's problems than she did. Surely she could throw a light on his murder, whether she'd witnessed it or not.

"How long has she been like that?" Sarah asked.

"Since they picked her up," Oakes said. "Maybe half an hour. Somebody called in her location. Probably an undercover. Guy knew about the BOLO."

"One of ours?"

"Does it matter?"

"I guess not," Sarah said, though she would have liked to have had the chance to interview the person who called in the tip. Odds were good he could have told her details that Tiffany herself didn't realize were important. Or that she wasn't willing to offer.

"Has she said anything?"

"Not yet. But don't get too excited." Oakes held out his hand. "She had this."

Sarah's euphoria vanished when she saw the small plastic packet filled with white powder. It figured. Just as her investigation was coming together, she found out her main witness was a meth head.

"Let her sit," she said in disgust. "I'll be in my office."

Goddard was waiting in the extra chair. He pointed to the clock over the door as the hands clicked to 12:46. "What took you so long?"

"Traffic." She peeled off her jacket and hung it over the back of her chair. "Where's your sidekick?"

"Oakes rotated him to patrol." He nodded to the medical examiner's reports on Sarah's desk. "You seen these?"

"Not yet. Give me the Cliff Notes version."

"Your Marsee was killed by a single gunshot to the forehead. Negative results for cocaine and heroin, and a blood alcohol level consistent with a guy who'd had a couple of beers. My guy was clean. M.E. ruled the cause of death was a gunshot to the back of the head."

No surprises there. "Times of death?"

"Fuzzy. Your Marsee's body temperature was skewed because of the open door. Mine because the body was outside for hours in a cold rain. Best she can do is narrow both down to plus-or-minus five hours."

"So we can't prove my guy died first." Another disappointment.

"No. But why would we want to?"

"I spent the morning talking to the human resources manager at Stratoco. Turns out, Lance Marsee was fired four months ago after he was caught faking test results. He was also a chronic gambler—he met Tiffany when she worked at Black Bear. But here's the kicker. Stratoco gave Lance a huge severance package when they fired him. We're talking hundreds of thousands of dollars."

"Hold on. The guy gets fired, and they give him a bonus? That doesn't make sense."

"It does if it's a payoff. Think about it. Stratoco knows their research is flawed, but they don't want the news to get out. Maybe they're using the data anyway; maybe they're worried about the damage a scandal would do to their reputation. Either way, the solution is the same: get rid of my guy and pay him to keep quiet."

"Okay, I'm buying it."

"Good, because it gets better. My contact told me the severance package was split in half. Four hundred thousand went into a trust fund, and the rest was dispersed in monthly installments, one hundred thousand dollars a month for the first four months. Guess who was the executor of the trust. *And* the beneficiary."

Goddard whistled. "My Marsee? You're kidding."

"I'm not."

"So if the medical examiner ruled that your guy died first," Goddard said slowly as he worked out the ramifications, "my guy could have killed your guy. He certainly would have had opportunity and motive. But if my guy died first, obviously not. So okay. The autopsies aren't going to help us. What about prints?"

"Ray's working on it. But our victims were brothers. Your vic's prints could be all over the trailer and mine in your guy's apartment, and it wouldn't mean a thing."

"What about your witness? The girlfriend? Heard they picked her up. Maybe she saw what happened, or has some idea."

Sarah shook her head. "The girlfriend is no good to us. She's a tweaker. We can't make a case off of anything she says. Who's the beneficiary to your Marsee's estate? That's the person we should be looking for. Because no matter which brother died first, if your guy was the beneficiary to my guy's trust, with both brothers dead, that person gets it all."

Goddard laughed. "This is getting confusing. 'My guy,' 'your guy,' and one of them really is a 'Guy.' Maybe we should give our vics numbers."

"Or switch to first names." Sarah smiled. "There's another angle we need to consider. Lance was caught faking test results. Our victims were brothers, so…"

"You think my guy—Guy—was up to something fishy, too? Just because they were related doesn't mean they were both crooked."

"Innocent people don't usually get hauled out to a shipyard and shot in the back of the head for no reason."

Goddard nodded. "True. I'll tell the techs to look for faked research or similar unethical activity on Guy's computer."

His phone buzzed. He checked the display. "Sorry. Voicemail from my wife. Better call her back. I'll catch up to you later."

He hurried out into the hallway. Sarah tapped her fingers on her desk, wondering if she should wait for him. That was the trouble with working alongside a family man—too many demands and distractions. Not that there was anything wrong with caring about your family, as long as it didn't get in the way of the job. Everyone who wore the badge had to make sacrifices. How many times had she had to leave Jack with Regi while she was working a case? It wasn't as though a homicide detective could keep regular hours.

There was something she could do while she waited. A quick internet search found Tiffany's old dupe, Desmond Whittaker, CEO of some corporate monster whose function Sarah couldn't begin to fathom. At least not without some serious research. But it didn't seem necessary. According to a piece in an online business magazine, Mr. Whittaker was no longer in the country, just as Jaycee had said. Sarah had never seriously considered him a suspect in Lance's murder—why would he want to go anywhere near Tiffany again and risk his reputation—but a year-long transfer to oversee the Paris division was a pretty strong alibi. She'd get a uni to ring around to confirm, but it looked like Whittaker was out of the picture.

She checked her watch. Evidently Goddard wasn't coming back. She stood up. Tiffany had been stewing in the interview room for forty-five minutes. Good a time as any to find out what her former star witness had to say.

# 19

Goddard punched in the number for his voicemail the moment he was out of earshot of Linden's office. He'd downplayed the urgency of the call because he didn't like mixing his personal life with his job.

Also Linden had a reputation for being so focused when she was working a case, she could get more than a little prickly if she got interrupted. But Kath hardly ever called him during work hours. And with just six weeks until the baby was due…

"John," her message said. "Don't flip out. I'm at the hospital. I'm fine, but—" her voice broke. "I'm having contractions. Please hurry."

His heart plummeted. They'd known all along that Kath's age increased the risk of a premature delivery. But a risk for something, even a higher one, didn't necessarily mean it was going to happen. He took chances every day. In his job, at home, driving to work. Life itself was a risk when you came right down to it, a precarious state of existence that anybody could lose at any time. No one had to tell a homicide detective how fine the line was.

Anyway, they'd done everything they could to prevent

Kath from going into labor early. No working long hours. No stress. Still.

He texted her to say that he was on his way and hurried to his office to grab his coat. "I'll be at Harborview Medical," he called to the desk sergeant as he sprinted out the door. "Family emergency."

"Emergency." The word rang in his head as he jumped into his car and peeled out of the parking lot. For most people, the idea of having to deal with an emergency would throw them into a panic. But for a police officer, emergencies were practically routine. Goddard knew how to keep a cool head under pressure. A cop had to. Kath sometimes got frustrated because he didn't freak out on the rare occasions when the girls got hurt. But how would that help the situation? Would an accident victim or a kid lost in the woods want the police officers who were helping him to panic? Goddard didn't think so. There were two kinds of people in an emergency: those who sat on their hands and waited for someone to tell them what to do while a building burned down around them, and those who got up and got everyone out. Guess which kind he was. Just because he didn't panic, didn't mean he didn't care.

As he drove, he ordered the next steps in his head. Get to the hospital. Assess the situation. Find out if Kath had actually gone into labor, and if she had, how long it was going to take. It was one-fifteen now; he had a couple of hours to see how the situation was going to play out before the girls got out of school. Depending on how things shaped up, he could call their grandmother from the hospital and she could go and stay with the girls if it looked like he wasn't going to make it home in time. Six weeks was definitely early, but he was sure everything would turn out all right. Harborview had an excellent neonatal unit. They'd chosen the hospital for that reason. The baby's condition might be dicey for a few days, possibly a few weeks, but they'd get through it if they had to. And without discounting in any way Kath's genuine panic, the whole thing might be a false alarm. Maybe what she thought were contractions was really indigestion. Kath had always had a tendency to worry.

He pulled up to the emergency room entrance and parked his car in the tow-away zone with the lights flashing. One of the perks of being a cop.

"Kathleen Goddard?" he asked at the reception desk. "Pregnant? Would have come in about a half hour ago?"

The white-haired volunteer consulted her papers. "It looks like she's still in triage. Are you a family member?"

"Her husband. I'm also a police detective." His hand was in his pocket ready to pull out his badge if he needed to.

"Certainly, Officer. Down the hall and turn right."

He hurried off in the direction she pointed. He didn't need her to tell him where the emergency room was. Goddard had escorted both prisoners and suspects to this same hospital emergency room on more than one occasion. The only difference was he'd never been here to visit his wife.

The hallway opened into a large room arranged with beds around the perimeter that were separated by curtains, with crash carts and medical equipment in the middle. Each bed was clearly visible from anywhere in the room except the bed directly beside it. In an emergency room, privacy took a back seat to medical attention. He scanned the occupants, found Kath, and hurried over.

"We have to stop meeting like this," he said as he leaned across the IV line feeding into the back of her hand to kiss her forehead. A corny line, but under the circumstances, it was the best he could do.

She smiled. "You got my message."

Her face was splotchy and her eyes were puffy like she'd been crying. He brushed back a strand of damp hair. "Of course. I came as soon as I could. How are you doing? How's the baby?"

"The baby is fine. We're fine. Really. The doctor did this test to see if there was protein in the birth canal. I guess that's how they can tell if a woman is really in labor or not. Turns out, it was a false alarm. I'm sorry I made you come all the way down here for nothing."

"It wasn't nothing. It could have been something. Better to be safe, than sorry."

"It's just that I really thought I was in labor. My back ached, and I was—well, leaking. I did everything the books say you should if you think you're going into labor early; I drank two glasses of water and rested on my side for an hour, and then I did it again. But it still felt like I was having contractions. So I came in."

"You did the right thing." Goddard patted her arm. Kath was always more up on this stuff than he was. He'd done the expectant father thing as much as he was able to. Gone with Kath to her prenatal classes on the nights he wasn't working, and read the books she left for him on his nightstand when he didn't fall asleep from exhaustion first—even though secretly, he wondered why, after two children, his wife felt she had to take childbirth classes again. It had only been nine years since Sophie was born. How much could things have changed?

"Are you mad at me?" Kath asked.

"Only for driving to the hospital by yourself. Next time, call me."

"I will."

"I mean it, Kath. None of this gallivanting off to hospital emergency rooms without me. Did the doctor say how long you have to stay?"

"Just for a couple of hours for observation. After that, he wants me to come in twice a week to get checked from now until the baby is born. And I'm supposed to call him immediately if anything changes, no matter what time of day or night. I suppose we'll have to figure out what we're going to do with the girls. Do you have any vacation time coming?"

As if he could simply walk away in the middle of a murder investigation and sit home for the next six weeks to babysit their daughters and hold his wife's hand. His responsibilities were far more complex than picking up and putting down a paintbrush. Ten years on the job, and Kath still didn't fully comprehend the demands on the life of a cop.

"I'll call my mother," he said. "She'll be thrilled to spend some time with the girls. Do you need anything while I'm here? Can I get you something to eat or drink? A bowl of ice chips?" Adding the last to show he'd been paying attention during childbirth classes.

She laughed. "You can feed me ice chips later. Hopefully in about six weeks."

He smiled and leaned over the tubing to give her another kiss. "It's a date. Meanwhile, I'm going upstairs for a few minutes. I'll be right back."

Goddard waved his fingers as he left the room, then went back to the reception area. He found the bank of elevators and pressed the button for the tenth floor. As long as he was at the hospital, he might as well drop in on Neil Campbell.

Compared to the "do what you have to do and who cares how much noise you make in the process" atmosphere of the emergency room, the silence in the burn unit was unnerving. Goddard actually considered taking off his shoes as he squeaked his way down the corridor. Instead, he walked almost on tiptoe, out of respect for the patients who might or might not be listening. Not all of them were being kept under sedation like Campbell. He knew, because he could hear some of them moaning.

He went straight to the nurses' station, avoiding looking into the rooms he passed as much as possible. It wasn't that he was squeamish; as a homicide detective, he couldn't afford to be. But even a glance into the patients' rooms felt intrusive. Each window framed a tableau of misery and suffering. Dark, disturbing, and above all, intensely private. If he was in this place, he wouldn't want strangers looking in at him.

The charge nurse was the same one who'd been on duty the night before. With her black hair pulled into a simple ponytail and straight-cut bangs, she looked almost childlike. She couldn't have weighed more than Goddard's fourteen-year-old daughter.

He held out his card and reintroduced himself, though he was reasonably certain she recognized him.

"I'd like to talk to Neil Campbell, if he's awake," Goddard said. "Has there been any change in his condition?" The burn unit hadn't called, so he doubted the answer would be yes; still, he had to offer her some reason for his spontaneous visit.

"No change. But honestly, considering how badly he was burned, for him, that's a good thing. His body needs time to rest, and to heal."

"Has he had any visitors?" Thinking of the tweaker he'd seen skulking outside Campbell's room last night. If the man knew Campbell through his drug activities, he might also know something about the trailer park half of the Marsee brothers' murders.

She shook her head. "No, just you and your partner, and the other police officer."

"Police officer?" Goddard's mind raced. As far as he knew, he and Linden were the only officers who'd stopped by. He supposed it was possible that the officer who'd landed the meth fire investigation had also come to the hospital to try to talk to Campbell. Then the pieces fell into place.

"Guy about this tall?" He held his hand over his head. "Scruffy looking, with a beard and a hoodie?"

"That's the one."

"Did he happen to tell you his name? What department he was with?"

"No, but hold on. I think I still have his card."

She dug through the charts and papers on the counter until she found what she was looking for. She handed the card to Goddard.

*Stephen Holder, King County Sheriff Department*, the card read, with an email address and a phone number at the bottom.

"Can I get a copy of this?" Goddard asked, handing the card back.

"Keep it," she said. "I won't be needing it."

Goddard slid the card into his wallet and headed for the elevators. This Officer Holder guy was good, he'd give him that. He'd had no idea last night that the tweaker he'd been talking to outside Campbell's hospital room was actually a cop. He couldn't have been very deep undercover, though—otherwise, he never would have presented himself as a police officer to the charge nurse. Deep undercover operations—the ones where officers completely cut themselves off from family and friends for years—were relatively rare. Mainly because they were so expensive. Most undercover cops slept in their own beds at night.

As he punched the elevator call button and waited for the elevator to arrive, Goddard bounced his fingers against the side of his pants and grinned. At last, he'd caught an honest-to-goodness break in his case. Maybe, just maybe, he was back on track this time for an easy solve. Technically, the trailer park murder was Linden's half of the investigation, but at this point it was safe to assume that the Marsee brothers' murders were linked. Goddard was confident that the undercover would be able to shed light on Lance's murder. Which meant he might have information on Guy Marsee's murder as well.

He exited the elevator at the lobby level. He considered going back to the emergency room to check in one last time with Kath. Then he thought about the business card in his wallet. Moving to a quiet corner of the lobby, he took out his cellphone.

# 20

Sarah stood alongside Tiffany in the corridor outside the morgue viewing room window. She could feel the woman trembling. She put a steadying hand on her shoulder. It was hard to say if Tiffany was shaking because she was nervous, or because she was jonesing. Probably both.

The interview had been a bust. No surprise there. From the moment Sarah learned that Tiffany was a meth head, she'd known what the outcome of the interview was going to be. Add in the fact that Tiffany was clearly reeling from the news that Lance had been murdered, and getting anything useful out of her was highly unlikely. Forty-five tedious minutes of Sarah asking questions she already knew the answers to and Tiffany responding with dissembling and non sequiturs. How many times in one interview could a subject say, "I don't know"? Answer: forty-seven, according to the transcript.

"You sure you're okay with this?" she asked. "Remember, you don't have to go inside."

It wasn't up to Sarah whether Tiffany identified the Marsee brothers from inside the viewing room or from out in the hallway—that was Tiffany's decision. That said, Sarah was just as happy to stay on the corridor side of the window.

Sarah didn't have a problem with the odor of antiseptic underlain with decay, but Tiffany was already in rough shape. Not everyone could handle the smell.

"I'm okay out here." Tiffany chewed on her fingernail and grimaced. "Let's just get this over with."

Sarah knocked on the glass to indicate Tiffany was ready and nodded to the medical examiner waiting between two gurneys. The M.E. lifted back one of the sheets.

Tiffany stiffened and turned away.

"Is it him?" Sarah asked.

Tiffany nodded. "It's him."

"It's who? I need you to say his name."

"That's Lance. Lance Marsee. My boyfriend," she added almost inaudibly. As if not speaking the words aloud could negate the truth.

"You're doing great." Sarah nodded a second time, and the M.E. lifted back the other sheet.

Tiffany's eyes widened. She covered her mouth. Despite the fact that the second gunshot victim's head was turned away from the window, it was obvious that a good chunk of his face was gone.

"Take a deep breath." Sarah squeezed Tiffany's shoulder. "Don't forget to breathe."

Tiffany gagged, swallowed, nodded. "And that's Guy," she said after a long pause. "Guy Marsee. Lance's brother. Can we go now?"

Sarah knocked once more on the glass, and the M.E. pulled both sheets back in place, then came over to the window and lowered the blinds.

And that was that. Sarah took the trembling Tiffany by the elbow and led her toward the stairs. The process of identifying a body was one of the few aspects of police work that took place almost exactly as viewers were used to seeing on television. But sometimes bodies were never identified. At present, there were ninety-eight John and Jane Does in Washington State alone. The elderly, the unmarried, the orphans, the childless, the recluses—sometimes there was no one to recognize them, to give them a name. Most police departments posted pictures of their unidentified dead to their websites and to missing persons databases. But too many cases remained cold.

As for the Marsee brothers, Sarah had been reasonably sure of their identities. But there were other reasons for bringing Tiffany to the morgue aside from making a formal identification. Her reaction could tell Sarah a great deal about her relationship to the trailer park victim. As Sarah led her back to the station lobby, she asked herself if Tiffany's grief at seeing Lance's body had been real. Had she cried enough? Too much? Had she been shocked to see both brothers shot in the head, or did she already know that was how they had been killed, and her reaction forced? It was hard to say. Sarah wasn't unsympathetic. For most people, losing a loved one and coming to the morgue to identify the body was one of the most traumatic things they would ever have to do. But Sarah's job required that she keep her emotions in check. It wasn't easy, but she did it for them. So she could find out what had happened to their dead.

"You can pick up Lance's things in a few days," Sarah told Tiffany when they reached the front desk. "Meanwhile, if you think of anything that could help us find out who did this, please give me a call. And don't leave the city. We might need to talk to you again." She handed Tiffany her card.

Tiffany shoved the card into her jeans pocket and sniffed as she shrugged on her oversized down coat. The desk sergeant pushed a box of Kleenex across the counter. Tiffany blew her nose, and headed for the front door. Sarah let her go. She'd gotten all she could out of Tiffany. For now.

* * *

Sarah put down her office phone and crossed the final entry off her list. No pawnshop in the Rainier Valley area had copped to having Lance Marsee's thousand-dollar tablet. The Surface Pro had not surfaced.

"Going home?" Lieutenant Oakes stood in the doorway later that afternoon with his trench coat draped over his arm. He tapped his watch. As if Sarah could forget.

"Soon." She smiled to show that she was okay.

He nodded and moved off.

She sat back. The late afternoon sun slanted through the windows across the hall from Sarah's office, picking out the dust motes swirling in the air and highlighting the fact that her work space was long overdue a serious cleaning. According to the weather report, a cold front was moving in, bringing with it the probability of high winds and freezing rain and snow. A snow event always put an extra burden on the department. It would be all hands on deck when it hit. But for now, Sarah was content to bask in the warmth of a few minutes of rare winter sunshine, leaning back in her chair with her boots propped on her desk.

The rest of the day was hers to do with as she wished. Jack had gone home from school with his best friend, Nick. Sarah was supposed to pick him up after supper on her way home from work. He and Nick were probably playing computer games, though Sarah hoped that Emily would shoo the boys outside and make them shoot a few hoops, soak up some sunshine. A play date, she would have called it in the past, though she wouldn't dare let Jack hear her call it that now.

Her office grew noticeably cooler as a cloud passed over the sun. She swung her legs off the desk and pulled Tiffany's interview transcript toward her. Paged through the transcript again until she found the only useful take away, approximately thirty-eight minutes in:

**Linden:** Did you know Lance's brother, Guy?

**Crane:** Yeah. They spent a lot of time at the trailer before Lance—you know.

**Linden:** What did they do when they were together?

**Crane:** I don't know. Mostly, they talked.

**Linden:** What did they talk about?

**Crane:** I don't know. Stuff.

**Linden:** Did they talk about sports? Music?

**Crane:** No, work stuff. They're both really smart. Lance was into space. He knew everything. He had this photographic memory. We used to play this game. He'd give me one of his books, and I'd open it and pick a sentence and read it to him out loud. Then he'd tell me the sentence that came before and after. He could really do that. He was amazing.

**Linden:** And his brother? Did Guy have a photographic memory too?

**Crane:** I don't know. He might have. Guy was more into numbers, though. Like that guy on the TV show?

**Linden:** So Lance was interested in space, and Guy was interested in numbers. Is that what they talked about?

**Crane:** I guess. They also talked about their secret project.

**Linden:** Their secret project?

**Crane:** They didn't call it that. That's what I called it. I knew it was a secret, though, because whenever they were talking about it and I came in the room, they'd get quiet. Sometimes I'd walk out and come back in again just to see them do it. It happened every time. It was funny. They were like little kids.

**Linden:** You must have overheard snatches of their conversation. Do you have any idea what the project was about?

**Crane:** I don't know. I only know that it was a secret. Can I smoke in here?

A secret project. Lance and Guy working on something they kept hidden from Tiffany was intriguing. Sarah had tried to circle around the subject later in the interview and dig deeper, but either Tiffany didn't have more to offer, or she wasn't telling.

She did confirm a few facts over the course of the interview: Guy had what sounded like an obsessive-compulsive disorder. Tiffany had met Lance at the Black Bear Casino. When the casino found out about their relationship, they fired her for violating their "no fraternization" policy. Lance and his fancy tablet were inseparable. The tablet that was still missing.

She also dug up a few new ones. Tiffany had never been to Lance's brother's apartment, though the brother was a frequent guest at her trailer. Lance was a neat freak who couldn't stand to see anything out of place. Since he'd moved in with her, he'd completely rearranged her trailer and taken over the cooking. Lance had never taken illegal drugs in any form, and was furious when she'd started using meth. Small details, possibly inconsequential, but at the beginning of a case, you had to treat all of your facts with respect. You never knew which ones might end up being critical.

Most importantly, Tiffany was not in the trailer when Lance was killed. Her alibi checked out. The food bank where she and her girlfriend Claire had gone during the hours in which the M.E. estimated Lance had been killed was the kind where people had to sign in with their name and the time and show an I.D. so the volunteers could make sure people didn't double dip. After that, they'd spent the rest of the afternoon at Child Protective Services with Claire's social worker, finishing with a visit to a walk-in clinic for a cut Tiffany had got when she tripped stepping off a sidewalk. Probably while high.

And yet as strong as it was, something about Tiffany's

alibi felt too neatly assembled. How many people could document a random afternoon so completely? And her activities for the rest of the evening were unverifiable. That Tiffany's initial interest in Lance was because of his money was fairly certain. If she also knew about the trust, she could have been maneuvering to put herself in a position to get it. Tiffany was no longer at the top of Sarah's suspect list, but she hadn't dropped off.

Sarah bound the transcript pages with a paperclip and slid them inside Lance's growing file. It was the drug use that got to Sarah. By all accounts, Tiffany had been doing all right for herself until she started using. She owned her trailer. She had a car and a job. Yes, her rich new boyfriend lost all his money and she lost her job afterward as a result. But she could have found another way out of her troubles. Gotten another job. Moved in with friends. Faced her problems head on and taken steps to get past them instead of running away. Instead of adding one more.

Still, all in all, it had been a good day. She understood now how a brilliant astrophysicist with a trending career ended up living in a declining trailer park. All she had to do was find out who killed him, and why.

# 21

"Hold your hands like this, half pint." Holder spread his feet and positioned his fists, one ready to strike, the other held back to protect his chest. Beside him in the living room of his sister's apartment, his nephew Davie did the same.

Davie was short for a six-year-old. It was too soon to know if he was going to get his uncle's height eventually or not, but he definitely had Holder's looks: shaggy dark hair, soulful brown eyes that made women want to hug him, baseball cap worn backwards to give him some 'tude. Little man was gonna be a real lady killer when he was grown.

His sister's boy looked up to Holder, and not just because Holder was twice as tall. He had to, what with no pops around. Holder liked hanging with his nephew. Davie was one of the people who made him feel real. Grounded. Like he was a good person.

"Now jab like that." Holder demonstrated. "Pow! Pow! Aww right! That's the way! Just like my man Bruce Lee. Gimme some skin!" They slapped hands and finished with a complicated series of hand maneuvers that made up their own special salute. "Now lemme see a kick."

Davie crouched and concentrated, picturing his foot

connecting with his target like his uncle had taught him, then kicked out with his right leg. Holder grabbed his ankle and dropped his nephew onto the carpet.

He laughed. "Gonna have to work on that move, son." He rolled Davie onto his back and pinned him to the floor with his knee. Davie wriggled and shrieked.

"Say uncle!"

Davie shrieked louder.

"Say uncle!"

"Uncle! Uncle! Uncle Steve!" Davie hollered, giggling.

"Stephen!" Liz called from the kitchen where she was cleaning up after a dinner of spaghetti and meatballs. No meatballs for Holder; he was doing the vegan thing. It was the same tone of voice she'd used to keep Holder in line when he was growing up. Liz was a tough, blue-collar girl who wouldn't take you-know-what from her brother—or from anybody else.

Holder rolled off his nephew, then held out his hand and pulled the boy to his feet. He messed up his hair, and picked up the baseball cap from where it had fallen on the floor and plopped it on Davie's head. His phone buzzed in his pocket. A text from Logic. His moms was off the warpath and it was business as usual. Time to get to work.

"You work on those Bruce Lee moves, now, you hear?" He zipped his hoodie and started for the door.

"Where you goin'?"

"I got to go to work, little man." Holder tugged affectionately on his nephew's cap.

Davie reached up to straighten it. "But we was gonna play Mario."

"We'll do that next time, 'kay?"

"You promised."

"Davie, stop arguing," Liz said from the kitchen.

"Lis'sen to your moms," Holder said. "Your moms is the

best. She's there for you, 24/7, 365. You feel me? 'Sides," he opened the door and tossed off a grin. "Some of us gots to make a livin', son. Them Nintendos ain't cheap."

Holder parked two trailers down from Logic's mom's and pulled out his cigarettes. He turned off the headlights and left the engine idling as he lit up. It was cold outside and getting colder. The music coming from the trailer told him the party inside was going strong. There was nothing stopping him from getting out and going in, but for some reason, he didn't feel like it. Not yet.

He took a drag, let it out. It was too dark to see Campbell's place, but he could smell it. He'd spent some time at the hospital again that afternoon. Holder wasn't sure why he felt compelled to keep going back. The charge nurse probably thought Holder had come to see her, but he didn't need to go to a hospital to score. And it wasn't like Campbell was going to wake up so Holder could lean on him to snitch. He supposed he went because it felt like the right thing to do. Like a vigil. If their places had been reversed, he would've wanted somebody to set up camp for him on the other side of the door.

The thing was, you never knew when your circumstances were going to change. One day, you're a bad ass makin' meth and terrorizing the trailer park, and the next, you're a crispy critter. People said it all the time: "If I'd only known, I'd've done X, Y, or Z differently." Well, fact was you couldn't know. All you could do was live in the moment, and you'd better appreciate that moment while you had it no matter how bad you thought it was, because the next one might be a whole lot worse.

Until yesterday, Neil Campbell had been one scary piece of work. The only time Holder had seen him show a shred of humanity was with his kid. But the real reason

Campbell scared people wasn't his temper. It was because he was so smart. As in master criminal, get-away-with-murder, nemesis smart. Like the villains you saw in movies and books. Campbell's brainpower might've been part of the reason why Holder had chosen him to make his case. Maybe a big part. Maybe Holder wanted to test himself. See if he could match wits. Like Moriarty and Sherlock. Whatever. It didn't matter now.

He smoked the cigarette down to the filter and stubbed it out. Grabbed the six-pack he'd brought. He locked his car because of the sleeping bag and the other homeless dude props he kept in the back. Holder spent most nights in the back seat, moving his car to different places so he'd look like a guy without a permanent address, even though his six-foot two-inch frame guaranteed he'd wake up in the morning with at least one leg still sound asleep. Keepin' it real. It was easier to act a part if you lived it.

He knocked on Logic's door and waited until Ridgeback opened it on a chain. Logic had a bouncer thing going on. Not that his parties pulled in crowds behind a velvet rope, but he didn't let just anybody in. Ridgeback had the look and the build of a bodyguard, and the attitude to go with it. Useful for when little guys like Logic needed to feel big.

"Who is it?" he heard Logic say from inside.

"It's Steve," Ridgeback called back over his shoulder. Like most undercovers, Holder used a variation of his first name. Less likely to forget or get tripped up that way.

"Let 'im in."

As if there was ever any doubt. 'Specially because Holder was the guy who always brought the beer.

He sauntered into the living room and put the six-pack on the coffee table, knocked fists with Logic reining over the party from his La-Z-Boy boy throne, glanced around. It looked like girls' night at Rainier Valley. Besides Logic and Ridgeback, there was Claire and Tiffany, and two other women he guessed were in their late teens or early twenties. The meth made them look older. Worn out and used up before they were hardly old enough to vote.

Holder was surprised to see Tiffany but was careful not to let on. She looked rough. Eyes red from crying, hair straggly like she hadn't run a comb through it for days. He hoped the cops hadn't been too hard on her. Must not've had enough to hold her, since they'd let her go.

"'Sup?" He squeezed between Claire and Tiffany and sat down on the sofa. Laid his arms across the back pretending like he was relaxed. Inside, he was tense. Something about the group was off. Something in the air. He could feel it. Like they'd been talking about him right before he came in. And the talk wasn't good.

"You tell me," Logic said.

"How'm I s'posed to know what you lame-asses are up to? I just got here."

"Yeah, but where you been?"

"At the hospital, fool. Checkin' on our human firecracker. Which none of you losers apparently thought to do."

And where he would have run into that cop again, he could have added, if he hadn't quickly ducked out of sight behind a corner. He thought about the message the dude left that afternoon on his cop phone back at his apartment. He didn't say how he got Holder's number, just that he could use Holder's help with the trailer park murder, which had Holder worried. Gil was Holder's contact. He shouldn't be giving Holder's number out.

"And before that?" Logic asked. He nodded to Ridgeback.

Ridgeback took a step toward Holder. Loomed over him and made sure that Holder could see his hands balled into fists. Bared his teeth like a pit bull gone too long without a fight.

Holder snorted. “Why don’t you stop playing Twenty Questions and tell me what you think you know?”

“This morning. When we was hanging under the bridge. The cops grabbed Tiffany. How’d they know where she was at?”

“How would I know? I was s’prised as you when they showed up. Had some weed on me, too.”

Logic aimed his finger. “I think you called ’em. I think you’re a snitch. Maybe you a cop. Ain’t no coincidence, you take off an’ the cops pull up.”

“Fool. I was takin’ a piss. When the po-lice came, I split.” Holder turned toward Tiffany, put on his most innocent grin. “You don’ think I’d call the cops on you, do you, darlin’?”

“I don’t know. Logic says you did.”

Ridgeback stepped closer. Holder took his arms down from around the girls. Leaned forward and tugged a beer can from the plastic ring using his good left hand, made like he didn’t know Ridgeback was itching to beat him into the floor. Sat back ready to smash the can into Ridgeback’s face the moment the gorilla made his move.

“Hey, baby. You got one of those for me?” Claire scootched into his lap and laid her head on his shoulder. She snaked her arm around his neck and stretched her face toward him and gave him a long kiss.

Holder got what she was doing. He smiled down at her like they’d always been a couple. Gave her the beer and leaned past her with his arm around her waist to get another for himself.

“Let me, baby,” Claire said as he fumbled to open the can with his left hand. She cracked the tab, then held the can to his lips. He took a long swallow.

“Hey, Ridgeback,” she purred sweetly as she snuggled deeper into Holder’s chest. “Be a doll and go get us some chips.”

Ridgeback blinked. Confused. Beaten. Still believing

in the righteousness of the beating he'd been about to administer. Knowing the moment was gone.

He dropped his hands and stomped over to the breakfast counter and grabbed a bag of chips and threw them at her. "I still think he's a cop," he muttered.

"Oh, honey." Claire laughed. "You see cops everywhere. My grandpa was a cop, and my brother *is* a cop. If my boyfriend was a cop, don't you think I'd know it?"

She lifted her face to Holder and smiled expectantly. Her teeth were white and straight. She hadn't been using long.

Holder leaned in for the kiss. He didn't know why Claire was lying for him, but he had a good idea of what she wanted in return. If that was all it took to keep his cover, he didn't have a problem playing along.

# DAY THREE

JANUARY 26, 6:45 A.M.

# 22

Linden was already in her office when Goddard arrived at the station at six forty-five the next morning. He wasn't surprised she beat him in. Goddard had been with the department for less than a year, but he was well aware of Linden's reputation. Once the other detectives heard that he and Linden were working together on related cases, they made sure he knew that Linden could get "intense." Goddard took that as a euphemism for "obsessed." He didn't necessarily see that as a bad quality. Whatever got the job done.

Anyway, a person had to be at least slightly unhinged to do what they did. It wasn't as though police work gave you any choice about which days you were going to work, or what hours you came in. Besides, when it came to putting your work ahead of your family and neglecting your personal life, he was the poster boy. Case in point: Yesterday, his wife had spent the better part of the afternoon at the hospital thinking she was about to have their baby. Yet here he was at work bright and early the next morning. Granted, he'd waited to leave the house until she was awake so he could check on her one last time, and he'd made her promise to call him if she felt so much as a twinge. Still. Pot, meet kettle. Given that he and Linden were working together as temporary partners until the Marsee murders were solved, it was just as well they were both black.

"I talked to the Marsees' lawyer," she said when he appeared at her door bearing a bag of Krispy Kremes and two Styrofoam cups. She eyed the bag pointedly. He shrugged it off. So what if his breakfast went straight to type? A lot of people liked donuts.

"Hatchett was telling the truth," she said, "at least about the trust fund. The fund checks out. The four hundred thousand is still there."

"I followed up yesterday on the tweaker I saw at the hospital outside Campbell's room." Goddard put the donuts on her desk and sat down in the extra chair. "Turns out, he's an undercover. I left a message on his voicemail asking him to call. If he's working the trailer park, he might know something about your vic. No telling when he'll get back to me, though. Those guys don't exactly keep regular hours."

"I wonder if he's the same guy who called in the tip on Tiffany. Oakes said the person knew about the BOLO."

"Probably. I'll ask him if you want. How'd it go with Tiffany yesterday?"

"About what you'd expect. She managed to I.D. the bodies for me, but the interview was a bust."

Goddard nodded sympathetically, then pushed one of the coffees toward her and pulled a handful of sugar and creamer packets from his pocket. "I didn't know how you take it, so I brought both."

"Black."

Same as him. He scooped up the condiment packets and dropped them in the trash.

"Guy didn't leave a will so he didn't name any beneficiaries," Sarah said, carrying on as if the conversation hadn't been interrupted. Focused. Goddard liked that in a cop. A partner who was easily distracted could get you killed. "The public administrator who gets assigned to the case will use some of the funds in the trust and from the sale of Guy's possessions to look for collateral heirs," she continued. "But if no one turns up, the money goes to the state."

"That takes care of one theory." Goddard hadn't really bought into the idea that an unknown beneficiary had knocked off both brothers, but they had to check it out before they could cross it off. "Anything else?" Judging by the crowded whiteboard and the papers scattered over her desk, Linden had been at it since at least four or five. Or maybe she'd worked through the night. It happened.

She walked over to the whiteboard. On it were two lists, one for each victim.

"Guy was older than Lance by four years," she said, pointing to each item as she summarized her findings. "Both brothers were geniuses, and both had photographic memories. It looks like Lance was the smarter of the two, however, because he graduated with a Ph.D. from MIT just one year after Guy, despite the age gap. Must have skipped a few grades. Guy took a job at GenMod Labs. A year after that, Lance went to work for Stratoco here in Seattle—maybe he wanted to be close to his brother. Both brothers never married, and they never had children. There are a lot of similarities during the early years since our victims grew up in the same household. But I tried to focus on what they've been doing during the last ten."

"Did your guy show signs of Asperger's?" Goddard asked. "The waitress I talked to at Guy's favorite coffee shop seemed to think he did."

"As far as I know, Lance's only issue was gambling."

Goddard reached into the Krispy Kreme bag for a second donut. There were two left. He held out the bag to Linden. She shook her head. Apparently she didn't sleep *or* eat when she was working a case. That was okay. They'd get more done that way.

"I did get one interesting piece of information from the interview with Tiffany," she said. "Apparently, Lance and Guy were working together on a project that they were keeping secret from her. Those were her exact words. A 'secret project.' She swore she didn't know what it was about, because whenever she came into the room when they were talking about it, they shut up."

"I don't know. Sounds pretty thin." Goddard licked the sugar from his lips and wiped his fingers with a paper napkin. "Could be just the paranoid imaginings of a tweaker."

"I considered that. But by that point in the interview, she was fairly lucid. And people don't generally notice things unless there's a reason to."

Which was true. How many times had he asked an interviewee to tell him anything they could remember, anything at all, no matter how inconsequential they thought it might be? If you let people tell you only what they *considered* important, you could easily *miss* something important.

"You know, this could fit with something the waitress at the coffee shop told me," he said. "She thought Guy was keeping a secret. She saw him sitting and smiling to himself for an extended period of time, something he never usually did. Odd enough for her to remember and mention it. Something that made him happy, was how she put it, like he was expecting something nice to happen. A payoff, or some other good news is the sense I got from her, though she didn't spell it out like that. I didn't think much of it at the time, but if you put the two together, it could be a start."

He went over to the whiteboard and added "Asperger's?" to the list under Guy's name, "gambling problem" under Lance's, and "secret project" under both. He stepped back and studied the board.

"There's one other thing that's still hanging," Linden said. "Lance's computer. Or rather, his tablet. One of his former coworkers at Stratoco told me Lance had an expensive Surface Pro. Tiffany confirmed he used it when he was living with her at the trailer, but it didn't turn up in the inventory list."

"Did you check local pawnshops? If the murderer took it, he or she might've pawned it."

"I already called around yesterday. I'll check again later today. See if anything turns up."

"Meanwhile, we should take a look at Guy's computer. If the brothers were working together on a project, there might be something on it. Ray should be about finished with it by now. Grab your coffee, and we'll go check it out. And bring your file on Guy. I'll bring Lance's."

Goddard followed Linden into the corridor, then paused in the doorway and looked back at the sack of Krispy Kremes on her desk. Thought about bringing the sack along. Then he thought about his own burgeoning belly. He went inside and dropped the sack in the wastebasket.

# 23

In Sarah's opinion, the tech guys at the station were unsung heroes. They rarely went out in the field; hardly ever left their cramped and cluttered offices. Some of the more devoted—some would say "obsessive"—practically never saw the light of day. But in an increasingly technological world, the work they did behind the scenes to support the cops out on the street was essential.

Most of the tech toys police departments invested in benefitted the officers in the field. Miniature cameras clipped to an officer's chest pocket to verify and record witness statements. Patrol cars with dashboard cameras. A city-wide WiFi system that enabled officers to know where their fellow officers were at all times in case they needed to call for backup. Flashlights with different preset wavelengths designed to detect hair, fibers, and body fluids at a crime scene. Thermal imaging. Electronic whiteboards. Diagramming systems that allowed crime scenes and collisions to be charted in minutes instead of hours. K-9 cameras. But when it came to pulling evidence buried in somebody's laptop, Sarah's favorite tech guy couldn't be beat.

She and Goddard positioned themselves on either side of

Ray's ergonomic office chair, effectively taking up all of the available floor space in the crowded office. Ray walked them through his findings.

"Here's what you need to know," he said, pointing to the screen. "Besides checking his emails, I also ran Guy Marsee's recent computer history, looking for files he'd viewed or changed and websites he visited. A lot of the activity is mundane, but check this out."

That was the other thing Sarah liked about Ray. Besides being good at his job, he always got straight to the point and never wasted time on small talk.

Ray clicked on a Google Drive doc that Guy had apparently created and then shared only with his brother. Sarah had no idea how Ray had broken Guy's password in order to access the file, and she didn't ask. She didn't need to know how the trick was performed in order to appreciate the magic.

The file opened as an Excel spreadsheet labeled "PKD Project."

"What's a PKD?" Sarah asked, knowing that Ray would have already found the answer.

He handed them each a printout he'd pulled from www.pkdcure.org—the "Polycystic Kidney Disease Research and Education Foundation" website, according to the printout's header.

Sarah read the opening paragraph out loud. "'Polycystic kidney disease (PKD) is one of the world's most common, life-threatening genetic diseases affecting thousands in the U.S. and millions worldwide.' Okay. Why are we looking at this?"

"This spreadsheet on polycystic kidney disease the Marsee brothers put together represents a great deal of work." Ray clicked rapidly through multiple pages so Sarah and Goddard could appreciate the extent of the file.

"Like you, I wondered why they were investigating this particular disease. Especially since neither one of them was a medical doctor. It took a little digging, but I believe I know. According to their death certificates, your brothers' parents both died in their early forties of polycystic kidney disease."

Goddard whistled. "Nice work." He turned to Sarah and raised his eyebrows. "Think this is our secret project?"

"Could be. Assuming there's nothing else significant on the computer, then it probably is."

"Just the usual," Ray confirmed. "No porn. A lot of online shopping. This is the only thing that raised any flags."

"Okay, then let's upgrade that 'probably' to a 'most likely.'" Goddard chewed on his thumbnail while he mulled over the information. "Don't you think it's odd that both parents died at such a young age from the same disease? I could see it if they died at the same time in a car crash. Or even if they both had cancer. But how common is polycystic kidney disease?"

Sarah flipped the pages of the printout Ray had given her. "Apparently it affects an estimated twelve and a half million people worldwide."

"Twelve and a half million. Okay, then I guess it's not impossible for them both to have it. Highly unlikely but not impossible."

"But did you catch that the disease is genetic?" Sarah asked. "I just remembered something. Guy Marsee's bank statements, the ones you got from his apartment—they were in his file when we first got together on this." Goddard wordlessly handed her the folder. She flicked through the contents, found the sheet she was looking for, and ran her finger down the entries.

"There." She showed the two men the statement, pointing at an entry. "I remember this. A big payment, four thousand dollars, made three months ago to Rockland Diagnostics.

They do genome mapping." She put down Guy's file and pulled Lance's from under her arm, rifling through it until she found a stack of bank statements held together with a paperclip. She removed the clip, split the stack into thirds, and passed one third to each man. "See if Lance Marsee had the same idea."

Ray and Goddard began flipping through pages, Sarah doing likewise. It was Ray who spoke first. "Here. A four-thousand dollar charge from Rockland Diagnostics, made two weeks after Guy's."

"That can't be a coincidence," said Sarah. "And at four grand a pop, I doubt they did it out of idle curiosity."

"You think the brothers wanted to know if they had inherited the disease?" asked Goddard. "If they were going to die young like their parents. How old were they again?"

"Thirty-six and thirty-two. If one or both of them had the gene for the disease, they would have been looking at maybe another decade at most."

"And Guy worked for GenMod Labs. An outfit that conducts genetics-based research. Their family history could be why he went into that field in the first place."

Sarah nodded slowly as the pieces came together. They always did. You just had to keep digging, keep following your instincts, keep following up. During the first phase of an investigation, all you had was facts. You put them on a whiteboard, studied them, rearranged them, looked for clues. Patterns. Connections.

"So three months ago," Goddard said, "Lance and Guy decide to get their genomes mapped or tested or whatever you call it to see if they carried the same gene that causes the disease that killed their parents. That still doesn't address why they were killed."

"Maybe they weren't only interested in knowing if they were going to develop the disease," Sarah said. "Maybe they also wanted to find a cure. That's what I'd do if I were in their position. Maybe that's why Guy was trying to access the trust fund. According to our timeframe, the tests were done one month *after* the trust fund was set up. It must have driven him nuts to see the money tied up like that. Especially after Lance had already burned through a similar amount. If I knew I had a terminal disease, and I was the beneficiary of serious money, perhaps enough to find a cure, I'd do everything I could to get my hands on it."

"Even murder?"

She shrugged. "Somebody shot Lance."

"Then who killed Guy?"

"We'll sort it out. For now, we need to confirm whether or not the brothers had the gene for the disease, and what that would have meant for them if they did. What the knowledge might have motivated them to do. Know anywhere we can get a crash course in genetics?"

"I know just the place," Goddard said. "I'll ring ahead, see if we can get a tutor on short notice. Meet me in the parking lot. I'll drive."

# 24

Sarah clenched her hands in her lap as she sat in the passenger seat of Goddard's four-door Ford Taurus. She hated being relegated to passenger status. Her obsessive need to be behind the wheel was well known at the station, even joked about on occasion. She knew what the others thought of her, but she couldn't help it; she just didn't like the feeling of someone else being in control. But GenMod was Goddard's show. And after the exhausting and unproductive day he'd put in at GenMod yesterday, he'd earned the right to take the lead role.

"What exactly do they do at GenMod?" she asked to distract herself as he hung a left into the parking lot without using his turn signal. Her fingers twitched as he drove past not just one, but two empty parking slots before finally pulling into a third.

"GenMod Labs specializes in research into human genetics, with the objective of understanding and curing inherited diseases by modifying the genes that are responsible." He pointed to a glossy trifold on top of the stack of papers stuffed into the console beside him and smiled. "Or so it says in their brochure."

"Genetic modification. GenMod Labs. Got it." Funny how easy it was to miss what in hindsight should have been obvious. She followed him through a set of revolving doors into an expansive lobby. High ceiling, leather seating, skylights above a fountain in the middle with enough foliage surrounding it to make a rainforest jealous. Just once, she'd like to see a corporate lobby that broke the mold.

"Morning, Megan." Goddard greeted the woman behind the information desk. "It is Megan, is it?"

The receptionist looked up and smiled. "That's right! What a great memory you have!"

Sarah didn't have the heart to point out that her nameplate was clearly visible on her desk.

"Are you back for more interviews?" the woman asked. She looked around hopefully. "Where's your partner today?"

"Today, I'm just chauffeuring the lady." Goddard smiled modestly and held up his car keys. "She's the real brains of the operation."

The receptionist turned expectantly toward Sarah. Sarah smiled back through gritted teeth. If the receptionist thought Sarah was going to toss back a clever quip or a banal rejoinder, she had a long wait ahead of her. Goddard might have the easy, joking way about him that for most people passed for genuine conversation, but small talk drove Sarah crazy.

"We have an appointment with Dr. Agnes Preston from Information Services," Sarah said stiffly. "She's expecting us."

"Of course." The receptionist filled out their visitors' passes. "She's on the fifth floor. Take the elevators and turn right. Room 527."

Dr. Agnes Preston turned out to be a small woman in her mid-sixties with long gray hair and a fading ankle tattoo.

Unlike nearly everyone else Sarah had seen roaming the halls, Dr. Preston was not wearing a white lab coat. Her flowing skirt, peasant blouse, and chunky turquoise jewelry struck Sarah as inappropriate, both for the work environment and the season. But with the Boho look in fashion, Sarah had noticed that a lot of women Dr. Preston's age seemed to gravitate toward the style. Maybe they felt they owned the look because they'd created it. Or maybe they thought wearing the styles they'd worn when they were in their teens and twenties kept them young. Either way, Dr. Preston pulled off the look remarkably well.

She waved them toward a pair of mismatched floral guest chairs flanking a small rattan table. Apparently her Bohemian tastes extended to her décor as well.

"I was so sorry to hear about Dr. Marsee," she said. "I assume you're here as part of the investigation. Please, tell me how I can help."

"Did you know Dr. Marsee well?" Goddard asked.

"Oh, no. Not at all, actually. I knew who he was, of course, everyone did. Such a brilliant man. But I didn't know him personally."

Goddard raised an eyebrow and shot Sarah a look that said *You see what I was up against?* At the same time, his phone buzzed in his jacket pocket. He took it out, checked the display, put it back, mouthed "sorry" and nodded to Sarah to continue.

"Dr. Preston," Sarah began, "can you please give us a quick overview of what you do here at GenMod Labs? I don't mean you specifically, I'm talking about the company's objectives and purpose. After that, we can address specifics."

"Certainly. But please, call me 'Angie.'" Dr. Preston propped her elbows on her desk and tented her fingers under her chin. She looked like a college professor getting ready to expound on her favorite topic. Sarah settled in for a long, dull, and quite possibly incomprehensible lecture on the finer points of genetic research.

"To understand what we do at GenMod," Dr. Preston began, "you first need to appreciate that almost every major disease afflicting mankind has some basis in our genes. Until recently, all doctors could do was treat the symptoms. Sometimes successfully. Many times not. But now that we can read and interpret the genetic code, we can isolate the mutated genes responsible for a specific disease, repair them, and thus offer a cure."

Sarah sat up straighter. Clear, concise, and to the point. A pleasant surprise. No wonder Preston worked in Information Services.

"Is GenMod looking into any particular genetic disorders?" she asked.

"Currently our scientists are investigating a broad range of genetic diseases. Hemophilia, cystic fibrosis, Huntington's disease, and sickle cell anemia are a few you're probably familiar with. But there are many more which aren't as well known."

"What about polycystic kidney disease? Is that on your research list?"

"It might be. If it's a heritable condition, odds are the answer is yes. I'd have to look it up to be certain."

"Thank you, I'd appreciate that. You mentioned mutated genes. Could you clarify how they factor into the disease process?"

"Certainly. There are two kinds of mutations. A mutation in a specific gene can be inherited from one or both parents. Or a gene can mutate later in life due to environmental and other factors. Mutations that are passed from parent to child are contained in the DNA of egg and sperm cells. This means that this type of mutation is present throughout a person's life in virtually every cell in their body. Someone who carries such a mutation has the *potential* to develop the disease, but whether or not they will still depends on many factors, including environmental influences, as is the case with cancer. On an individual level, predicting who will come down with a disease and who will not is very complex."

"Sounds like we're all walking time bombs," Goddard remarked. "Doomed from the day we're born."

"Yes and no," Dr. Preston said. "In truth, only a small percentage of mutations cause genetic disorders. Most have no negative impact on our health or development whatsoever. For instance, your lovely red hair," she said to Sarah, "is actually the result of a gene mutation, the Melanocortin-1 receptor, or MC1R gene. For people with brown, black, or blond hair, this gene produces a protein called melanin, which colors the hair and allows the skin to tan. In redheads, the mutated MC1R gene produces pheomelanin instead, which accounts for the characteristics we typically see in redheads, including pale skin and freckles."

Goddard grinned. Sarah could guess what he was thinking: *Linden's a mutant.* She smiled back. If being a mutant meant being an individual, he'd get no argument from her. Anyway, she'd always taken pride in the uniqueness of her red hair. Worldwide, only half of one percent of Earth's population had it.

"And here's something else to keep in mind about mutations," Dr. Preston continued. "There are a very small percentage of mutations that actually have a positive effect. For example, a beneficial mutation might generate a protein that *protects* an individual from disease rather than causes it. And because the mutation is genetic, the advantage would be passed to that individual's future generations. To a pharmaceutical company, these positive mutations are incredibly valuable because they have the potential to form the basis for an entirely new drug or treatment. They can be worth billions."

Goddard whistled.

"How long would it take to develop a genetic-based treatment for a specific disease?" Sarah asked. If both brothers had the disease, but if they or someone were actively looking for a cure, knowing the timeframe would help. How much would it cost? was the other question. Investing $400,000 toward a treatment that would ultimately be worth billions wasn't a bad return. Especially if the new treatment also saved your life.

"It's not quick, if that's what you're thinking. The process takes years—even decades to develop. There are clinical trials to be conducted, approval from the Food and Drug Administration to be obtained before the treatment can be brought to market. At GenMod, we're not looking for immediate results. We have to think far into the future."

"Would additional funding speed things up?" Sarah asked.

"Well, naturally that would help."

"So let's say—hypothetically—that someone discovers a genetic mutation that has the potential to cure a major disease. How much money are we talking to develop a treatment? Ballpark estimate, of course."

"Many hundreds of thousands, certainly. Millions, most probably. But given the current state of the economy, your hypothetical person would have a hard time finding funding at all, no matter how attractive their project. Everything after the 2008 economic downturn is struggling. Before that, genetics research was moving so quickly, it was like a race. Now it's almost impossible to find a venture capital company willing to risk funds on experimental research. Even GenMod has had to withdraw funding from a number of worthy projects. It's quite tragic. While the development of a cure is on hold for lack of funding, people are dying. There's also the issue that there's less call for research into the rarer disorders. Fewer cases means fewer sales down the line, even if a cure is found. But that's an issue for economists and politicians. Does that help?"

"Immensely," Sarah said as Goddard's phone buzzed again. "We appreciate your time."

Dr. Preston took out a business card and handed it across her desk. "If you have any other questions, please don't hesitate to call. I'm happy to do whatever I can to help your investigation. Poor Dr. Marsee. Such a nice man."

As they waited for the elevator to take them back to the lobby, Goddard took out his cellphone. He checked the display, and returned the phone to his pocket.

"Is everything all right?" Sarah asked.

"Fine. I'm expecting a call, is all."

"So what did you think of our visit?"

"I definitely think we're moving in the right direction." He ticked the points off on his fingers. "One or both Marsees had or might have had a genetic disease that was likely to kill them by the time they reached their mid-forties. GenMod may or may not have been working on a cure for their particular disease. Either way, the process of finding a cure would go a lot faster with more money."

"Money Preston says would be extremely difficult to obtain. But did you catch what she said about the financial potential? Perhaps the Marsee brothers weren't hoping just to develop a cure to save themselves. Maybe they were also hoping for a significant financial return. We've really got to get a look at their test results. If they were looking for investors, or going to put their own money in the project, then they must have felt they were onto something."

"I'll get on that as soon as we get back."

"And I want to talk to Tiffany again. See what Lance might have told her about his parents; find out if he was worried about getting sick."

"You know, this whole terminal genetic disease issue could explain why Guy and Lance never married or had children. I'd sure think long and hard about bringing a kid into the world if I knew the chances were high the kid would inherit a disease from me that was going to kill him. To say nothing of the fact that I wouldn't be around to see him grow up."

Sarah nodded. She couldn't imagine her life without Jack. Or what his life would be like if anything happened to her.

The elevator chimed and the doors opened, revealing a tall man with a shock of white hair.

"Dr. Rutz," Goddard said. "Good to see you again."

Rutz acknowledged Goddard with a nod and stepped to the side. Sarah expected Goddard to push the conversation as chatty people tended to do, but they rode the rest of the way to the lobby in silence.

As the elevator doors closed behind them, Goddard snagged Rutz's arm and pressed his business card into his hand. "I'm glad I ran into you again. I believe you left this behind yesterday. Please, if you think of anything that might help our investigation, give me a call."

The man slid the card into the notebook he was carrying without comment and hurried off.

"Was he that talkative during the interview, too?" Sarah couldn't resist asking as they crossed the lobby and stopped at the receptionist's desk to turn in their visitors' passes.

Goddard shrugged.

"I saw you talking to poor Dr. Rutz," the receptionist said as she noted the time on her sign-out list. "It's so sad."

"What's sad?" Sarah asked.

"Just that Dr. Rutz and Dr. Marsee were so close, and now Dr. Marsee is gone. I'm sure he's taking Dr. Marsee's death harder than he's letting on."

Goddard's head snapped back toward the elevators. Sarah's did the same.

Rutz was gone.

"Are you sure they were friends?" Goddard asked, his voice controlled. "Not just acquaintances? No one else I talked to yesterday mentioned it."

"Well, maybe 'friendship' is too strong a word," the young woman said. "But I've seen Dr. Rutz and Dr. Marsee meet up in the lobby, and then walk across the street together when they go for coffee. And once when Dr. Marsee's car was in the shop, Dr. Rutz gave him a ride to work for almost a week. They might not act like friends in the usual sense—probably because they're both very private people. But there was definitely something between them." She gave Goddard a smug smile. "People think all a receptionist does is answer the phones. But I see everyone's comings and goings. I know who's going to lunch with whom, who's late getting back… who's having an affair with a coworker… Believe me, I could write a book."

"Maybe you should," Sarah said. "For now, let's test that all-knowing superpower of yours. Do you know where Dr. Rutz was going?" Pointing to the corridor down which the man had disappeared.

The receptionist smiled. "Sure. That's easy. It's ten o'clock. Dr. Rutz always goes to the smoking room for a cigarette."

# 25

"I can't believe GenMod has a smoking room," Sarah said as they started down the hallway. In the era of the Big C, cigarette smokers were pariahs. A company that was actively pursuing a cure for cancer that also provided an indoor space for their workers who hadn't yet kicked the habit spoke volumes to the regard they had for their employees.

"And I can't believe I bought Rutz's B.S.," Goddard said through gritted teeth. His face was redder than Sarah had ever seen it. He looked like he was going to have a heart attack—or punch his fist through a wall. "Everything that came out of that man's mouth yesterday was a lie. 'I only sat down with him when we happened to run into each other at Starbucks.' 'I don't know where he lives.' 'I've never been to his apartment.' That boy's got some serious explaining to do."

Sarah didn't answer. So Rutz had lied during yesterday's interview. So what? People lied all the time. You couldn't let your emotions get away from you. People screamed at you, lied to you, sometimes they even assaulted or shot at you. No reason to get bent out of shape about something that was just part of the job.

"Let me take the lead this time," she said. "Rutz doesn't

know me. We don't have a history, so I can ask him things you can't. Better yet, let me talk to him alone. You go back and talk to the receptionist. Find out what else she knows. She likes you." What Sarah didn't add was that she would get far more out of Rutz if the conversation wasn't confrontational.

"You sure?"

"I got this. That receptionist knows more than she's letting on. I'm sure you can charm it out of her."

"Okay. But remember, Rutz is smart. He has a photographic memory. He's going to use that against you."

"I got this."

"Okay, then good luck." Goddard took a deep, calming breath and pulled out his cellphone. He checked his messages, and then started back toward the lobby. Sarah pursed her lips as she watched him go. It wasn't like Goddard to let his emotions get the better of him to such an extent. She wondered if his overreaction had something to do with the way he kept checking his cellphone. Problems on the home front, most likely. In which case, he needed to be careful.

She followed the receptionist's directions down the hallway and opened the third door on the right. To her surprise, instead of the dingy, windowless cubicle she had been expecting, the door opened to a large atrium attractively decorated and overflowing with lush vegetation. Carcinogen-absorbing vegetation, she presumed. A dozen workers were scattered around the room sitting at café tables, most in pairs; a few, including Rutz, sat alone. The room barely smelled of smoke; no doubt because the smarter-than-your-average-corporation had invested in a top-of-the-line air exchange system.

She pulled out her detective shield and made a beeline for Rutz, showing him the badge and sitting down at his table without waiting for an invitation.

"Dr. Rutz, I'm Detective Sarah Linden, SPD Homicide. I'd like to ask you a few questions about Guy Marsee."

Rutz took a long drag from his cigarette and exhaled slowly in her direction. The gesture seemed so deliberate, it was almost as if he assumed she was a non-smoker and was trying to annoy her. She reached inside her jacket for her cigarettes and lit one of her own.

He arched his eyebrows. "I'm sorry. I don't want to be rude, but I honestly can't see what's to be gained by more questions. I already told your partner everything I know."

"Actually, Dr. Rutz, you and I both know that isn't true. Yesterday, you told my partner you barely knew Guy Marsee. Today, we found out that not only were you friends, you even carpooled to work."

Laying her cards face up on the table. Betting on the fact that if Rutz was as smart as Goddard seemed to think he was, he'd respond better to a direct approach than if Sarah came at the subject sideways. A good interviewer needed to be able to size up the interviewee in a matter of seconds and adjust accordingly. Sarah was good.

Rutz clucked his tongue. "It's that nosy secretary, isn't it? The one who runs the front desk. Marsee and I didn't 'carpool,' no matter what she might think. I gave him a lift to work once is all, when his car was in the shop. As I told your partner yesterday, you couldn't be friends with Guy, even if you wanted to. He had the social skills of a flea."

He'd actually said "amoeba" according to Goddard's interview notes, but Sarah let it go. "So you've been to his home."

"Of course I've been to his home. How else was I supposed to pick him up?"

Rutz shook his head in obvious disgust as if her question marked her as too stupid to live. Or at least as too stupid to remain in his exalted company. She didn't let it bother her.

She knew her own abilities, and it didn't matter what this pompous snob thought. Better that he underestimate her.

"Did he ever invite you up to his apartment?"

"Never."

"What about his friends or family? Can you fill in anything about them? You must have talked about something as you drove to and from work."

"You'd be surprised how little we said." He arched his eyebrows. "Not everyone feels compelled to fill dead air with mindless chatter, you know. As I told your partner, I simply didn't know the man."

"Only you did."

Sarah started as Goddard came up behind her. He grabbed a chair from the table next to theirs, sat down, and handed Sarah his cellphone. She read the display, then rephrased her question.

"Dr. Rutz. Are you *sure* there's nothing about your relationship with Guy Marsee you're not telling us?" Giving him one last chance to come clean.

Emphatically, he shook his head. "Nothing."

"In that case, Dr. Rutz, you might want to look at this." She held out her hand and showed him the article Goddard had pulled up on his cellphone. "To refresh your memory," she couldn't help adding. The corner of her mouth turned up on a small smile. Rutz wasn't nearly as smart as he wanted them to believe. Too bad for him that his photographic memory had been set to selective recall.

Rutz took the phone and read the display. His shoulders sagged. Wordlessly, he laid it on the table.

Sarah took out her handcuffs. "Dr. Rutz, I need you to stand up and put your hands behind your back. You're under arrest for obstruction of justice. You have the right to remain silent. Anything you say can and may be used against you. You have the right to have an attorney. If you cannot afford an attorney, one will be appointed for you."

The murmur of background conversation stopped. Heads swiveled as the workers grasped the import of the words they'd overheard. Mouths gaped in disbelief as Sarah and Goddard marched the handcuffed Rutz out of the room.

# 26

Goddard was a genius. Never mind that the man sitting on the other side of the interview table probably had an I.Q. that was three times his and Linden's put together. Right here, right now, Goddard was the true genius in the room. Dare he say it? The *only* genius. Because with a simple Google search done from his smart phone while he was cooling his heels in GenMod's lobby waiting for Linden to finish Rutz's interview, Goddard had discovered what was quite possibly the only piece of information in existence that proved beyond a shadow of a doubt that Rutz was lying.

And it was so ridiculously easy. A quick internet search of "Marsee + Rutz" and up popped an article from a university alumni magazine. An article revealing a link between Rutz and the Marsees' parents. A link Rutz couldn't deny. It was too early to claim he'd broken the case—a lot would depend on what Rutz had to tell them next—but Goddard couldn't help feeling as though they were about to.

"Help us understand," he began per the unspoken agreement between him and Linden that his initiative had earned him the right to take the lead in the interview. "Why didn't you tell us you were the Marsee brothers' godfather?

Don't you want to help us find out who killed them? Don't you want closure?"

"Closure." Rutz spat the word back at him as if Goddard had fed him a mouthful of dirt. With his unruly white Einstein hair, he looked every bit the famous scientist's twin, although twice the size. A very angry twin. "There's no such thing as closure. Closure is nothing but a rhetorical concept, a made-up term. A myth. What people are really looking for when they talk about finding closure is a release from the pain. But no amount of knowing or not-knowing can change how someone feels when they've lost a loved one. Closure isn't something we *need.* God knows it's not something that's going to make us *feel better.* Closure is merely a concept that funeral home directors and forensic pathologists and wrongful death attorneys and psychics use to exploit people's grief. There's a reason we grieve. We grieve because we miss the person who died. Sometimes we even miss the things about them we didn't like. Expecting someone to move on after a death minimizes the validity of their emotions. I *know* what killed the boys' parents. That knowledge does *not* make me feel better. Why should it be different for them?"

"Then tell us about their parents," Goddard said smoothly. He didn't have a problem with Rutz's oratory; much of Rutz's impromptu speech rang true for him. His own mother's murder was the reason he'd quit his internship at the Art Institute of Chicago after he graduated from art school to become a cop. Not a day had gone by in the years since that he didn't think about her at least once.

Rutz sat back with his lips pressed together and crossed his arms over his chest. Classic body language indicating his speech was finished.

"You were their godfather," Goddard continued. "No one knows the Marsee brothers like you did. Help us close our investigation. If not for yourself, then for us. So *we* can move on."

Rutz didn't answer. For a moment, it looked like the interview was going to be over before it had hardly begun. Then Rutz sighed deeply and closed his eyes. Goddard waited. After long moments, Rutz opened his eyes and began to speak. His voice was barely more than a whisper. Goddard and Linden had to lean over the table in order to hear.

"Bob and Janet Marsee and I were friends long before the boys were born," Rutz began. "Before Bob and Janet were married, in fact. Both Bob and I fell for Janet. She really was quite wonderful."

He stopped, savored the memories of the woman whom Goddard presumed was Rutz's first love, then went on.

"It wasn't long, however, before it was clear that Bob was going to come out the winner. By the time they married, I had accepted the situation and our friendship continued. I was Bob's best man at their wedding. Naturally, when the boys were born, their parents asked me to be their godfather. Unfortunately, as it turned out, it was the boys' great misfortune that Robert Marsee was their father instead of me."

"How is that?"

"Because both Bob and Janet carried the gene for polycystic kidney disease. I'm sure you must know enough about genetics to realize that when both parents are carriers of a genetic-based disease or condition, the odds that their offspring will contract the disease as well become astronomical. Of course, back in the early years, we had no idea of what was coming. Bob was adopted, and knew nothing about his birth parents, and Janet's died when she was a child. Until they started showing symptoms, it was a pretty idyllic family setup. Both parents university professors; Janet an anthropologist, Bob a nuclear physicist. The boys were already showing signs of their abilities, and were included in the weekly faculty dinner parties, where they could listen to some of the country's most brilliant minds debate everything from chaos theory to the body politic. They were also encouraged to participate when they got older. Loving parents. Doting godfather. The boys had it all."

"But Camelot didn't last."

"It never does, does it? The first crack came when the boys were ten and fourteen and Bob and Janet separated. Bob had fallen ill by then. It was a terrible time for all of us. Polycystic kidney disease is an absolutely horrific illness. The body just keeps producing cysts. There's no cure, no way to stop it. The cysts are noncancerous, and they vary in size, so a person might be forgiven for thinking the disease is something a person could live with. But as the number of cysts accumulate and the cysts fill with fluid, they grow to an enormous size. A normal kidney weighs less than a third of a pound. The kidney of a PKD sufferer can weigh as much as thirty pounds. Can you imagine the pain? To say nothing of the suffering the victim goes through on their way to eventual kidney failure."

Rutz ran his hand through his wild hair. "Janet couldn't cope, couldn't stand to see Bob go through all that. She was weak, and she dealt with it in the worst possible way. Left him, left the boys, took up with one of her students. I suppose she was desperate for something to distract her—she was starting to show symptoms herself—but it ended badly. Her lover got her pregnant and then left her high and dry, and an alcoholic into the bargain. She went downhill pretty soon after the baby was born. A boy."

Beneath the table, Goddard's leg twitched with excitement. The boys' mother had a son by another man? Lance and Guy had a half-brother? Goddard was careful to keep his expression neutral. He could feel a similar tension vibrating off of Linden, could almost see the gears turning in her brain. No doubt thinking of the four hundred thousand dollars in Lance's trust. Thinking that if the half-brother was alive, he would stand to inherit. And that if he knew about the trust, he had a motive to kill them both.

"Did Lance and Guy know they had a half-brother?"

"They did not. After Janet left, Bob made sure they never saw her again. After everything she put them through, he didn't want her in their lives. Her or her bastard son.

"I realize that sounds harsh," Rutz continued, "but what we did was in the boys' best interests. Janet was drinking heavily. Bob and I had to shield the boys from that. At first, we told them that she'd gone for an extended visit to their grandmother. Then when Bob died, I told them Janet had died at her mother's. I didn't let them go to Bob's funeral. I was worried that Janet would show up, but as it turned out, she was already gravely ill. She was dead within the year. From then on, I was the only constant in the boys' life."

Rutz paused and lifted his chin. "Judge me if you will, but to this day, I believe I did the right thing. The boys went to live with Bob's parents until they came of age. The grandparents were as disgusted with Janet as I was, and were only too happy to continue the deception. And really, what did it matter? After we knew that Janet also had polycystic kidney disease, her early death was a given. It was only a matter of time. The boys received a substantial inheritance when their grandparents passed away, but how can money compensate for the loss of your family? How can it give you *closure*?"

Rutz glared. Goddard tipped his head to concede the point. If he'd been in Rutz's position, who was to say he'd have done differently? The picture Rutz painted of the Marsee brothers' background was enlightening. Children of privilege, both financial and academic. On top of the world, until they weren't. Guy must have used his share of the inheritance to purchase his extravagant apartment, even if he couldn't quite afford to stock it with real works of art, just good imitations. Given what they knew about Lance, it seemed safe to presume that his share of the inheritance had been donated to the Black Bear Casino.

"Is that why Guy became a data analyst? He was following in your footsteps because he looked up to you as his substitute father?"

"Perhaps. I like to think so," Rutz admitted. "Regardless, Guy was well-suited for the work. He had a gift for numbers that was truly extraordinary. You've heard of the term 'autistic savant.' Although Guy wasn't autistic; his disorder was more along the lines of Asperger's syndrome, not that he was ever officially diagnosed. Which was the real reason he found it difficult to make friends."

"Let's go back to their half-brother," Goddard said. "How old would he be now?"

"Lance was four when his mother left, five when his brother was born. That would make the half-brother twenty-seven."

"And you're certain that Lance and Guy knew nothing about him?"

"Absolutely. As I've already told you, it was better for everyone that way. He was adopted, but I kept track of him during his early years. As it turned out, the boy was deeply flawed."

"Deeply flawed? How?"

"The boy was just wrong. He wasn't like other children, no empathy, no kindness. Cold. And he seemed to enjoy hurting others, both mentally and physically. I wouldn't be surprised if today he has a criminal record. He may even be dead."

"So you're not in touch with him? When was the last time you saw or spoke to him?"

"I really couldn't say. Years, certainly. I have no idea where he might be now."

Except… for the first time during the lengthy interview, Rutz did not look Goddard in the eye. He'd licked his lips when he said it had been years since he'd talked to the half-brother, then unconsciously scratched the bridge of his nose.

Rutz was lying.

"Are you sure you haven't been in touch with him?" Goddard pressed. "You'd swear to it under oath? I'm warning you, Dr. Rutz. We have ways of finding things out. You really don't want to lie to us." Again the unspoken implication.

Rutz sat up straight, offended. "I'm not *lying*. I received one phone call several months ago at his instigation. That can hardly be construed as being 'in touch.'"

"He called you. What did he want?"

Rutz waved his hand dismissively. "He had some cockamamie idea that he'd found a way to cure polycystic kidney disease, if you can imagine that. As if better minds than his weren't already at work on the problem. He wanted me to invest in his scheme. Frankly, I was surprised that he even knew the name of the disease that killed his mother. But as it turns out, he wasn't a stupid man. Judging by our conversation, he was every bit as intelligent as his half-brothers. At any rate, I turned him down flat. I don't have that kind of money, wouldn't have given it to him if I had. And it's absolutely true that I have no idea where he is today or what he's doing."

Rutz lifted his chin, challenging Goddard to accuse him of lying again.

"Does this half-brother have a name?" Goddard asked.

"Campbell. Neil Campbell. And now we're done. Charge me, or let me go. Either way, I want my attorney."

# 27

Sarah faced off with the nurse in charge of the burn unit at Harborview Medical. Barely five feet and pretty as a model, the nurse was the kind of woman who was smart and determined enough to get where she was despite the double handicap of her small size and good looks.

"It's absolutely imperative that I speak with Mr. Campbell," Sarah said. "Call a doctor. I want to speak to someone in authority."

"There's no point, the doctor won't consider removing Mr. Campbell's sedation. I'm sorry. We have to consider what's in the best interest of the patient."

"And I have to consider what's in the best interest of my investigation. This man has vital information regarding a murder." *Possibly two.* Never mind the fact that he might well have committed them both.

The woman drew herself up to her full height. The look she gave Sarah could have crumbled a marble statue.

"I don't think *you* understand," the nurse said. "Mr. Campbell has suffered second and third-degree burns over eighty percent of his body. If he wasn't in an induced coma he'd be in agony. He could die."

"That's exactly my point. I need to hear what he has to say now."

"And I told you that waking him up is not my call. It's up to his doctor."

"Then get his doctor."

The nurse shook her head emphatically and put her hand on the desk phone. Making sure Sarah saw it. Letting Sarah know she was ready to call security if Sarah didn't back down.

Sarah clenched her fists and turned away. She stomped off down the corridor and rode the elevator down to the lobby. Walking quickly, she exited the building through the double doors and found the smoking area in an outdoor courtyard next to the parking lot. She lit up and paced back and forth, trying to organize her thoughts.

Campbell was Lance and Guy Marsee's half-brother. Highly intelligent, and—if what Rutz had said about his character was true—completely without conscience. A lethal combination? Quite possibly. The AFIS search she'd done before coming to the hospital revealed that Campbell had been in trouble with the law repeatedly. His juvenile records were sealed, but just the fact that he had a juvie record spoke volumes. His adult rap sheet included a baker's dozen of minor and not-so-minor charges, including a prison stretch for assault with a deadly weapon. Thinking that he was capable of murder was not a stretch.

She tossed the cigarette and ground it under her foot, then went back inside and rode the elevator to the tenth floor. She hoped the charge nurse had had a chance to cool down enough to change her mind. Sarah's was the voice of reason. She wasn't asking the nurse to wake up Campbell herself. Only to call a doctor.

Sarah's hopes climbed higher when she stepped off the elevator and saw that a different nurse was behind the counter. Pleasant-looking, grandmotherly, rotund. She smiled sweetly and showed her badge.

"I need to speak with Mr. Campbell in room 1011," she said. "It's very important."

"I'm afraid that won't be possible. Mr. Campbell is unconscious."

"I understand that. I need someone to wake him up."

Gray Hair looked surprised. "I can't possibly authorize that."

"I'm not asking you to. Please. Just call Mr. Campbell's doctor. This is a police matter. It won't take long, but it's important. I just need to ask Mr. Campbell a few questions."

The nurse pursed her lips as she considered Sarah's request. For a moment, Sarah thought she was home free when the nurse nodded and laid her pen on top of a stack of patient charts. Then: "Let me go ask the charge nurse what she thinks. Wait here. I'll be right back."

And back on the merry-go-round they went.

Sarah leaned against the counter. A not-so-subtle message for anyone who happened to be looking that she was planning to stay until she got her way. Nothing was more important right now than interviewing Campbell. She'd camp out in the waiting room day and night, get a death-bed confession if she had to.

The gray-haired nurse returned. Sarah could tell immediately from her expression that nothing had changed.

"No dice?" she said pleasantly. Making an effort to maintain a semblance of cordiality.

"I'm sorry," the nurse said with a shrug. She looked sincere. Not that that was going to help Sarah's case. "I promise, we'll call you the moment Mr. Campbell is able to talk with you. I was wondering, though. Do you happen to know if Hugo is all right? I'd like to be able to tell him when he wakes up."

"I'm sorry. Who?"

"Hugo. Mr. Campbell's little boy. Before we put Mr. Campbell under, he kept asking for him, wanting to know if Hugo was all right. I suppose he thought the boy was also burned in the fire. Of course we told him his son was fine, even though we didn't know either way. But when he *does* wake up, I'd like to be able to tell him the truth."

Sarah had to press her lips together to avoid lashing out. She was beyond frustrated. This woman wouldn't help with her investigation, yet she expected Sarah to take on the additional chore of finding out what had happened to Campbell's boy? Still, she supposed it wouldn't hurt to get on the nurse's good side. If she agreed to look into the boy's whereabouts, maybe this woman would cooperate as well. Give a favor, get a favor in return.

"I imagine he's in foster care," Sarah said as pleasantly as she was able. "If you like, I can look into it."

"Oh, would you? That would be wonderful. I—"

She broke off and looked down. Sarah followed her gaze. Behind the counter, a row of lights had begun to flash. At the same time, the speaker system crackled to life. Code blue.

"I'm sorry," the nurse said. "You have to leave. Now." She ran off down the hall. Sarah ran after her. An orderly passed them, pushing what Sarah assumed was a crash cart. She ran faster. Followed the cart to room 1011.

"You can't be in here," the charge nurse shouted as Sarah ran into Campbell's room.

"This man is a witness in my investigation! I need to talk to him! *Now!*"

"Get her out of here!" the charge nurse shouted.

A pair of orderlies grabbed Sarah by the arms and muscled her out into the hallway. She pushed past them as soon as they released her and ran back. They followed her in and grabbed her again. Shoved her back into the hallway. Held onto her arms.

"You can't go in there," one of the orderlies said. "Stay here. Let us do our job. You don't want him to die, do you?"

"Of course not." Sarah shook her head. The orderlies let go. They went back inside Campbell's room, and shut the door.

Sarah moved to the window. A man straddled Campbell on the bed doing chest compressions. Someone else jabbed a needle in his arm. Sarah caught a glimpse of the monitor before the charge nurse came over to the window and jerked the cord and the blinds fell.

Flatlined.

# 28

Goddard drummed his hands on the steering wheel on his way to Rockland Diagnostics as he sang along with the Blues Brothers tune blasting from the CD player. *Oh baba don't you wanna go, back to that same old place, sweet home, Chicago-o-o…* drawing out the last note of the chorus as the song finished in a happy riot of drums and cymbals. A cheerful, foot-tapping, sing-along song, all sunshine and blue skies that was perfectly suited to his mood. Never mind that the real sky overhead was so foreboding; it looked like the rain that had dogged him since he left the station was going to change to snow at any second. Goddard didn't care. Not even a hurricane could spoil his good mood.

He still couldn't believe his luck. Or his inspiration, or his brilliance, or his genius, or his intuition, or whatever you wanted to call his discovery of the link between Rutz and the Marsee brothers. Without it they would never have known that Neil Campbell was the Marsees' half-brother. It seemed a fair supposition that Campbell had found out about the brothers' "secret project" and had tried to get Rutz to buy in. Otherwise how could you explain the coincidence? Both Campbell and the Marsees looking into a cure for a rare disease at exactly the same time? It couldn't be chance.

It never failed to astound him how a random query, a chance encounter, a word spoken at the right time, could blow a case wide open. Or how one small variance could make all the difference. If Rutz had been the boys' official guardian instead of their godfather, he and Linden could have uncovered that fact easily enough through the usual channels. But Rutz as godfather was an obscure detail that under normal circumstances wouldn't even make it into print beyond a notice in a church bulletin at the time of the boys' christening. Whether it was sheer dumb luck that the article in the online alumni newsletter had linked their names, or whether it was fate, didn't matter. The important thing was that Rutz had wanted to keep the relationship hidden. He'd almost succeeded. Almost.

As for why Rutz had been determined to conceal that particular detail to the point where he barely acknowledged being acquainted with Guy Marsee, Goddard could only guess. Whatever the reason, he certainly wasn't swallowing the whole "it doesn't matter who killed them" B.S. that Rutz had tried to feed him. Goddard had a theory, one he hoped would grow legs after he interviewed the technician at Rockland Diagnostics who'd run the Marsee brothers' DNA, and it had nothing to do with how Rutz felt about closure.

He turned into the parking lot, detouring around a pothole that could have doubled as a duck pond. He thought about the questions that Rutz's interview had raised. Was Rutz lying when he said the two halves of the family didn't know each other? Were all three brothers working together on the PKD project? Was the picture Rutz had drawn of Campbell as a conscienceless man a fabrication? If the answer to any of those questions was yes, then maybe he and Linden had it backwards. Maybe, instead of being a suspect, Campbell too was a victim. Maybe it wasn't chance that his trailer exploded the same day the brothers were shot. In which case, he and Linden needed to take a long, hard look at the esteemed Dr. Nelson Rutz.

He locked the doors of his aging Crown Vic and hurried with his head down against the rain toward the building. There was waterfront, he reflected as he splashed his way through the puddles, and then there was *waterfront*. This was definitely the downscale kind. Rusty cranes. Empty loading docks. A sliver of gray water barely visible between a row of corrugated sheet metal warehouses and swaybacked wooden buildings. Not an area of the city where he would have expected to find a state-of-the-art genetics testing lab. Still, Goddard preferred neighborhoods like this to the downtown waterfront's renovated glitz and glamour. The peeling paint and neon signs reflecting in the puddles on the crumbling sidewalks spoke to him more eloquently than winding boardwalks and trendy shops.

No name on the front of the building. No doubt keeping a low profile to keep thieves and degenerates away. Making it look like there was nothing special going on inside, when in reality, the building was probably full of thousands, maybe even millions of dollars' worth of equipment.

He tugged open the door. Inside, the no-frills approach continued. No fancy lobby, no perky receptionist, just a cluster of desks crowded into a common workspace. Which was all very progressive and democratic, but figuring out which person he should approach to ask for the technician he'd spoken to on the phone was going to be a problem. Goddard stood awkwardly near the door with his hands in his pockets. Just as he was considering calling out the man's name to see who looked up on the off chance that the technician was in the room, a young man at the desk nearest to him came to his rescue. "Who are you looking for?"

"Jason Weirs. He's expecting me."

"Ah. Jase. He's in the back." The young man pointed toward a set of double doors.

Goddard pushed one open and found himself in a large room that could have doubled as the set for a science-fiction movie: rows of gloved technicians wearing disposable white caps seated on lab stools working with ridiculously technical-looking equipment. Over the hum of vent fans he could hear music. Bob Marley.

The technician nearest to him was wearing headphones. Apparently he wasn't a fan of reggae. Goddard tapped him on the shoulder, and the man pulled out one ear bud. Goddard could hear a woman singing tinnily about love.

"I'm looking for Jason Weirs."

"Jase!" the man called. "Cop here to see you."

Was it that obvious? Goddard was wearing a trench coat, but that was because it was raining. On the other hand, the undercover at the hospital had made him right away. No matter. Jason Weirs was expecting a cop. No harm, no foul.

"Jase!" the man called again. "Get up here. You got company."

"Be there in a sec," an unseen voice called back. Moments later a slight man with a halo of curly red hair appeared. Goddard guessed him to be in his mid-twenties. The technician pulled off a latex glove and shook Goddard's hand, while Goddard tried not to stare. If he'd thought Rutz's hair was outrageous, this kid's could have won the mad scientist lookalike contest hands down. Goddard couldn't decide if the young man was trying to imitate his favorite theoretical scientist or a rock star.

"Thanks for seeing me," he said. "I'm hoping you can clarify some of what we discussed over the phone."

"Sure thing. Happy to help." Weirs led Goddard to his workstation and pulled up a second lab stool. Goddard hefted himself awkwardly onto it.

"Like I told you on the phone," Weirs said as he hopped agilely onto his own, "I'm not sure what more I have to offer." Subtext: *I wish I hadn't told you as much as I did.* Too late for that. Goddard was going to get the results of the Marsee brothers' genetics testing out of this kid if he had to—to… He tried to think of a threat to illustrate his determination that was suitably dire, and smiled. If he had to shave the kid's head.

"I appreciate that," he said smoothly, "and believe me, I'm not here to give you the third degree. I'm just looking to better understand the process to see how it might tie into my investigation. This whole idea of genetic testing—" he waved his arm to encompass the lab "—is fascinating to a layperson like me. At some point, we're going need to see the Marsee brothers' test results, but don't worry. I'm not going to put you on the spot. We'll get a court order for that."

The court order compelling the lab to release the results of the Marsee brothers' genetic testing was in process—at least Goddard hoped that it was. It seemed as though the closer Oakes got to his retirement, the more erratic his cooperation became. The detectives working under him never knew if he'd approve a request or deny it. Oakes hadn't been particularly impressed with Goddard and Linden's "secret project got the brothers killed" theory. But Weirs didn't need to know that. And besides, the best lies always contained an element of truth.

"Okay, well then, sure," Weirs said, clearly relieved. "As long as you understand that I have to maintain our clients' confidentiality, that's great."

"On the phone you told me that you ran both Marsee brothers' DNA."

"That's right. The lab always runs familial DNA using the same technician. When there's just one test involved, reading the results is pretty straightforward. But when there are two related test subjects, we always use the same person. Sometimes we can spot extra details that way. Anomalies. Whatever. It's pretty interesting stuff."

Goddard could think of a million things that would be far more interesting than reading the bars on a DNA chart, but he let it go. "Have you worked here long?"

"About ten years."

Goddard would have guessed that ten years ago the kid was wearing diapers. It was unnerving to realize that he was fast approaching the age where he was older than most of the professionals he dealt with.

"So tell me, when a person shows up at Rockland and wants to have their genome mapped, what are they looking for?"

"Lots of different things. Some people aren't looking for anything specific at all—it's just curiosity. There's this thing people do where they get the results blown up to poster size and hang them on their wall. Like a family portrait, but at the genetic level. It's pretty cool. But most of the time, people get their genomes mapped because they're looking for something specific. Paternity tests, or markers for disease, or chromosome abnormalities. We do more than a thousand different tests at Rockland, and more are being developed all the time."

"Fascinating," Goddard said again. This time, he actually meant it. No lack of new things to learn over the course of doing his job. "I understand that the Marsee brothers had their complete genomes mapped. Is it unusual to do full workups on brothers?"

"Not really. We do a lot of sibling comparisons, especially for twin studies."

"But most genetic testing is done with a narrower focus, say to screen for a specific disease?"

"That's right. You'd be surprised how many people

want to know if they have the gene for Huntington's or Alzheimer's. It doesn't necessarily mean they'll develop the condition. But it's a possibility. Some people want to be able to plan for that."

"The Marsee brothers' parents died from polycystic kidney disease. Is this the marker they were looking for?"

"That's correct. Both brothers had the mutation. PKD2, the gene is called."

*Bingo.* This kid may have been able to run circles around Goddard when it came to extracting and reading DNA, but when it came to extracting information from an interview subject, nobody could beat his technique. "And so for them, the fact that they had the gene meant their chances of getting the disease were very high."

"Right again. I explained this to them when I sat down with them together to discuss their results. But the Marsees insisted they weren't sick."

"I understand the symptoms of polycystic kidney disease don't show up until adulthood."

"That's true. But both brothers were well within the age range where the symptoms should have been obvious. They wanted me to look at the results again to see if I could figure out why, and long story short, in going over their genomes a second time, I discovered that the mutated gene that should have caused the disease was *itself* mutated, if you follow me. Genetically speaking, the brothers had the disease. But for all practical purposes, thanks to the double mutation, the potential for the disease had been cancelled out. It's pretty exciting. I'm working on a paper."

The young man beamed. Maybe he thought his discovery was going to put him on the fast track for a Nobel. Maybe it already had. Goddard made sure to look suitably impressed.

"Just to be sure I understand you," he said, "you're saying the brothers carried a double mutation—an anomaly that no one else has—that in effect cured them of polycystic kidney disease?"

"That's the gist of it. And what's really cool is that extracting this gene and then injecting it into others who carry the normal mutation for PKD could prevent them from developing the disease as well. The potential was enormous. I still can't believe both brothers are dead. I know they were hoping to use their DNA to develop a treatment. But unless their relatives object, there's no reason someone else can't follow through. That's the cool thing about working on the molecular level—you don't need much of a sample."

"What if the brothers have no living relatives?" Goddard asked. "Could someone else use their DNA to develop a cure?" Thinking that perhaps he should add the knowledgeable and enthusiastic young man with the clown hair to his suspect list.

"Really? They have no living relatives? That changes things. You can't just take people's genetic material and use it without their permission, you know. Your DNA belongs to you. It *is* you. The laws are there for a reason. Otherwise, we're back to grave robbing and Dr. Frankenstein. I don't suppose there's a will?" Said almost wistfully, as if he couldn't bear the idea that the possibility of a cure had died with the Marsees.

"We're looking into that. One last question. Did someone named Neil Campbell also have his genome mapped recently?"

"If he did, I really couldn't say. Not, you know, without a court order." Realizing he'd already said too much.

"I could get a warrant," Goddard said smoothly, "but I wouldn't have to bother you again if you could just take a few more minutes and look it up now." Making it seem as though giving up the information was inevitable, and the technician's convenience was the only issue.

"I guess I could check." He worked the keyboard, pulled up a database, then scrolled through a list of names. "Yep, there it is," he said, pointing. "Looks like another familial pairing."

"Familial?"

"There are two entries for Campbell, a Neil and a Hugo."

"Campbell's a common name. There must be thousands in Seattle. How do you know they're related?"

"I don't one hundred percent, but both tests were carried out on the same day and have the initials 'J.G.' against them. That means both tests were carried out by the same tech, John Galloway. As I said before, we try to use one tech for familial runs. Of course, I'd have to go deeper into their records to know for sure, but again, I'm really not comfortable doing that without a warrant. Sorry."

"That's okay. I appreciate your time."

Goddard shook the technician's hand, left his card on the workstation, and stood up to leave. Or rather, he slid down. He rubbed his aching rear. How could people stand to work on lab stools all day?

As he unlocked his car door and slid in, his phone buzzed in his pocket. He flipped open the phone. Linden. Perfect timing. He hit redial and tapped his fingers against the steering wheel as he waited for her to pick up. He couldn't wait to hear what Neil Campbell had to say.

# 29

Holder woke feeling as though he were walking in a dense fog. Somewhere in the distance, a trumpet was playing. Reveille. He groped to make sense of it, then came awake one degree further and realized the trumpet was the alarm on his cellphone. The alarm tone was a joke. His sister had used the same tune as his wakeup call when he was fifteen and it was her thankless job to see that he got to school on time. He'd never told her that he still used it.

He rolled over and reached out to turn off the alarm. Instead of cool plastic, his hand touched warm skin. Somebody else's skin. He cracked open one eye.

Claire.

He raised himself up on one elbow and reached over her to shut off the phone. The phone was on a coffee table. And the table wasn't his.

He rubbed his eyes and blinked away the sleep fog, then raised his head and looked around. Skanky living room. Smelly plaid sofa. Logic's trailer.

Claire stretched and draped her leg across his. "Mmm," she murmured as she snuggled in. As if two people sharing a sofa could get any closer.

Holder slid out from beneath her and sat up with her legs across his lap. He'd messed up big this time, for sure. It didn't matter that Claire was wearing underwear and he was fully clothed. Not that he had anything against—well, anything. But he was supposed to be undercover. He was supposed to be working. He wasn't supposed to be waking up in his target's trailer with a mostly naked woman and absolutely zero memory of whatever had happened during the previous who knew how many hours. His head felt like a balloon that had been stuck onto his body. He wondered if he'd been drugged.

He checked the time. Almost noon. The party last night had been a late one. Snatches of the previous evening came back: Logic trying to get him to take a hit off the meth pipe, Ridgeback itching to beat him into a pulp. Claire pretending to be his girlfriend and saving him from the beating. Maybe Ridgeback had gotten back at him by slipping him a roofie. It was possible. The trailer was a regular pharmacy.

Holder's jacket was on the floor. He reached down and dug through the pockets for his lighter and a cigarette. The rain beating against the front windows sounded like gunshots, more sleet than rain. It looked like there was a full-on storm coming. A shaft of light slicing through a crack in the curtains stabbed his eyeballs like daggers. He shut his eyes.

"Baby?"

"Darlin'." His tongue felt thick. Like it didn't belong to him. He'd definitely been drugged.

He slid her legs off his lap and stood up, arms out for balance. Congratulated himself when he remained standing. "You hungry? I'm gonna see if there's anything to eat in this dump. I make a mean *huevos habaneros*."

"A what?"

"An omelet with hot sauce."

"Oh."

He went around the breakfast counter into the kitchen. Moving around made him feel better. Plus the nicotine helped. He picked up a coffee pot to fill it with cold water. The pot was so stained it looked like it was made of brown glass instead of clear. He added an extra scoop to hide the bitter taste the crud was going to leach into the brew and turned on the pot. Checked the fridge. The shelves were fully stocked, a happy surprise—until he remembered the size of Logic's moms.

Holder whipped up the eggs with a teaspoon of water and dumped them into a hot iron pan.

"Smells good, baby," Claire said from the living room.

"How do you like your coffee?"

"Cream and two sugars."

Like they were playing house. Only Claire wasn't his wife or even his girlfriend and it was somebody else's house. He carried two steaming cups into the living room, then went back for the plates. Balanced them on his good arm like a waiter and put them down in the space she'd cleared on the coffee table between the platters of last night's half-eaten hot dogs and Logic's meth pipe and stash tin. A milk crate filled with tangled game controllers at one end of the coffee table, piles of dirty laundry on the other. Logic's moms might've cleaned the place *sometime* during the last century. Or not.

Claire leaned over the coffee table and forked a mouthful of eggs. "Mmm," she said between bites. The same sound she'd made when she woke up beside him. Seems his ranking on the pleasure scale was the same as a plate of scrambled eggs.

"I was thinking about Hugo," she said when she finished. She sat back on the couch with her legs tucked beneath her and picked at a scab on her knee. "What's going to happen to him now?"

"CPS prob'ly scooped him up. They'll be lookin' for a foster moms."

"I wish I could take him. He's so little and cute."

Holder s'posed that was so. There'd been a couple of times when he was at Campbell's trailer, playing the part of Logic's crewman, where the little guy was hanging around watching the grownups and sucking his thumb.

"I'd take him if Campbell doesn't make it. Somebody needs to take care of him. I could be a good mother. I have a kid, you know."

Holder did not know.

"He stays with my mom. Because of his asthma. Wait—I have a picture." She got up and crossed the room and came back carrying her purse. Opened her wallet and handed Holder a school photo.

"Cute." Dark hair, big eyes, wide face like his moms; maybe five or six years old. He handed it back. "So what you doin' hangin' here? Wouldn't you rather be home wakin' up with your kid?"

Her face shut down. She stuffed the photo back in her wallet. Holder supposed he shouldn't have offered an opinion. It was none of his business where she woke up or what she did. It was just that the picture of the little boy got to him. Something about his expression reminded Holder of himself. He'd grown up on the streets, and it hadn't exactly been a party. This boy had a moms. All she had to do to be there for him was to go home.

"I've only been doing crank a month or so," Claire said, almost defensively, looking across the room at nothing and picking at her knee. It struck Holder how young she was, how young she still looked, despite the drugs. Still a teenager. He had to play this carefully. "Before that I was only smoking weed and drinking. I ran into an old friend I used to hang with when I went to another school, and I found out he was a dealer. Pretty soon, I started selling weed for him. To get money for beer. I liked drinking best.

I didn't want to get into crank. I wanted to keep things safe. I heard stuff, you know? Then one night, I was so drunk, I was sick. My dealer said a line of crank would sober me up, so I tried it, and it did. I asked if I could get some more, and he said sure. I kinda wanted to see what it was about by then anyway, you know? 'Cause everyone would talk about it. After that, I could drink as much as I wanted to because that line would sober me up. Got a smoke?"

Holder shook a cigarette from the pack and handed it to her. She lit it and took a long drag.

"I know people think I'm just a crankhead, or a bag whore. That I'll do anything for a hit. But they don't understand. When you're tweaking, it's the most amazing feeling in the world. You have all this energy, you feel like you can do anything. Like you're big and powerful. Everything is brighter and better, like you're living in a fairytale, only the fairytale is real. Once you've experienced that, all you want is to go back again and again."

She shrugged. Picked up the glass pipe from the coffee table, tore open one of Logic's magic packets, and poured the powder in.

Holder's phone buzzed on the coffee table. He picked it up. Claire looked over his shoulder at the display.

"Who do you know at Harborview Medical?" Said in the tone of voice that wives had been using since the beginning of time to make their guilty husbands toe the line. Something about the way she asked made Holder wonder if she'd somehow found out about the cute nurse at the burn unit. In Holder's experience, women seemed to have a way of picking up on things like that. Especially women who'd made up their minds that they were your girlfriend. Even though there was nothing going on between him and Claire. *Serpico* meets *Fatal Attraction*, anyone? He could see how some guys ended up with a wife and a family they hadn't planned on or even wanted. Sometimes it was easier to just do as you were told than to cross your woman once she'd made up her mind that you were the marrying kind.

"I asked the hospital to call me if Campbell woke up. I didn't expect to hear so soon. Guess the poor bastard's gonna make it after all."

Claire nodded and sat back. Holder put the phone in his pocket and settled his arm around her shoulder as she packed the pipe and flicked her lighter. He was okay with playing house as long as it suited his undercover role, though he still couldn't get over how quickly she'd established them as a couple. Yesterday morning when they were under the overpass, she'd been coming on to Ridgeback and Logic. Now less than twenty-four hours later, him and her were as good as married. No wonder Ridgeback had doped him.

He thought about giving Claire a kiss, watched her flick the lighter and hold the flame under the pipe bowl, and decided not. He felt restless and bored. Lately it seemed as though the sum total of his life had devolved into hanging out in Logic's trailer. Back when he was working his way into the group, there had been some exciting times. Tense moments. Close calls. Now that he'd been accepted, the lack of a challenge was turning his brain to mush. Holder wasn't sure what he expected when he'd signed on as an undercover. Not a life of non-stop James Bond adventure, but definitely nothing as mind-numbingly boring as hanging with the same sorry group of people twenty-four seven; watching movies with them, playing video games with them, drinking with them, getting high with them. Getting drugged by them. That was a new one. Most undercovers only got beat up or robbed.

He ached for the kick of being out there. He wanted to take risks. Get shot at. Arrest somebody. Make 'em pay. Make a difference. He got that long hours with no action was part of the job. Some cops stayed under for years working a single case. And Holder was good at it, without a doubt. But he wanted more. Something a little higher on the interest scale than watching grass grow.

"Aren't you going to listen to the message?" Claire asked.

He pulled out his phone and looked at the display. Got up and went out into the kitchen before he played it on the off chance that it actually *was* the charge nurse. Listened to the message, and felt like he'd been punched in the chest.

"What's wrong, baby?" Claire asked when he came back into the living room.

"It's Campbell." Holder shook his head. "He's dead."

"Aw, man. I'm really sorry to hear that. I know he was in a bad way, but I really hoped he'd make it. What about his little boy? What's going to happen to him now?"

What indeed? One more child lost. He'd planned to turn Campbell, but the man might still have ended up in prison, albeit on a reduced sentence. The kid would have gone into foster care just the same.

Suddenly, he'd had all of Claire and the drugs and the sleazy trailer park that he could stand.

"Why should I care what's gonna happen to him? Fool's only gonna grow up to be another sorry ass tweaker. Coulda done the world a favor and checked out with his pops." He zipped up his hoodie.

"Where you goin', baby?" Like she thought she had a right to know.

"Out," he snapped. Like the henpecked husband he was pretending to be. And some people thought that women were the weaker sex.

He felt better as soon as he was outside. Logic's place was too claustrophobic, that was all, what with the dope fumes and the spoiled food stink and the cigarette smoke. He pulled out his keys, got into his car, and drove. He didn't know where he was going, and he didn't care. He just needed to get away.

He pulled off onto a dirt access road that led to the river and parked under a bridge. The underpass was vacant. Most days the place was lousy with junkies and street kids, but it was too windy and cold for hanging out today. He lit a cigarette and took a deep drag and stared and smoked. The gray water suited his mood. It was hard to say why Campbell's death bothered him so much, but it did. Even though he knew Campbell's life going forward wouldn't have been the same, at least he would have been alive. Alive was always better than the alternative.

He took another long drag. Blew it out. Let the nicotine take the fight out of him. He shouldn't let the people he was working with get under his skin. It didn't matter what they said or did. He was just doing a job. Logic was a dope dealer and Holder had set out to take him down. End of story. Meth was a hard addiction, and Holder was doing his best to stop it. A person would have to be a fool to give it a try. A meth high was so intense, once you'd experienced it, nothing else compared. Like Claire had said, meth got you believing you were a better person than you were before you started using. It made you happy, even as it cut you off from your family and friends. No room for them in your new and improved life. No time to worry about it. All a meth head cared about was their next hit. They were probably glad that everyone from their old life stayed away so they didn't have to deal. All they had to do was find a way to get high every day.

That was why he wanted to get Logic. Take him down. Dealers like Logic were at the center of a spiral that grew larger and pulled everything into it until it touched more people than you could count. The scum at the bottom of a whirlpool that sucked everything down. Holder thought about the twenty-something from his last assignment. She'd known she was three months pregnant, and still she took crank almost every day. She had another kid that she was breastfeeding. She claimed the crank didn't hurt her unborn child. Never mind the breastfeeding baby who could've overdosed on his mother's milk.

Families were the fallout. That was the real reason Holder did this job. So kids like Neil Campbell's could have something better. He hoped the little dude got adopted. He was young and cute enough to have a chance at a new set of parents. Even one parent would be enough. Somebody like his sister. Davie would like to have a little brother. He wondered if he could talk Liz into signing up.

He crushed the cigarette in the ashtray and started the car. Drove up the embankment and onto the highway and turned back toward Rainier Valley. Because he had to. But also because he wanted to. Because he was the bad-ass Dutch dude givin' the sea the finger.

# 30

Sarah drove straight from the hospital to Rainier Valley. After the phone call in which she broke the news about Campbell and Goddard brought her up to speed on what he'd found out about the brothers' test results at Rockland Diagnostics, she wished more than ever that she'd had the chance to interview Neil Campbell before he died. She was almost certain that he'd known about the Marsees' secret project. Perhaps the three men were even working together. Just because Rutz claimed the Marsees didn't know about their half-brother didn't mean it was true. Rutz had lied to them on more than one occasion. Rutz had an agenda. She and Goddard just had to figure out what it was.

Meanwhile, if Campbell had hidden his identity from his half-brothers and was indeed all Rutz had described—a man without conscience or empathy—and if his DNA also carried the double mutation, it was certainly possible that Campbell had killed Guy and Lance in order to take over the project. Sarah bit her lip at how close she'd come to finding out the truth, and clenched the steering wheel until her fingers went numb, as if physical pain could somehow dissipate her anger. She was bitterly disappointed. Sarah had a reputation for being cold and unemotional, but the truth was, every day, she had to fight to keep her emotions in check. She felt everything deeply. Too deeply, according to her lieutenant—and her shrink. But she couldn't help it. When you were a cop—a cop who made judgment calls that affected people's lives—there was always a case that ate away at you, the worry that you'd got it wrong, locked up the wrong guy. The poet said that to err was human. But how could you forgive yourself when your mistake put an innocent person's life on the line? And people wondered why she was so driven.

This time, she'd been so close to a solve she could feel it, like a twist in her gut or an ache in her bones. If she could have talked to Campbell, even if only for a few minutes, if she could have extracted a confession from him, she would have been at the station right now filling paperwork instead of hitting the interview trail yet again. Talking to someone who had known both Neil Campbell and the Marsee brothers was a poor substitute, but it was all she had.

The gloves were off. No more "I can't remember" and "I don't knows." This time, Sarah would get her answers.

The rain was mixed with sleet by the time she turned into Rainier Valley. Sarah followed the now-familiar decaying streets to Tiffany's trailer. The crime tape was gone, the front door closed. The trailer looked abandoned. Empty houses had a certain air about them that was easy to spot, hard to explain. Tiffany's trailer had that look. More importantly, there was no red Toyota in the driveway. Wherever Tiffany was staying, it wasn't here. Sarah supposed that if *she* had been in Tiffany's shoes, she wouldn't have wanted to sleep in the trailer where her boyfriend was killed. She wasn't worried that Tiffany had skipped out on her. How far was a penniless tweaker going to go? She was probably off somewhere getting high. If so, Sarah would find her. The cops had picked her up once, they could do it again.

Sarah checked her watch. Almost noon. Aside from a pack of feral toddlers breaking up the ice in the puddles at the end of the street, the park was quiet. Kids were in school, their parents at work, hookers and other denizens of the night were still asleep.

She lit a cigarette, then sat back and watched the kids stomp and shriek as she waited on the off chance that the Toyota might return. A person could take these same kids, she reflected, dress them in clean clothes and put them in a different environment, like a field trip to a concert or a museum, and anyone looking at them would still know they were poor trailer park trash. There was an indefinable something about their appearance that went beyond their mothers' inexpert haircuts and their ragged clothes. A combination of poor nutrition and negligent parenting that left an indelible mark.

Sarah had that mark. The brand had faded over the years, but it was still there. Outwardly she had put her less than perfect upbringing behind her, but inside, she still sometimes felt like that frightened little girl. It wasn't her fault. Sarah had been five when her mother left. CPS found her in the apartment after she'd spent the night alone in the dark because her mother hadn't paid the electric bill. Child Protective Services must have come five or six times before that. Each time, Sarah tried to hide the truth. Even at that age, she knew a foster house was going to be worse. Most of them were. She'd run away a half-dozen times after that. But it was her mom who started it all when she gave Sarah up.

She smoked the cigarette down to the filter, then got out of the car. Pulled her jacket hood over her head and made her way through the rain up the broken sidewalk. Knocked on the door. Waited. Waited some more. Turned around and scanned the street as if by looking long and hard enough, Tiffany would magically appear.

Her gaze was drawn to the trailer across the street. The one that had hosted the meth party last night. A lamp glowed weakly through the living room curtains. The woman she'd talked to when she was canvassing the neighborhood the day Lance's body was found had been hooked up to an oxygen tank. Odds were good she'd be home. Old people and the housebound made great witnesses. They had nothing better to do than spy on their neighbors' comings and goings all day.

She crossed the street. Fresh tire tracks in the driveway and a dry spot on the pavement indicated a car had recently been parked there. She threaded her way through the yard junk—a patio table and chairs *sans* umbrella, broken bicycles, and a kid-sized plastic basketball hoop setup minus the net—then climbed the steps to the covered porch. A clay flowerpot in the corner was tipped over and broken, spilling a desiccated cactus onto the unpainted porch boards. Empty beer bottles lined the railing. Through the thin trailer walls, she could hear a television, along with the rhythmic click and hiss of an oxygen machine.

"Mrs. Gallagher? Jackie?" Sarah knocked on the door, waited, then knocked again. "Mrs. Gallagher? It's Detective Linden. I'd like to ask you a few questions."

"Tyler, someone's at the door!" a woman's voice called. "Tyler, get the door!"

Sarah waited. At last heavy footsteps shook the trailer's floor. Clearly Tyler wasn't the helpful type. The doorknob rattled as someone fumbled to unlock it, then Jackie Gallagher peered out. High side of forty, stringy hair, bloated face, oxygen tube shoved in her nose. She was wearing the same ratty housedress she'd had on the first time Sarah interviewed her.

"I already told you everything," she said. The door started to close. Sarah quickly stuck her foot in the gap.

"I realize that, Mrs. Gallagher. And we appreciate your

help." Said with a smile, though in truth, the woman had offered Sarah's investigation no assistance at all. "I'd like to ask you about the trailer fire across the street. We believe the two incidents might be related."

"Hmph." The door closed, the chain rattled, and then the door opened wider. "I wouldn't be s'prised. Nuthin' but trouble in this dump."

"How well did you know Neil Campbell?"

"I seen him around."

"And his little boy? Hugo?"

The woman nodded. "Blond. Always with his daddy."

"What did Neil do?"

The woman snorted. "What do you think? He cooked meth."

"Right. We know that. I mean when he wasn't cooking. Did he have any friends in the park? Maybe spend time at the trailer next door? At Tiffany's?"

The woman snorted again. "More like she spent time at his."

"What do you mean?"

The woman laughed. Unattractively. And her breath smelled. Sarah took a step back.

"I mean those two were a couple long before the new boyfriend moved in." She nodded smugly and winked as if there were more to the story.

Confirming the account from Tiffany's coworker, Jaycee. "And after? Did the three of them do things together?" Thinking about the secret project.

The woman's eyes narrowed. Going in for the kill. She took her hand out of her housedress pocket and held Sarah's gaze as she slowly rubbed her thumb against her fingers.

Sarah pretended she didn't see. If cops had to pay for every bit of information they needed to solve a case, the SPD would quickly go broke. "Please try to remember. It's important."

The woman frowned and put her hand back in her pocket. "Yeah, they were together a lot. Like one of those menageries."

"A menagerie?"

"You know, a threesome."

A *ménage à trois*. Sarah tried not to smile. She took out her phone and pulled up a picture of Guy Marsee. "Tell me, did you ever see this man with them?"

The woman took the phone, squinted at the picture, and handed it back. "Can't say. Maybe." She waited. Sarah waited too. In a contest of wills, she always came out the winner.

"What's he drive?" the woman asked at last.

"A white Prius."

"Yeah, I've seen that car. It's always parked over there." Pointing across the street. Not to Tiffany's trailer, *but to Campbell's.*

Before Sarah could stop her, Jackie shut the trailer door. She heard the chain rattle back into place. Sarah turned around and started down the porch steps. Her mind was reeling. She'd expected that Guy Marsee would come to the trailer park to visit his brother, Lance. Tiffany had said as much: that they were working on a project together, something secret that they wouldn't talk about in her presence. But what was Guy Marsee doing at Neil Campbell's?

"Who was that?" she heard a man's raised voice from inside the trailer as she continued down the sidewalk. High-pitched. Whiney.

"Why'n't you answer the door yourself?" the woman responded. "Then you'd know."

"'Cause I ain't your lame-ass slave, bitch."

"Yeah, but you're livin' in my house. Show some respect, boy. You don' like it, you can get out."

Their voices faded. The last thing Sarah heard was Jackie's boy yelling, "Yo! You hit me. You in a world o' hurt now!" followed by a thud. Something being thrown? Someone falling?

She crossed the street and leaned back against her car door and shook out a cigarette. Took a drag as she studied the two trailers, one half destroyed, the other seemingly abandoned. Sarah now knew that the half-brothers had known each other—perhaps more intimately than either she or Goddard had guessed. The question was, did they know they were half-brothers?

# 31

Goddard had nothing but admiration for the undercover making his way through the food line ahead of him in the hospital cafeteria. Undercover work was a tough gig. It took a certain personality to pull it off, a combination of fearlessness and street smarts that not every officer possessed. An undercover had to be believable in their assumed persona, to strike the right balance between being too friendly and too aloof. Weariness and stoicism made a more convincing criminal.

Kings County Sherriff Department Officer Stephen Holder had texted a reply to Goddard's voicemail, suggesting a meet. Goddard had had to drive a steady ten miles an hour over the speed limit all the way back from Rockland Diagnostics in order to make the appointment, but it was worth it. An undercover's life was so erratic that you had to adjust to their schedule, or you might not get another chance.

"Thanks for agreeing to meet with me," Goddard said as he paid the cashier for their meals and scanned the room looking for an empty table.

"Nothin' I like better'n hospital food." The undercover winked. "Long's you understand this is off the record, we're cool. I can't swear to anything I'm gonna tell you in court."

"I understand. Let's sit over there." Goddard pointed to a table in the corner, away from the large plate-glass windows that were open to the hospital's main corridor. The undercover wasn't likely to run into any of his street pals here, but you couldn't be too careful.

Holder must have been thinking the same, because he sat in a chair with a view of the door. The lunch crowd was dwindling; maybe a couple dozen people, mostly hospital workers, remained in the room. The undercover kept his hooded sweatshirt on. Keeping it real. The look he was cultivating, scruffy hair, neatly trimmed goatee, cigarette tucked rakishly behind his ear, was definitely working for him. If Goddard had tried to wear the same get-up, he would have looked like a clown. Goddard noted the charge nurse from the burn unit who had given him Holder's business card eating nearby, looking at the undercover. Holder saw it too, and winked.

"What I really need is information about four people," Goddard said after he'd finished half his burger and Holder had wolfed down all of his. The undercover had thrown the cafeteria staff for a loop when he'd asked for a burger with no meat. "Tiffany Crane, Lance Marsee, Guy Marsee, and Neil Campbell. Tiffany owns the trailer where her boyfriend, Lance Marsee, was killed. Campbell's the guy from the meth fire next door—you know he's dead, right?"

"Yeah, I got the word."

"And Guy Marsee is Lance's brother."

Holder nodded. "I know who they are 'cept the last one."

"You might have seen him. We have reason to believe he's been to the trailer park. Guy Marsee is blond like Lance and about the same height and build. Drives a white Prius."

Holder brightened. "Yeah, I seen the car. Not too many Priuses at Rainier Valley."

"So what can you tell me about these four? I'm most interested in their relationships, how well they knew each other, that sort of thing."

"Well, let's see. Campbell was a cooker, but I 'spose you already know that. Tiffany's his girlfriend. They've been together 'bout three years now. I haven't been working the park that long, but that's what they tell me. She spent a lot of time at his place. Said she was babysitting the boy, but a lot of the time, Campbell was there too, so you know." He shrugged. "Actions tell a different story."

"But she found a new boyfriend, right? Lance Marsee? The guy who got shot in her trailer?"

"Nah, he wasn't her boyfriend. He thought so, but she still had a thing for Campbell big time. That girl had it bad. She'd do anything for him."

"Even murder?"

"Nah, I didn't mean that. Just that she was his drudge, his gofer. Like those Manson girls. When Campbell said 'jump,' she didn't ask how high; just climbed onto the nearest bridge and flew."

"What do you figure Campbell got out of their relationship? Besides the obvious."

"Control. That's what he got off on. Dude was one cold mother. Getting people to do what they didn't want to made him feel big. Like Tiffany. All she wanted was him, but he made her come on to the rich guys at the casino. He didn't care about the stuff they gave her. Just that he'd made her do something she didn't want to. That's how she hooked up with Lance. Campbell picked him out for her himself." Holder laughed. "Only I guess he never figured on her bringin' the dude home. Man, I never seen him so mad. It was the first time she'd ever really stood up to him. He got back at her, though. Turned her into a meth head. One taste and she was gone. Like I said, control."

"And you're sure about all of this?"

Holder nodded. "I keep my ears open. A lot of what people say is bull, but I got eyes. I know what I see."

"So Campbell was a control freak. What about his boy, Hugo? Was he rough with him?" Linden had filled him in on what she'd learned about that particular detail. They made a good tag team.

"Nah, he loved that little man. Campbell was one mean mother, but you'd never know it when he was around his kid. Kid's bedroom was a regular Toys R Us. And whenever he cooked up a batch of meth, he always put the kid in the car."

As if that made him a good father. Though it did prove, Goddard supposed, that no one was either all good, or all bad. He thought about his own soon-to-be-born son. Kath had the nursery set up. Blue wallpaper with teddy bears on it. Teddy bear lamps, teddy bear bedding in the crib, teddy bear mobile. Goddard had wanted to do up the room with a baseball theme, but Kath preferred teddy bears.

"What about the boy's mother? Does she come around?"

Holder shook his head. "She took herself out of the family photo when Hugo was a baby. Decided she didn't like being a moms and just walked away. Gave Campbell full custody before she disappeared. I dunno what'll happen to the little dude now. Doubt she's gonna be there for him, you feel me?" Holder looked pensive as he took a long slug of diet Coke. "Anyways, we done? I got places to go, people to see."

"Just one more thing. That Prius. You wouldn't happen to remember where it was parked when you saw it? Which trailer?" Trying to nail the detail Linden had gotten from the woman across the street, that on at least one occasion, Guy's Prius had been parked in front of Campbell's trailer.

The undercover raised his eyebrows. His forehead creased and his brows furrowed as he tried to remember. "Hells, I dunno. On the street. In front of Tiffany's trailer, I guess."

"Was it always parked there? In the same spot?"

Holder shook his head and shrugged. "Sorry. I didn't know there was going to be a quiz."

"Okay," Goddard said. He couldn't fault the guy for not noticing. It was an obscure detail. Possibly not even important. "Thanks for meeting with me. Appreciate your help."

Holder touched his finger to his forehead, picked up his tray, and carried the contents over to the trash. Goddard noted he chose the trash bin closest to the attractive charge nurse. He shook his head. Holder, Louis… these young guys with their hormones, always thinking about just the one thing. Goddard sighed and picked up his tray to follow. He wasn't that many years older than Holder and Louis, but sometimes it felt like a million.

# 32

Goddard was already in his office when Sarah got back to the station. His office looked a lot like hers: standard-issue furniture, whiteboard, wooden coat rack in the corner, cardboard filing boxes stacked three-high on the side table and on the floor. Family photos on the shelves behind him instead of on his desk. Looking down on him rather than looking back. Sarah wondered if the "out of sight, out of mind" placement had been done consciously, or if there were bigger issues in play. Decided it didn't matter as long as he could stop checking his phone for messages every five minutes.

Still, nobody was perfect, Goddard was an okay partner; they'd accomplished a good day's work. And the day wasn't yet over.

Lieutenant Oakes appeared at the door. "You got your warrant," he said, handing Sarah the folded paper. "Happy hunting."

She turned to Goddard. "We still have a couple hours of daylight. Ready to head back out?"

"Why not? Let's go."

Sarah slid the warrant into her jacket pocket while Goddard put on his coat. Even in death, Neil Campbell retained his constitutional rights, but she and Goddard had established the likelihood that Campbell had known about the Marsee brothers' PKD project solidly enough to list him as a possible murder suspect on a warrant application. Now that they had the warrant in hand, they could legally search the sections of his trailer that hadn't been destroyed by the meth fire, perhaps turn up some more evidence to link the two halves of the dysfunctional family.

The lines of investigation they were following were not as neat and tidy as Sarah would have liked. If the two Marsees and Campbell were working together using their unique genetic material to develop a treatment for PKD, why did Guy's computer show only himself and Lance with access to their Google Doc? And if the three men *weren't* working together, how had Campbell found out about the project? She hoped a search of his trailer would turn up answers. At the very least, there should be something about the project on Campbell's computer. Although finding the murder weapon would also be a much-needed break.

"There's one thing that's still bothering me in all of this," Goddard said once they were settled in Sarah's car. "Our man Rutz. First he tells us he doesn't know Guy Marsee outside of work. But it turns out that he's Marsee's godfather. After we catch him out, he narrates a six-volume book about the family history and tells us about the half-brother. He insists the two halves of the family don't know each other, but then we find out that they do. He's a smart man. Surely he doesn't think he can hide this stuff forever. So what's his game? Is he just trying to mess with us? Slow down our investigation? If so, why?"

"I don't know," Sarah said. "But I'm sure we'll find out." "Game" was the right word to describe Rutz's behavior. He was toying with them. Like he thought he was smarter, or perhaps he shared Campbell's obsessive need to be in control, as described by Goddard's undercover source. But the reasons for his behavior didn't matter. Persistence on their part along with careful detective work would bring him down. It always did.

She pulled out of the parking lot and turned toward Rainier Valley. As she did, her cellphone rang. She handed it to Goddard without checking the display. The rain had been intermixed with sleet all day, and the roads were slick. She didn't need to get into an accident when they were getting so close. "Can you take this?"

"Sure. Detective Goddard," he answered. "Uh-huh… right… Yes, please." A pause. Then, "That's great. Thanks. You've been a big help."

He closed the phone and handed it back. "That was Dr. Preston, from GenMod. Remember when you asked her if GenMod was working on a cure for PKD, and she said she'd look into it? Well, it turns out, they are. Or rather, they've just started. The project is still in the application stage because it hasn't yet been approved."

"Let me guess: Guy and Lance Marsee's names are on the application."

"You're half right. Their names are on the application, but the application was submitted on their behalf by our good friend, Dr. Nelson Rutz." Goddard grinned.

"So that means—"

"He knew about their project. And because he also knew about Campbell, that means—"

"—Rutz is the connection. That's how Campbell knew about the brothers' plans: Rutz told him. So Rutz was lying when he said he hasn't been in contact with Campbell other than that one phone call."

Goddard nodded. "So that brings us back to the same question. What's his game?"

"I don't know," Sarah said again. "But I have a feeling we're about to find out."

* * *

Campbell's trailer had been one of the nicer homes in the park. The kind that was called a "double-wide," hauled to its final destination in halves and then joined together. With a pitched roof built over both, the result was a reasonable approximation of a house. Sarah had seen the two halves of a double-wide being pulled down the highway once when she was a kid. The idea of a house traveling down the road had been novel enough all on its own, but the fact that she could see right through the plastic sheeting stapled over the opening to the inside was utterly fascinating. Like looking into a life-sized dollhouse. Living room. Kitchen. Bedroom. Hallway. She remembered wondering if there were dishes in the cupboards and clothes in the closets. She'd giggled when they drove past the bathroom and she saw the toilet. The foster couple hadn't appreciated bathroom humor and had washed Sarah's mouth out with soap.

Campbell's front door was again covered with a sheet of plywood. Sarah wondered how long this second sheet would last. Either the explosion had blown the door out or the firemen had broken it in. Someone was bound to pry the plywood off before long. After that, the whole trailer would be picked clean. Assuming the non-Marsee half of Campbell's family didn't lay claim to his belongings first and empty the trailer before the vandals had their way with it and the squatters moved in.

Sarah and Goddard picked their way through the charred debris and frozen puddles to the back yard. The back door was unlocked. Campbell hadn't exactly been planning to leave his home for the last time on a stretcher.

The odor inside the trailer was appalling. No telling what toxins they were breathing in. The blaze had started in the kitchen, but it looked like it had taken the fire department a while to get the fire under control, because the flames had done a number on the living room as well. Most of the fake-wood paneling was either charred, or missing, and the ceiling had fallen in. Broken and blackened asbestos ceiling tiles blanketed the remains of a blue leather sofa and a plate-glass coffee table.

The melted carpet stuck to Sarah's shoes. It felt like she was walking in quicksand. She picked up a framed photograph from the floor. It showed a man and a boy holding hands, Neil and Hugo Campbell. Now she came to think about it, she hadn't known what Campbell looked like. She'd only seen him after the fire, his face mummified in hospital bandages. The picture showed a blond man with the same sturdy build as the Marsee brothers. More athletic, like he'd spent less time in front of a computer and more time working out. The boy was also blond, about two or three, and definitely Campbell's son. Sarah could tell not only by the physical resemblance, but by the way the boy looked up at his father's face.

"What a mess, huh?" Goddard remarked. "Let's check the bedrooms."

The first bedroom they came to had clearly belonged to Hugo. Even knowing that Campbell had indulged his boy with every toy and gadget imaginable, Sarah wasn't prepared for the sheer quantity of toys and stuffed animals. If a father's affection could be measured by his offspring's possessions, Hugo had been well loved. Most of the techno-gadgets were for an older child. The Marsees had been raised by university professors, plenty of intellectual stimulation, at least according to Rutz. Apparently Campbell was continuing the tradition. She hoped that whoever was looking after Hugo would come back to the trailer and box up a few of his things before they were stolen or thrown away. Everything in the trailer smelled of smoke, but stuffed animals could be washed. She hoped they'd pick out the ones that were the most worn.

Campbell's bedroom was at the end of the hall. The bedroom where he and Tiffany had been a couple. Up to the day that Campbell blew himself up, according to Goddard's information from the undercover. Sarah couldn't stop thinking about her interview with Tiffany. The woman had cried through the interview, cried when she identified Lance and Guy's bodies. Naturally, Sarah had assumed her grief was for her murdered boyfriend, Lance. But all along, her tears had been for her real lover, Campbell. It was hard to accept that Sarah had been so completely deceived. All she could offer in her defense was that Tiffany was a consummate actress. She'd convinced Lance and who knew how many other high-rollers that she loved them. Now that she knew the truth, Sarah couldn't wait to talk to the woman again. They'd call both her and Rutz back to the station as soon as they'd assembled their evidence.

The bed was made, an interesting indicator of Campbell's personality. How many single dads took the time to do that? Sarah herself couldn't claim to be so tidy.

"Check the closet," Goddard said as he pulled on a set of gloves and pulled open the drawer of the nightstand. Sarah put on her own gloves and opened the closet's bi-fold doors. Campbell had evidently favored jeans and polo shirts. The jeans were pressed and hung on hangers. She took a flashlight from her pocket and shone it over the shelf above the hangers. Folded sweaters and baskets that turned out to contain socks and underwear sorted by color and rolled neatly into balls. Goddard's report had said that Guy was a neat freak. Apparently the neatness gene ran in the family.

"You finding anything of Tiffany's?" she called over her shoulder. Placing Tiffany in Campbell's bedroom would give Sarah leverage at their next interview.

"Not yet. Room's pretty clean. But I've got Campbell's laptop. It was in his nightstand."

On the floor of the closet were two cardboard boxes with the flaps folded and tucked. She pulled one into the middle of the room where the light was better. Old textbooks: *Introduction to Physical Anthropology*, *Appreciating Diversity*, *What Does it Mean to Be Human?* Probably belonged to Campbell's anthropologist mother.

She pulled out the second battered box. It contained family photos, and Sarah pulled out a handful. At first, she thought she was looking at pictures of Campbell when he was a child. But most of the pictures showed *two* blond-haired boys, not one. She picked out another handful. Boys playing at the beach, on a swing set, coming down a park slide. They looked to be around four years apart. Guy and Lance.

In the bottom was a clear Ziploc bag full of yellowed newspaper clippings and faded report cards. She opened the bag, paged through a few. Sat back on her heels. All of the clippings pertained to Campbell's half-brothers. Not a single one of them mentioned Campbell himself.

She spread the clippings out over the bed. "Goddard, come here. Look at this."

Goddard studied the assemblage. "What am I looking at?"

"These clippings. Science fair projects, awards won, report cards and SAT results and—" she picked up a more recent clipping "—an announcement of Lance Marsee's induction into the National Academy of Sciences. These are all about the Marsees. Campbell has been watching them, monitoring them, *stalking* them for years. Decades. He knew everything about them."

"While they knew nothing about him." Goddard whistled.

"Maybe," Sarah said. Whether or not the Marsees knew they had a half-brother was still open to debate. But there was no doubt now that Campbell knew all about them. The sheer quantity of material set her nerves on edge. Sarah didn't have this many mementos of her own son.

"No wonder he used Tiffany to come on to Lance," Goddard said. "He had to have known about Lance's gambling problem. Tiffany worked at the Black Bear. It was the perfect setup."

"But why?" Sarah waved her arm at the clippings spread over the bed. "He already knew everything there was to know about them."

"Everything except the exact details of their 'secret project.'"

Sarah nodded. "Of course. Campbell finds out about the project through Rutz. He wants to know more, but he can't approach the brothers openly without revealing himself. So he uses his girlfriend as a conduit."

"The undercover said Campbell was furious when she brought him home to live with her. Bet that wasn't part of the plan."

"I'm sure it wasn't." Sarah picked up a handful of clippings and started packing them into the box. "Let's get these back to the station."

As she followed Goddard back through the living room, Sarah glanced into the kitchen. The table had been knocked over in the blast; its surface was scorched and charred. Campbell had sat at that table, crushing the pseudoephedrine tablets, mixing the chemicals, shaking the soda bottle, and for what? A few grams of meth. The undercover told Goddard that Campbell had turned Tiffany on to meth after she brought Lance home to live with her in order to re-exert his control. But there were easier ways of obtaining the drug than making it yourself, especially in a place like Rainier Valley. Campbell was a smart man. He had to have known that cooking meth was a risky business. Again according the undercover, that was why he'd locked his boy in the car. So why was he doing it? It was possible he was cooking simply for the thrill of it. People did stranger things to get their adrenaline pumping. Or he might have been cooking out of hubris, thinking he was too smart to be the guy for whom things would go wrong. Or maybe he was cooking because he needed the cash—a great deal of it—for a certain "secret project." He couldn't have been taking such a risk just to supply one addict.

She thought about the boy, Hugo, shivering in the car while his dad cooked up a batch of meth. Some father.

"I'll catch up with you in a sec," she said to Goddard, and went back down the hallway to Hugo's bedroom. She looked over the menagerie on the boy's bed, selected a faded yellow rabbit that was flattened on one side and missing an eye, then hurried back out.

She stuffed the rabbit into her jacket pocket and followed Goddard out to the car. The cardboard box of mementos was already on the back seat, along with Campbell's laptop. She hoped the tech guys would be able to find some answers on it.

Sarah put the key in the ignition and reached into her jacket for a cigarette, then looked over at Goddard watching her and thought better of it. He'd only recently quit smoking. She didn't want to make it harder for him. Now that she was considering cutting back, it was becoming painfully clear just how much of an addiction she had. Never mind what it was doing to her lungs, she hated the idea of being dependent on a chemical. And at the end of the day, was she really all that different from Tiffany? Addiction was addiction. Just because her substance was legal didn't make it right.

"Got another of those Nicachews?"

Goddard reached into his coat pocket and handed her two. Sarah unwrapped one and popped it into her mouth. Taking a final long look at the sad remains of Campbell's trailer, she drove off.

# 33

Sarah dropped off Goddard next to his car in the station lot. She had an hour before it was time to pick up Jack from his after-school program. She thought about going inside and catching up on paperwork. Instead, she pulled back out of the lot and drove across town to a familiar two-story red-brick building. A building where Sarah had spent far too much time during her childhood. From the outside, the Child Protective Services Administration offices looked like a school. A fenced-in playground surrounded by trees—maples and oaks with thick, low branches that begged to be climbed. Bicycle racks and cement park benches, a garden bordered by rhododendrons and a grape arbor. A pleasant enough setting for the social workers who worked here and the children they looked out for during the spring, summer, and fall. But in winter, the bare branches reflected in the tiny panes of the metal-frame windows made the place look like the prison Sarah had often felt it was.

She parked in one of the visitor slots, then took a deep breath and got out. So many memories. None of them good. She patted the stuffed rabbit in her pocket, then opened the building's front door and went into the lobby. Instantly, she was nearly overwhelmed. The sounds. The smells. The same plastic chairs lined up around the edges of the room that she remembered from when she was a child. She crossed the room and knocked on a sliding glass panel. Waited until the receptionist behind the frosted glass pushed one of the panels to the side.

"Hi, there," Sarah said pleasantly. "I'm Detective Sarah Linden." *Whose name is somewhere in your computer files*, she could have added. "I'm looking for information about a child who was brought in a couple of days ago. Hugo Campbell. He's two or three years old. Blond. His custodial parent had to be hospitalized after he was burned in a house trailer fire."

Sarah deliberately left out the fact that Campbell was burned in a meth explosion. No doubt the details were in Hugo's case file, and the caseworker would be well aware of the circumstances, but not everybody needed to know.

The receptionist consulted her computer screen. "I'm sorry. Hugo's caseworker is out in the field for the rest of the day. Can you come back tomorrow?"

Sarah could. Except that tomorrow, she'd be busy following up on other aspects of the case. Who knew where the investigation would lead her, or when she'd have a chance to get out here again? She just wanted to find out where Hugo had been placed so she could bring him his favorite toy.

"That's okay. I don't really need to speak with the caseworker. I just need to see Hugo. If you'll give me the address..."

Still smiling. The problem was, cop or no cop, it was entirely up to this woman whether she would cooperate with Sarah's request or not. Legally, Sarah had a right to the information, even though she wasn't actively involved with the case. But Child Protective Services and law enforcement didn't always get along. Both agencies wanted the same thing in theory, and that was to do what was in the best interest of the child. But CPS saw their role as reuniting families wherever possible, while the cops wanted to see the bad guys put away. Visitation between the child in foster care and his or her parents was particularly tricky. CPS maintained that visitation was vital to the child's sense of continuity and belonging even when removed from an abusive home. As bad as the child's home life might have been, it was the only one they'd known. But law enforcement worried that parents would use the visitation time to coach the child, or pressure them to change their story. Often, they were right. "I'm sorry. I really can't tell you more than that."

Sarah forced a smile. Breaking into Fort Knox was probably easier than extracting information from Child Protective Services. Waterboarding might help. She pulled the toy rabbit from her pocket and laid it on the counter. Her ace in the hole. "I just wanted to give him this. It's his favorite."

The woman practically melted. "That's so sweet of you!" She reached out and took the toy before Sarah could react. She was still smiling as she wrote Hugo's name on a piece of paper and used a rubber band to fasten it around the rabbit's neck. "I'll make sure to give it to Hugo's caseworker tomorrow. She'll make sure it gets to him."

Sarah smiled through gritted teeth. There was nothing for her to do but let the woman have it her way. Sarah was profoundly disappointed. She was also angry. She recognized that her reaction was completely out of proportion to the offense. Even so, what was wrong with people? How hard would it have been for the woman to give Sarah Hugo's address? All she'd wanted was to give the stuffed rabbit to Hugo herself. Make that one small connection. Let him know somebody cared.

She was about to leave when she had an idea. "Could I please have a piece of paper? I'd like to write Hugo a note to go with it."

"Of course." The receptionist tore off the top sheet from a pad of paper and handed it to Sarah, along with a pen.

*Your bunny's been looking for you!* Sarah wrote. *Give him a big hug! Love,*

She hesitated.

*Daddy.*

Sarah was running late by the time she got to Jack's middle school. Everyone was driving slower than normal because of the icy roads. Jack got testy if she didn't pick him up on time. Sarah couldn't blame him. What kid wouldn't rather be at home than hanging around at school a minute longer than necessary?

She texted him to let him know she was outside, then lit a cigarette while she waited.

He appeared a few minutes later. The scowl on his face was visible from the street. He opened the rear passenger door and tossed in his backpack, then slammed it shut and slid into the front seat. "God, Mom. I can't believe you're late again."

"Better late than never." She smiled. Jack did not.

"I bet you were at that stupid trailer park again."

Jack had her cop's instincts, without a doubt. Sarah didn't know whether to feel proud or annoyed. When he was littler, she used to be able to slide things past him. Now he was quick to call her to account.

"Buckle up," she said as she pulled away from the curb.

He rolled his eyes. "I'm not a baby."

"I know. It's just that you're growing up so fast, sometimes, I forget you don't need me to tell you what to do. Listen, what do you say we grab some McDonald's on the way?"

"I'd rather have Wendy's. Their fries are better. I haven't liked McDonalds since I was like, ten."

Letting her know he couldn't be so easily bought. His assertiveness didn't bother her. Teens were supposed to push back. It was just part of the process. Where communication broke down was when parents took it all too seriously. You had to cut your kids some slack. Give them a chance to find their way. No reason to get bent out of shape over something that in ten or twenty years neither of you would even remember.

"Wendy's it is." She reached out to ruffle his hair. Congratulated herself on her most excellent mothering skills when he didn't pull away.

"How was school today?" she asked.

"It was okay."

Which was about all the conversation on that topic she was going to get.

"I'm thinking Scrabble tonight. What do you say? We'll turn on the fire, make some hot chocolate. It'll be fun."

"Maybe."

By the time Sarah inched her way through the mile-long line at the drive-thru, the on-again, off-again sleet that had been threatening all day turned to snow. Jack didn't seem to notice the treacherous road conditions as he bobbed his head to whatever music was playing on his headphones and munched his French fries.

At last they pulled into their driveway. Sarah peeled her fingers from the steering wheel, suddenly aware how hard she'd been clenching. She picked up the nearly empty fast-food bag and got out of the car. Jack followed her, twirling like a little boy with his mouth open and his head tipped back to the sky as he caught the big, fat flakes. Sarah smiled and did the same. As soon as Jack saw her, he stopped.

Sarah sighed. As she started up the steps, the motion sensor turned on the porch light. She looked down, and sighed again, then picked up the frozen bouquet of roses Rick had left on her front steps and carried it into the house.

# DAY FOUR

JANUARY 27, 5:30 A.M.

## 34

The power was out when Sarah woke up. She went into the kitchen to start a pot of coffee, filled the reservoir with cold water, spooned the coffee into the filter, and only then did she notice that the microwave display was off.

She walked over to the doorway and flipped the room's light switch. Nothing. Given yesterday's storm prediction, she supposed she shouldn't have been surprised. Luckily, her stove was gas. She filled the kettle, then dug through the lower cabinets for the French press someone had given to her one year for Christmas. She carried it over to the window so she could see well enough to read the directions on the box and figure out how to use it.

Rick's roses lay on the counter. The leaves were curled and the petals had turned to mush. She felt bad about the wasted money and effort. The roses were too far gone to try to revive them, but it didn't seem right to just throw them away. A dilemma which could have been a metaphor for their relationship, but she didn't want to go there. She pictured Rick standing on her porch last night, knocking on her door, waiting who knew how long for an answer, getting none, and then leaving the roses thinking that surely she'd be along shortly to bring them inside.

On the other hand, he didn't have to leave them behind and risk their being ruined. He could have taken the roses home with him and come back again later—or called before he came over in the first place to make sure that she was home. Instead, he'd put her in a position where she'd been made to feel guilty. She gathered up the flowers and threw them in the trash.

Outside, it was just starting to get light. Beneath the streetlights, the snow was falling in fat, wet flakes. The air had the thick, muted quality that came with a heavy snowfall. The light was softer. Sounds were muffled. She could hear a plow scraping pavement several streets over, but that was all. The crews would have worked through the night to keep the main roads open and the buses running, but side streets like the one she lived on didn't get cleared. She craned her neck to see her driveway. Her car looked like a giant marshmallow. Too bad her condo didn't have a garage. Even a carport would have helped. But those units were more expensive, and on her cop's salary, this was all she could afford.

The kettle whistled. Sarah read the instructions on the box again, then carefully followed them to the letter. As it turned out, making a cup of coffee with a French press was not as difficult as the directions made it seem. She carried the cup into the living room, feeling a pleasant sense of accomplishment, and sat down on the couch with a fleece throw wrapped around her shoulders and her bare feet tucked beneath her. She thought about the Marsee case as she sipped. She and Goddard had made good progress with their investigation yesterday, but today was going to be a bust. She'd badly wanted to bring in Rutz or Tiffany this morning for questioning. But now thanks to the storm, she'd be doing well if she managed to dig herself out and get to the station. Once she was there, it would be all hands on deck. Most likely, she was going to have to spend the day working accident assist or traffic control. At least with the city shut down by the storm, neither of her persons of interest were going anywhere.

Her phone vibrated. She reached over to where it lay on the coffee table and picked it up. A text from Goddard: *Wife had the baby last night. We got our boy! Bringing cigars. See you in a few.*

She smiled. She couldn't remember exactly when Goddard had said the baby was due. It seemed early, but from the tone of his text, it sounded like everything was all right. She texted back her congrats, then called the station.

"Linden here. I'll be there in about an hour," she told the front desk. It was going to take at least that long to clear the car, not to mention getting Jack up and dressed.

"Thanks for checking in. I'll let them know." The officer sounded tired, like he was just coming off shift. Or maybe he was pulling a double. "Everyone's in this morning, all leave cancelled. Seattle got socked."

What was she going to do with Jack? No schools would be open on a day like this, but she didn't want him home alone, no matter how grownup he thought he was. She polished off her coffee and went to get dressed. Long underwear, jeans, a thermal undershirt, thick wool sweater, and two pairs of wool socks beneath her oiled-leather work boots. Wherever she ended up working today, it was practically guaranteed it would be outside.

She went down the hall to wake up Jack. His room was as dark as a cave. She opened the mini blinds and sat down on the edge of the bed.

"Jack. Wake up." She shook his shoulder. "It's time to get up."

He groaned and burrowed deeper into the covers. She pulled them off him. "Jack. You have to get up. You have to come with me to the station."

"What about school?"

So now he suddenly cared about school? "School's closed. We have a snow emergency."

He pulled the blankets over his head. "Then why can't I stay here? There's nothing to do at the station."

"Because the power is out. You'll freeze. Besides, there's nothing to do here, either. We'll be warm at the station. I might even let you raid the vending machines." She shook his shoulder again. "Come on. Get dressed."

Sarah waited in the hallway until she was sure she had heard him get out of bed, then went to the front closet. She buttoned her police jacket over her sweater, added a hat and a scarf, slipped her phone into her jacket pocket, pulled on a pair of gloves, and went outside.

Seattle had indeed gotten "socked." Six inches of snow had fallen while the city slept. Sarah knew from her white-knuckle drive home last night that there was a layer of ice underneath. No doubt the governor had already declared a state of emergency. It wasn't just the treacherous roads that were the problem. The weight of all that wet snow was going to break tree branches, pull down power lines, collapse roofs. And the snow was still coming down.

She waved to a neighbor across the street who, like Sarah, was also standing on her porch admiring the transformation and wondering where to start, then picked up a shovel and began clearing the steps.

Her phone buzzed in her pocket. She took it out and flipped it open. Another text. An AMBER Alert. A toddler was missing from a foster home. Hugo Campbell.

She dropped the shovel with a clatter and dashed inside. She pulled off her hat and scarf and tossed them on the coffee table. Her hands trembled as she punched in her lieutenant's number.

"What do we have on the missing child?" she asked

without preamble. Hugo's disappearance had to be connected with her case. Every crime had a ripple effect. And sometimes, the ripples built into a tsunami.

"Snatched or wandered away from the front yard of the foster home," Lieutenant Oakes replied. "What's your interest?"

"Hugo is Neil Campbell's son. My suspect in the Marsee brothers' murder."

"Then get your ass down here," Oakes said. "We're gonna need what you know."

Sarah shut the phone. What did she know about Hugo that could help the police get him back? Not much. His father was dead, and his mother had been out of the picture since Hugo was a baby. He'd been sent to foster care and his favorite toy was a flattened yellow rabbit. She could think of only two people who had a direct connection to the boy who might or might not have had a reason to take him. Not coincidentally, the same two people she'd wanted to bring in today for questioning.

But if Tiffany or Rutz had kidnapped Hugo, the question not only was, "*Where* had they taken him?" but "*Why*?"

# 35

Goddard had never seen the task force bullpen in such chaos. Or so empty. The snow emergency had cut the department's resources to a fraction of what they normally would have been. All available officers were either on their way to the station, or already on out call directing traffic, rescuing stranded motorists, cleaning up accidents. A skeleton mission control crew had been hastily thrown together to locate the missing toddler that consisted of himself, Linden, Lieutenant Oakes, and three uniformed officers. Others would be joining them as they became available, but right now, they were it. Seven people to find one little boy.

"Okay, listen up," Lieutenant Oakes called out over the radio chatter and the buzz of conversation. "We've got a snow emergency, and we've got a missing kid. He might have wandered off, but the yard is fenced, so the foster mom doesn't think he did. Until we know otherwise, we're calling it a snatch." He nodded to one of the uniforms, who started passing out glossy photos along with a fact sheet. "The kid is two and a half," Oakes said. "Name's Hugo Campbell. Linden's got more for us."

Linden stood up. Goddard would have smiled if the

situation hadn't been so dire. She had so much winter gear on, she looked like she was ready to head off to the Klondike. This was his first Seattle winter after six years in L.A. Compared to her, his standard-issue police department outerwear had him seriously underdressed.

"Hugo's father, Neil Campbell," she began, "is the number one suspect in two open murders. Yesterday he died from burns he suffered in a meth explosion; that's the reason his boy is in foster care. We have two persons of interest in the case. The first is Tiffany Crane, who lives in Rainier Valley trailer park, although she hasn't been seen recently. Her live-in lodger was one of the murder victims. Our other lead was a work associate of the other victim, Dr. Nelson Rutz."

"Do you think one of them took the boy?" one of the uniforms asked.

"We don't know," Linden said. She looked at Goddard to confirm her response. He nodded. "Given what we know about both of them, it doesn't seem likely," she continued. "But considering that the boy's father was the suspect in an open murder investigation, it also doesn't seem likely that the boy was grabbed by a stranger, or that he just wandered away. Especially since we're in the middle of a major snow storm."

"Which one of your suspects should we be looking at?" Oakes asked. He waved his hand around the empty room. "We don't exactly have a lot of manpower here. Give us your best guess."

Linden shook her head and looked again at Goddard. He chewed on his knuckle as he thought.

"Rutz," he said. Not because he thought Rutz was the more likely suspect of the two, but because he had to pick one, and Rutz would be easier to find. Tiffany had been in the wind since her interview with Linden. All things being equal, meaning he really couldn't see either of them taking the boy, Rutz was as good a place as any to start.

"Okay," Oakes said. "Put out a BOLO for both suspects' vehicles. All Seattle, all King County. Goddard, you and Linden go talk to the foster mom, see what you can get out of her. Then follow up on Rutz. Gonzales and Reid, you go to Rainier Valley and see if you can find Tiffany Crane. The rest of you, stay here and man the phones."

Phones that had been ringing almost from the moment the announcement went out. Since the AMBER Alert system had been established nationwide, the program had recovered hundreds of missing kids. Television, radio, highway billboards, social media, and text alerts marshaled an army of eyes and ears that sometimes resulted in the perpetrator releasing the abducted child just from hearing about the AMBER Alert through the media. Goddard had taken several calls during the half hour he'd been waiting for Linden to get to the station. Apparently the city was crawling with little blond boys wearing navy blue snowsuits and Power Ranger boots.

"I'll drive," he said as he and Linden grabbed their jackets and headed for the door.

"I got it," she replied. Probably thinking that because he'd moved up from L.A., he didn't know how to drive in ice and snow.

"Fine." Goddard was a perfectly capable winter driver, but he wasn't about to debate the issue. Not now. He didn't care who drove as long as they got there.

"Your boy'll be okay?" he asked.

"Jack will be fine. He's got his cellphone and a handful of quarters for the vending machines, along with instructions to stay in my office and not bother anyone. Don't worry. He knows the drill."

They hurried down the hall and through the lobby, buttoning their coats and pulling on their gloves as they went. Goddard brushed away the snow that had accumulated on Linden's car in the half hour since she'd parked, while she got in and started the engine.

"What's the address?" she asked as she turned the defroster and the windshield wipers to "high."

Goddard consulted the handout. "2023 Pineview. Over in Northgate."

Linden entered the address into the car's GPS. At the highway, she followed the instructions and turned right.

"Careful," Goddard said as they came to the first intersection. The traffic signal was out. A utility van that hadn't been able to make the stop was sliding through.

"I got it." Linden steered the car to the right, aiming for a spot slightly behind the van's back bumper so that by the time her car arrived at that point, the utility van would be gone. The vehicles missed each other by inches.

"Nicely done," he commented.

"The trick is not to jerk the wheel," she explained. "If you do, you'll throw the car into a spin. Not necessarily a bad thing if you want to make a tight turnaround, but usually a maneuver to be avoided."

A detail Goddard happened to be aware of, but he let it go. She could lecture him on the finer points of winter driving if she wanted to. He didn't have anything to prove. Goddard was utterly lacking in the competition gene—probably because he lived in a household of women. A situation that was about to change now that he had a son. He smiled. The men in the Goddard clan would still be outnumbered, but he was looking forward to some male bonding. Tools. Cars. Baseball. Definitely baseball.

*His son.* He smiled again. He was still reeling from the baby's birth. The experience had been incredible on so many levels, he hardly had words to describe it. A part of him had been terrified at the idea of the baby coming early. But a bigger part was fascinated by the birthing process. It really was a miracle, especially when you saw it for yourself. Kath had been a trooper. He'd done his part; helping with her breathing and wiping her forehead and adjusting her pillows, and yes, feeding her ice chips when she asked for them. In a way, the birth had been the easy part. It was the moments immediately afterward that were terrifying. Would the baby draw his first breath? Would he draw the next one? What about the one after that? He and Kath had held their own breaths until they heard their son's first cry. The nurses gave them a minute to marvel over their newborn before they whisked the child away.

The doctors' predictions were guarded, but optimistic. Goddard wasn't overly worried. He wasn't being fatalistic. It was just that whatever happened next was out of his hands. In a sense, it had been from the start. You had to accept that some things were out of your control or you'd drive yourself crazy trying to change them. Which was another reason he didn't mind letting Linden take the wheel.

"Do you think Rutz did it?" he asked, dragging his thoughts away from his newborn and back to the present.

"Honestly? No. I can't see it. Rutz is a liar, and we know he has an agenda, but he's a smart man. He can't possibly believe he could get away with taking the boy. And really, why would he?"

Why, indeed? Linden was right. It didn't make sense. The best theory that Goddard could come up with was that with the two full-blooded Marsees and the one half-blooded Marsee dead, Rutz was somehow planning to use the boy's DNA to continue the PKD project. But even Goddard knew that was a stretch. The boy was just one-quarter Marsee. The odds that he carried the double mutation were—well—twenty-five percent. Possibly less. Goddard had never been particularly clever with numbers. All he knew was that even if his best-guess theory was true, there were far easier ways for Rutz to carry the project forward than kidnapping the boy. Heck, if DNA was what he was after, all he had to do was steal the kid's toothbrush.

"What about the boy's mother?" he said. "Maybe she decided it was time to take an interest in her son."

"If she did, then she has ridiculously bad timing. Anyway, how would she know where to find him? I was at Child Protective Services yesterday trying to make arrangements to see Hugo, and they wouldn't even give *me* the address of his foster home. If they're not forthcoming to the police, I can't imagine them doling out that kind of information to a woman who gave up all rights to her son."

Linden had gone looking for the boy? Goddard would have loved to know the reason why. But he knew Linden well enough to know that nothing good would result if he were to pry.

"We'll figure it out," Goddard said. "Whoa! Watch out!"

A fallen tree that had only become visible as they crested a hill lay across the road. Linden took her foot off the gas and steered carefully around it, only to immediately have to swerve around another. It occurred to Goddard that he really should be at the hospital with Kath and his son instead of out in the blizzard risking his life looking for somebody else's boy. Though at this rate he might end up in the hospital sooner rather than later.

"Take a right at the next intersection," he said, taking on the role of navigator so Linden could keep her eyes on the road. He counted off the house numbers. "There. On the right. Should be that big blue house."

Linden pulled over to the curb. There was one other patrol car, presumably the officers who'd called in the report. Under normal circumstances, the street would have been crawling with cops. It was Hugo Campbell's great misfortune to have gotten kidnapped during a blizzard.

"What have we got?" Linden asked the uni standing beside the patrol car. Goddard assumed the man's partner was inside with the foster mother.

"Kid was snatched out of the front yard."

"Anybody see it happen?" Goddard asked.

"Just the other kids. The foster mom, Jean Schute, was in the house. Our oldest witness is five years old."

Five years old. Another unlucky break. Five was too young to be a reliable witness by anyone's calculation. Could this case get any worse?

The uni opened the gate. The chain link fence surrounding the front yard was around three and a half feet tall. Tall enough to keep the kids in, easy enough for an adult to reach over. The kids had done a number on the yard. Snow trampled and beaten down from a thousand little footsteps around a half-finished snowman—at least Goddard assumed that was what the lopsided lump was going to be. In another part of the yard it looked like the mom had been showing the kids how to make snow angels. Someone had cleared a path up the sidewalk the width of a shovel.

"I got this," Goddard said as they climbed the steps to the front porch. Linden had a history with foster homes, and it wasn't good. He didn't know the specifics, only that she carried a chip on her shoulder the size of a fireplace log as a result. He moved around her and knocked on the door.

The woman who opened to his knock was younger than he expected, maybe in her late twenties or early thirties, wearing jeans and a T-shirt stained with what Goddard recognized as baby spit. She looked like she'd been crying. Goddard could guess what Linden was thinking: *Probably crying because she just lost a big chunk of her monthly check.*

"Mrs. Schute? I'm Detective John Goddard. This is my associate, Detective Linden. We're with the SPD. May we come in?"

"Of course." The door opened directly into the living room. The uni's partner was seated on the sofa. She stood up as they came in. Goddard waved her down.

"Please. Sit." The foster mother indicated two matching armchairs and took a seat on the sofa.

Goddard assessed the room. Modest, but clean. A room that said the owner was more interested in providing for the kids than making a statement with decor. A laundry basket in the corner full of Fisher Price toys. One wall covered with kids' drawings hung at kids'-eye height. A stack of Disney movies in the console under the TV. Seemed like a nice enough place.

"Can you tell us what happened?" he asked.

"Like I told the other officer,"—she nodded toward the uni on the other end of the couch—"the kids were playing in the front yard, everybody seemed to be having a good time, when all of a sudden, I heard Gabby scream. I ran to the front window. The kids had been yelling and throwing snowballs ever since I let them out to play, but this scream was different. I knew right away that something was wrong. I thought maybe one of the kids had gotten hurt. Gabby tends to freak out at the sight of blood. Her mother—well, never mind."

"Gabby is the oldest?"

"That's right. She's five."

"How many other children were in the yard?" Goddard asked.

"Three besides Gabby. Nathan, Sammy, and Hugo. Nathan is mine. Then there's the baby. She was inside with me."

"And their ages?"

"Nathan and Sammy are four. Hugo is two and a half."

"Thank you. I just want to be able to picture the scene. So Gabby started screaming, and you ran to the window. What happened next? Did you see anyone with the children?"

"No. Only the children. I don't think the boys even understood that anything was wrong. The only reason they were crying was because Gabby was screaming."

"And what did Gabby tell you?" Goddard smiled and waggled his fingers at a little girl with red hair and pigtails who was peeking around the edge of a doorway. She ducked back.

"That she was making snowballs, and when she looked up, Hugo was gone. That's it. That's all she knows." The woman pulled a Kleenex from the box on the end table and dabbed her eyes.

"Can we talk to Gabby? She might remember something that will help." Goddard remembered well how imaginative his own girls had been at the age of five, but there was always an off chance that the girl might say something useful.

"Gabby!" the woman called. The child's footsteps pattered away down the hall. "I'm sorry," the woman said and followed after. Goddard heard her promising ice cream. A moment later she came back leading the child by the hand.

"Hi, Gabby," Goddard said, and waggled his fingers again.

The woman nudged her forward. "Say 'hello' to the police officer, Gabby."

"Hello," the little girl mumbled. Looking at her shoes. Not sure if she should speak or not. Goddard remembered teaching his own kids about stranger danger. On the one hand, you told them never to talk to anyone they didn't know, and on the other, like in situations such as this, you urged them to speak up. No wonder some kids didn't know how to act around adults.

"It's nice to meet you, Gabby." He stayed seated so that he and the girl were eye to eye. "I have a little girl just like you. Her name is Sophie."

"Does she have a brother?"

"As a matter of fact, she does. He's very little. He was just born yesterday."

"I had a brother."

"Hugo?"

"No. My real brother. His name is Tyler. My dad put him in a box."

The foster mother shook her head. Warning Goddard off. If Gabby freaked at the sight of blood, Goddard hated to think what kind of box she was referring to.

"Tell me about Hugo," he said.

"He's nice. I like him."

"Now Gabby, this is important. Did you see anyone else in the front yard? Did anybody talk to you or to Hugo?"

She looked down at her shoes again, and nodded.

"You saw someone in the yard?"

She looked up and bit her lip. Looked between Goddard and her foster mother, and then nodded again.

"I saw a big man. A *really* big man. Big like this." She put her hand above her head and stretched up on her tiptoes. "He had big white hair."

*Rutz.* Goddard couldn't believe the girl hadn't said anything about it before. Children were unpredictable, but this was such a key detail, he wished they'd known about it sooner.

"And he had a long white beard," the girl went on. "And a red coat. And reindeer. He had reindeer. And presents. Lots and lots of presents!" The little girl waved her arms and twirled happily as she warmed to her story.

Goddard smiled. No reason to spoil the child's moment. He glanced over at Linden. She was scowling. "Thank you, Gabby. That will be all. You've been a big help." He patted the girl's head. She giggled and ran down the hall.

"I'm sorry," the foster mother said.

"It's okay. She's young. Don't worry about it." Goddard stood up, shook the woman's hand and gave her his card. Linden stood as well. "If you think of anything else, please give me a call. And don't worry about Hugo," he added. "We'll get him back."

A promise he probably shouldn't have made, he reflected as he followed Linden down the sidewalk to the car. But a little boy was in trouble. Goddard had been charged with bringing him back. What else was he supposed to say?

# 36

Holder had almost finished doing the first aid thing on his burned hand when he caught a report on his police scanner. A boy had disappeared from the front yard of a foster house. Blond, thirty inches tall, two-and-a-half years old, last seen wearing Power Rangers boots, a red scarf, red mittens, and a navy blue snowsuit. Name: Hugo Campbell.

He froze. It couldn't be. She wouldn't. *She couldn't.*

Yesterday's conversation replayed instantly in his head. Claire talking about how much she loved Hugo. That she'd take care of him if anything happened to Campbell. "I'd take him," she'd said.

*I'd take him.* And now she had.

He felt like he was going to puke. Claire was a sweet kid. Totally messed up as far as the meth use was concerned, but she wasn't the first person to get caught up in something that she couldn't control. But this—taking Hugo from the foster home was an absolutely crazy thing to do. As in "lock me up and throw away the key" crazy. She had to have been totally out of her mind on crank to try a stunt like this. He couldn't even ask "What was she thinking?" because she wasn't. She'd just gotten an idea and acted on it. He had to find her before the cops did. And yeah, he got the irony.

He finished taping off the bandage, then grabbed his service weapon from the breakfast counter and stuck it in the back of his jeans. His right hand was useless, but he could hit a target reasonably well with his left.

Claire as a target. No. *He* was the one who was crazy. He could never shoot her. He shouldn't even go looking for her. Gil had warned him not to get involved. He should let the cops handle it. Let it play out without him.

But the little dude was in trouble. And Holder knew where he might be. He couldn't look away any more than he could when the little man was well on his way to becoming a crispy critter. Gil was just going to have to deal. Holder didn't become a cop to look the other way.

He took his service weapon from his jeans and put it back on the counter. Tried to think of where Claire would go, and realized that other than Logic's place and the underpass by the river, he had no idea where she hung out. Claire had always been one of the secondary players. A tweaker who came around with Tiffany once in a while. He hadn't paid her much attention until she'd started coming on to him.

Claire was friends with Tiffany. Tiffany might know where Claire had taken the boy. He'd have to play it cool. He couldn't let her know why he was asking *because* Claire and Tiffany were friends. Friends helped each other. Looked out for each other. Lied for each other if they had to.

He shrugged on his jacket and grabbed his car keys. Hurried down the hallway, opened the front door of his apartment building, and stopped. The weather dudes had been talking about a big storm, but he hadn't been expecting this. His car was buried to the point where he wouldn't have known it was there if he hadn't parked it yesterday in his usual spot. Even if he managed to dig the car out, there was still the problem of driving it down the unplowed streets. His car was as heavy as a tank, which was good, since it wouldn't slide around so much on the ice and snow. But it rode low. With six inches of wet snow on the ground and more coming down, he'd be scraping bottom all the way. He'd be lucky to make it to the end of the block. But he had to try. For Claire, and for Hugo. He went back inside for a broom.

Ten minutes later he tossed the broom on top of the junk in the back seat and headed out, gunning and fishtailing through the empty streets toward Rainier Valley. Another ten had him at the trailer park. As he started to turn left, he saw that the end of the drive was blocked with snow, thrown up by a passing plow. He revved the engine and stepped on the accelerator hoping to blast through, hit the snowbank, and immediately got stuck.

He got out and dropped to his hands and knees to take a look. There was no way his vehicle was going to move without a tow. The undercarriage was resting on top of the snow. The wheels weren't even touching the ground.

He got back in the car, shut off the engine and took the key out of the ignition. Not that anyone else would be able to drive the car away, but still. The park had a reputation. He locked the car and started walking in the direction of Tiffany's trailer. His car was blocking the park's entrance, but that didn't matter. He seriously doubted anyone was going to try driving in or out. And if they did, well, his vehicle would serve as a warning.

He shoved his hands into his pockets. His cheeks stung, his eyes watered and his jeans were soaked. Good thing he didn't have far to go. He thought about Hugo. Wherever the little dude was, he hoped he was inside out of the storm.

Two blocks to Tiffany's street. He turned down it and wiped his eyes with his jacket sleeve and raised his head and saw that her car wasn't there.

Strike two. Or was that strike three? He'd lost count. He

studied the tire tracks in her driveway. It looked like her car had backed out, gotten stuck, and then managed to drive off. The tracks were filled in. The car had been gone for a while. Which explained why she'd been able to drive out of the park when he hadn't been able to drive in.

He slogged up the sidewalk and knocked. "Yo, Tiff! You in there? Open the door. It's Steve." He didn't expect an answer. Just being thorough, like a good cop.

Except that the door opened. Claire. Thank god.

She smiled and leaned over and kissed his frozen cheek. "Hey, baby! You came to see me!"

Higher than he'd ever seen her, her eyes glazed and unfocused, her hair tangled and matted, wearing nothing except a wide-necked T-shirt that had slid off one shoulder.

She giggled and opened the door wide. He stepped inside and quickly closed the door behind him. Not that it was going to make much difference. The trailer was freezing, almost as cold as outside. Dark, too, what with the curtains closed. He flicked a light switch. Nothing happened. Of course the power was out.

"Got a smoke?" she asked. Jittery, rubbing her arms. She was so high she didn't even know she was freezing. If he hadn't come along, she might've died from hypothermia.

"Put some clothes on. Where are your clothes?"

She looked down at her bare feet and legs, then giggled and reached up to grab the cigarette he kept behind his ear. He pulled her hand away. Her hand was so cold.

"Go put some clothes on, darlin'," he said again. "You're gonna freeze."

"What? Oh. No, I'm okay." She started shaking. From the meth, or from the cold, or from both. He headed for the bedrooms. There had to be something of Tiffany's that she could wear.

"How come you hangin' out here?" he called out to keep

her talking, so she wouldn't lay down on the couch and go to sleep and never wake up. Makin' conversation like he wasn't in a trailer with a tweaker who may or may not be hiding a kidnapped little boy. "Where's Tiff?" He opened the dresser drawer. Pulled out jeans and a sweatshirt. Looked in another drawer and found a pair of socks. Looked in the closet for a little boy, found nothing.

"I don't know." Claire's voice drifted back from the living room. "She was gone when I got here."

Holder went back into the living room and handed her Tiffany's clothes. "Put these on. I'll be right back."

He searched the rest of the trailer. If Claire had been hanging out for most of the night, it was doubtful that Hugo would be here. The timing was wrong. Still, he had to check. He looked in the other bedroom and the bathroom. Called Hugo's name. Softly, so Claire wouldn't catch on to what he was doing. Loud enough for the boy to hear.

Nothing. He went back to the living room. At least he'd proven that Claire hadn't taken the boy. Wherever the little man was, it wasn't here.

Outside, he heard voices coming up the sidewalk. Footsteps on the porch. A knock on the side of the trailer that was so loud, it startled them both.

"Police!" a man's voice called. "Open up!"

# 37

It took Sarah and Goddard twice as long as it should have to drive from the foster home to Rutz's home. When the GPS directed them to a modest two-story in a neighborhood that a realtor might have described as "mature," but which was in reality declining, Sarah was surprised. She'd expected a high-ranking GenMod employee to live somewhere better. An outsider wouldn't have seen anything amiss; tree-lined streets, tidy houses. But Sarah saw trees in need of trimming, roofs requiring shingling, porches gone too long without paint.

She pulled up in front of a white clapboard identical to every other on the street and studied the house, trying to reconcile this humble home with the overbearing and presumably generously compensated Dr. Rutz. Decided this had been the Rutz family homestead and the doctor was its last caretaker.

No tracks in the drive, and the sidewalk had not been shoveled. If Rutz was home, he hadn't gone out today.

"How do you want to play this?" she asked.

"You can take this one," Goddard said.

"Am I good cop or bad cop this time?"

"Oh, bad cop. Definitely bad." He flashed her a grin.

They got out and started up the sidewalk. The snow was deep. The bottoms of Sarah's jeans were soaked in no time. At least her boots were keeping her feet dry. She stepped carefully over the snowy porch boards and knocked on the door.

The door opened almost before she could take her hand away.

Rutz was wearing a burgundy velour running suit. Or more accurately, a "lounge suit," given that he didn't look like he'd done anything more athletic than going out to the mailbox and back for years. Clearly, he hadn't been outside today and he wasn't planning on going anywhere. Sarah was ninety-nine percent certain they weren't going to find a little boy in his house. But maybe he could give them a lead on who *had* taken Hugo.

"Dr. Rutz," she said. "May we come in? We need to ask you some questions."

"I told you I wasn't going to speak with you any further without my lawyer."

"I understand. However, it's a matter of some urgency. We'd appreciate your cooperation. We'll only take a minute."

"Please," Goddard added from behind her. "A little boy needs your help."

Rutz raised his eyebrows, then opened the door and stepped to one side.

"Thank you," Sarah said. Resting her hand lightly on her holstered weapon as she entered the house. Rutz was a person of interest and not a suspect, but you could never be too careful. Every house had a back door. Rutz might make a break for it. Someone else might have used the door to come in.

"What's this about a little boy?" Rutz asked after Goddard shut the door. Keeping them standing in the foyer. Not inviting them into the house any further than he had to. Sarah could see a living room to the left, a dining room lined with bookshelves to the right, and a flight of stairs straight ahead of them leading to the upstairs; three small bedrooms and a bathroom, if she didn't miss her guess. A narrow hallway alongside the staircase led to the kitchen in the back of the house. Sarah had lived in a half-dozen houses just like this one.

"May we sit down?" She gestured toward the living room.

"You may not. Get to the point." *And then get out.* Sarah could have read the subtext even if Rutz hadn't been glowering. Her hand went to her gun again, just lightly resting her thumb on the grip. Rutz towered over her. He looked like a purple whale. A very angry whale.

"Hugo Campbell is missing," Sarah said evenly, watching carefully for Rutz's reaction. "We have reason to believe he's been kidnapped."

Rutz drew in his breath. Not an obvious gasp, but enough for Sarah to notice. An indication that he didn't know about the kidnapping? Perhaps. But more importantly, it was obvious that he knew Campbell's son personally, had some kind of relationship with him.

She pressed. "We need your help."

"I can't imagine how I could help you." He drew himself up stiffly. "I don't know anything about the boy."

"The boy's father is dead," Goddard said. "Please. We don't have anywhere else to turn. Anything you can tell us about Hugo will help."

"Neil is dead," Rutz repeated. A statement of fact, as if the outcome were inevitable. Given the extent of his burns, Sarah supposed it was. She noted his use of Campbell's first name.

"All right." He led them not into the living room, but down the narrow hallway to the kitchen, a brightly lit, cheerful room with faded yellow gingham curtains framing a window over the sink that looked out into the back yard. Sarah looked to see if the rug in front of the back door was wet to determine whether anyone had gone in or out. It was not.

"What can you tell us about Hugo?" she asked after the three of them were seated at a small wooden table.

"Not much. I was aware that Neil Campbell had a son, but I've never seen the boy."

Sarah didn't challenge the lie. "Can you tell us anything about the boy's mother?" she asked. "We're thinking this might be a parental abduction."

"I doubt she took the boy. Hugo's mother left as soon as he was weaned. The last anybody heard, she'd joined a biker gang in Florida. She's never sent so much as a card."

*Bingo.* Rutz's disdain for Hugo's mother had just proven he'd had far more contact with Neil Campbell than he'd led them to believe. The truth always came out. You just had to wait for it, ask the right questions. And he thought he was smart.

She shook her head and clucked her tongue at Hugo's mother's unmotherly behavior. Let him think they were sharing a moment. "I understand. I have a son. I could never stay away." She paused. "Let's go back to something you told us when we last met. You mentioned the boy's father had contacted you recently wanting you to finance his research project. Do you think Hugo might have been kidnapped in connection with that?"

"I don't see how."

"If Campbell needed money… let's say he borrowed from the wrong people after you turned him down…" She let the sentence trail off, then picked it up again. "Guy was found dead in a shipyard. Shot in the back of the head. Looks to me like the brothers went to the Mob for financing and got in too deep."

"It was Campbell." Rutz practically spat the hated name. "He's the one with the unsavory connections, not Guy or Lance."

"So the three brothers were working together."

"They were."

"To develop a cure for polycystic kidney disease. The disease that killed the Marsees' parents. The disease for which they carried a unique genetic mutation that prevented them from developing the disease. A mutation from which they hoped to develop a treatment. A very lucrative treatment in which you also saw potential, so you brought the project to GenMod."

Rutz's mouth dropped.

"We warned you not to lie to us, Dr. Rutz. Your name is on the research application. You knew about the project. You have not been straight with us."

Rutz's shoulders sagged. He ran his hands through his hair, laid his head on the table, rested his head in his hands.

"The brothers are dead," she went on. "All three of them." Ruthless. Going in for the kill. Not an ounce of sympathy for the man who had tried to derail their investigation not just once, but several times. "Thus the project died with them. No one can use their DNA to develop a treatment without their permission. They can't give permission because they're dead. There's just one way the project can go forward."

Rutz raised his head.

"Let's say Campbell's son also carries the genetic mutation. Let's say someone kidnapped the boy so they could obtain a sample of his DNA. Maybe they're planning to raise the boy as their own, to take care of him now that his father is gone. Maybe they're a good person, and they have only the best of intentions. Maybe they're planning to become his guardian, or his *godfather*."

"That's preposterous!" he sputtered. "I would never take the boy!"

"Prove it," Sarah said. "Let us search the house."

Rutz stood up, gestured widely. "Be my guest."

Sarah nodded, and Goddard moved off. She remained in the kitchen and kept eyes on Rutz. She could hear Goddard methodically searching the house, walking through the upstairs bedrooms, looking under beds, checking closets. *Closets.* She shuddered. She remembered another little boy, another closet… She pushed the thought away.

Goddard returned to the kitchen without a little boy, but carrying a plastic bag. He pulled out a teddy bear. It was dusty but the tags were still attached. The toy was nothing like Hugo's favorite stuffed rabbit. This bear was untouched. Unloved.

*A teddy bear*. Rutz didn't have children.

"Want to tell us about this?" Goddard tossed the toy carelessly on the table.

Rutz picked it up. He ran his hands over the toy and set it up carefully on the table. "It's my fault. My fault."

"What?" Sarah pressed. "What's your fault?"

"Lance. Guy. I killed them."

Sarah's gut clenched and her adrenaline pumped. Confession time. She and Goddard traded looks. Waited.

"How did you kill them?" she asked.

"I thought… I thought that the project could bring them together. I thought that after so many years apart, the boys could work together. They shared a mother. The disease killed her. Threatened them. They were all so smart… All of them. Lance and Guy were geniuses in their own right, but Neil was the smartest of all." Tears streamed down his cheeks as he ran his hands through his hair. There was nothing comical about the gesture now.

"So I introduced them. I told Lance and Guy about their half-brother and suggested they meet. Of course they were excited, but understandably, there was also some resentment that they hadn't been told sooner. I told them—" His voice broke. "I actually told them, 'Better late than never.'" He shuddered, drew a deep breath. "Of course, as it turned out, 'never' would have been preferable. I should have known that Neil hadn't changed. He couldn't. Once I told him about the project and explained its potential, he had his genome mapped, as well as his son's. Hugo doesn't carry the beneficial mutation, but Neil did. That was the moment my dear boys' fates were sealed. He killed them. Shot them both. He lured Guy to the shipyard under the pretext of meeting with an investor and shot him in cold blood. Then he shot Lance in that woman's trailer. Neil killed them, but it may as well have been me. I'm the one who set events in motion."

"How do you know Neil killed them?" Sarah asked. "Did Neil tell you what he'd done?" The confession would be hearsay, but it would be admissible in a court of law now that Campbell was dead.

Rutz shook his head, clucked his tongue in disgust. "Neil would never do anything that straightforward. He was the most cunning and manipulative person I've ever known. I told you he was deeply flawed, and I meant it. It was the woman who told me about the murders. His girlfriend, Tiffany. The heartless bastard took her with him when he killed my boys. To keep an eye on her. To make her watch."

*Tiffany.* Tiffany had witnessed both murders? The revelation was incredible. Difficult to believe. And yet, as she looked at the broken man weeping at his kitchen table, Sarah knew it was the truth.

She picked up the stuffed bear. "Did you buy this toy for Hugo? Did you take the boy? Are you hiding him somewhere?"

Rutz sat up straight. Vehemently, he shook his head. "No. No. I told you. I don't have any idea what's happened to the boy."

"Then why do you have this? You don't have children. Why do you have a new teddy bear?"

Rutz's eyes filled with tears. He took the bear from

Sarah. Fondled the store tags. Stroked the bear's fur. "It's not new, it's just never been used. I bought this years ago," he said softly, almost to himself. "I bought it the day Hugo Campbell's father was born. The day I promised his mother that I would be his godfather and watch over him, just as I did her other sons. This bear was meant to be Neil's."

Rutz lifted the toy to his cheek, then laid his head on the table and held the bear close as he wept for the disastrous consequences of the events he had set in motion. For the deaths of his favored godsons. For Campbell. For the deaths that he had caused.

# 38

After Sarah and Goddard brought a tearful and handcuffed Rutz to the station, after they shunted him off to an interview room to cool his heels and he asked for his lawyer again, after she checked in with the task force (which had grown to over a dozen officers and detectives in her absence) and stopped by her office to make sure Jack hadn't eaten himself into a sugar coma, Sarah was still turning around Rutz's revelations in her head. She could hardly believe that Tiffany had witnessed the Marsee brothers' murders. That Tiffany was such a consummate actress, she'd sat across from Sarah at the interview table and boldly hidden everything she knew. Tiffany could have won an Oscar for her innocent victim performance. Sarah wasn't sure now if anything Tiffany had told her was true. Maybe she wasn't even a tweaker. Maybe the whole scratching-her-arms-'cause-I-need-a-fix jitters was an act as well.

She was itching to interview Tiffany again. Her gut said that the woman was the key to finding Hugo. Not only because they had no viable suspects left; Sarah was convinced that Tiffany was still holding back. Possibly "Tiffany Crane" wasn't even her real name. A woman who could fool who knew how many men into thinking she was madly in love with them no doubt had more than a few as-yet unplayed tricks up her sleeve.

But Tiffany was still in the wind. The officers who'd gone to talk to her while Sarah and Goddard followed up with Rutz had hauled in a man and a woman they found in Tiffany's trailer for narcotics possession, but Tiffany herself was nowhere to be found.

As she stood in the hallway outside the interview rooms, Sarah reminded herself that patience was one of her strong suits. In time, all would become clear. All she had to do was follow the right leads, ask the right questions.

Rutz was in one interview room, and the woman from Tiffany's trailer was in the other. The man the officers had brought in with her had been released. As it turned out, he was the undercover cop who was working narcotics in the trailer park, the one Goddard had met and who had helped shed light on the strange dynamics between Tiffany and the men in her life. The officers at the station had roughed him up at his request and held him long enough to make the collar seem believable before they turned him loose again. Sarah hoped the ruse was sufficient to maintain the officer's cover. It was too bad their investigation had put a fellow officer at risk, but it happened. Undercover cops got picked up along with the bad guys. Especially when an undercover was good. It sounded like this one was.

The woman, Claire Seinfeld according to the booking sheet, looked up as Sarah came in. She was pretty. Dark hair, dark eyes, wide face and mouth, pale skin. Her eyeliner was smudged, and her hair was a rat's nest, but once she was cleaned up, she'd have been more than presentable. Of course, she'd have to get clean on the inside as well before anyone would give her a second look. If this woman wasn't a tweaker, Sarah didn't have a son named Jack.

"Claire?" she said. "It is 'Claire,' isn't it?"

The woman nodded. Hesitant. Timid. On guard, like she was expecting a trick.

Sarah smiled. "It's a pretty name. Claire, I'm sure I don't have to tell you that you're in a real jam." She picked up the incident report. "Possession. Six grams of methamphetamine. That's a Class C felony. Those charges aren't going to go away."

"Help me," the woman said. "I have a little boy. I can't get locked up."

"I can't promise I can get you released, but I'll do my best." Should have thought of your kid before you started using, Sarah wanted to say. "But first, you have to help me."

"Anything. I'll do anything." Claire rubbed her arms, bit her lip, scratched the backs of her hands, picked at her lip, shivered. Sarah bet the woman would do anything Sarah asked her to, all right—as long as the payoff was a hit of crank.

"I'm looking for Tiffany Crane," Sarah said. "Your girlfriend. You are friends, aren't you? That's why you were in her trailer?"

Claire nodded. "She lets me stay there sometimes. When I don't have anywhere else to go. But I don't know where she is. She took off. She said she was going out to get some dope, but I don't think that's what she did, because we had plenty already." She stopped, suddenly realizing that admitting to the drug possession charge probably wasn't the smartest move she could have made. Sarah wasn't about to tell her that the detective she was talking to couldn't have cared less about the drug charge. Their conversation was being recorded. Might as well make it easy for the officers who'd brought her in to follow up.

"Did you and Tiffany often get high together?" The routine questions and plodding pace were necessary, but frustrating. Sarah itched to move the interview along. Her gut said that Tiffany's disappearance and the kidnapping were connected. She needed to find Hugo, and fast. Seventy-five percent of the kids who didn't make it after they were abducted by a stranger were killed within the first three hours. Hugo had been missing for two. Before Rutz's revelations, Sarah would have said that Tiffany wasn't capable of hurting the boy. Now, nothing was off the table.

Claire nodded. "Tiffany and me started using at the same time, about a month ago. We were friends with one of the dealers in the park, and he gave us some stuff. Good stuff, too. His best. He liked us. Or rather, he liked Tiffany. Most men did." Claire shook her head as if she were in awe of Tiffany's powers of attraction. At least Sarah knew now that Tiffany's meth addiction was real.

"Was the dealer Neil Campbell?"

"No, no. Neil was Tiffany's boyfriend. The dealer was somebody else."

So Neil hadn't got Tiffany hooked to keep her in line. One crime that couldn't be laid at his door. Unless he'd got this dealer to do it for him. Sarah could have asked for a name, but let it go. She wasn't interested in a drug collar, and anyway, most likely, Goddard's undercover friend was probably already on it. "And Tiffany used to babysit for Neil's little boy, right? What's his name again?"

"Hugo. Isn't that the cutest name? I just love that little boy. When his daddy died..." Her face clouded.

"When his father died, you wanted to take care of him," Sarah supplied. "I don't blame you. It's only natural. Poor little guy. No mother. No father. Do you think Tiffany wanted to take care of him, too?"

"Maybe. I don't know. Steve asked me that too."

"Steve?"

"My boyfriend. The guy who was with me when we got picked up. Can I go see him?"

The undercover was sleeping with this girl? That was a new one. Normally undercovers played it safe, didn't get involved. Sarah wondered what Claire would think if she told her that her boyfriend was a narcotics officer with the King County Sherriff Department. Hoped for the undercover's sake that she never found out. A woman deceived could be almost as vengeful as a woman scorned.

"What did you tell him when he asked if you thought Tiffany wanted to take care of Hugo?"

"I told him what she told me. Tiffany said she didn't love Neil anymore, but that she still loved Hugo. That she would always love him. And that she would always watch out for him. Especially if something happened to his dad. She said that, like, a month ago. In a way, it was kind of creepy. It was almost like she knew Neil was going to get hurt."

There was a knock on door. Sarah went out into the hallway.

"It's going well in there." Goddard nodded toward the interview room. Sarah was annoyed at the interruption, but held her tongue. Goddard seemed tense, distracted. Like there was something more he wanted to say. Probably wishing he was at the hospital with his wife and baby instead of being stuck at the station. He definitely needed to learn how to compartmentalize.

"What do you think?" she asked.

"I think Tiffany's got the boy. The question is, where would she take him?" Goddard was still looking at the woman in the interview room. Granted, she was pretty, but there was a time and a place for girl-watching, and this wasn't it. Although there was something in his expression that Sarah couldn't pinpoint. Now that she thought about it, there was no lust there, more like regret, perhaps anger.

She shook the thoughts away. It didn't matter what Goddard thought about the tweaker girl. She pursed her lips as she replayed the details of her interview with Tiffany, combing it for clues. She moved on to the conversations she'd had with Ms. Crowd at the casino and Tiffany's coworker, Jaycee. Tiffany's Facebook postings, the online photo albums filled with pictures of company picnics and outings with her casino friends, the photo of her with Lance.

Suddenly, she grinned. She knew where the picture had been taken. It wasn't a random location. It was someplace special. A place that Tiffany knew would be empty. A place where she might have taken the boy.

"Grab your coat," she said to Goddard. "I have an idea."

Goddard didn't answer. He was still staring at the woman in the interview room, studying her like he felt sorry for her, like he was trying to get inside her head so he could figure out what made her tick. Why she did what she did.

Sarah tugged impatiently on his sleeve. They didn't have time to stare pensively at loser tweakers like they were your long lost sister. They had a little boy to save.

# 39

"What do you think she's planning to do with the boy?" Sarah asked as she crossed Magnolia Bridge, a high, arched span across Smith Cove that connected the hilly, forested peninsula northwest of downtown Seattle to the city. They were on their way to the country house owned by Tiffany's former dupe, Desmond Whittaker. The house to which, according to Jaycee, Tiffany still had the key, and which would be standing empty, its owner thousands of miles away on a different continent. She and Goddard had driven most of the way absorbed in their own thoughts.

"You interviewed her," he responded. "You must have come away with some sense of her thinking."

"After what Rutz told us, I'm not sure anyone can know what's going on in that girl's head. Imagine, she saw Campbell kill both men—one of them her boyfriend, or whatever Lance really was to her—and she said absolutely nothing."

"Campbell must've had some hold on her, is all I can say."

"Rutz described him as a master manipulator. Tiffany's coworker told me that Tiffany would do anything for Campbell. And in a sense, she did. By coming on to wealthy men at the casino in order to get stuff for Campbell to fence, she was basically a prostitute. It's almost like he was a cult leader."

"A cult with a following of one."

"I guess once you find the perfect disciple, one is all you need."

"Tiffany's lucky he didn't make her pull the trigger."

Or maybe he had. Unless and until they found and tested the murder weapon, all they'd have to go on would be her word, and Sarah now knew how reliable that was.

"I can tell you this much," she said. "I think Tiffany Crane is a great deal smarter than we're giving her credit for. I think she lied to us when she said she didn't know about Lance's project. I think she and Campbell hatched their plot together. Maybe they planned to kill the Marsee brothers from the beginning. Maybe after Campbell blew himself up, she saw her chance to carry on the project by herself, and that's why she took the boy. Because she needed his DNA."

"But according to Rutz, Hugo's DNA doesn't carry the double mutation."

"Tiffany doesn't know that."

"Maybe. We really can't assume anything about what she does or doesn't know. But if she's as smart as all that, how can she possibly think she'll get away with kidnapping the boy?"

Sarah shrugged. "Kids fall through the cracks all the time. Think of the child abductions where the kid turns up ten, twenty years later under a new name and a new identity with no clue that the person who raised them wasn't their mom or dad. Maybe Tiffany figured we'd think he just wandered off. Got lost in the storm and disappeared. Or maybe we're giving her *too* much credit. Maybe taking the boy was just something she did on the spur of the moment. Her girlfriend Claire said they were high last night." Megalomaniac or fool, it didn't make much difference which category fit Tiffany if the end result was the same.

At the mention of Claire, Goddard's face darkened.

"What?"

"Nothing. Just drive."

Which thanks to the storm, was easier said than done. Sarah had driven off the bridge into a foot of snow—twice as much as there had been at the station. Thanks to the weather phenomenon the TV meteorologists called the "Puget Sound Convergence Zone," it wasn't unusual for some parts of Seattle to get dumped on while other areas saw rain or even sunshine.

"Accident." Goddard pointed to the road ahead. A pickup truck and a minivan had apparently tried to defy the laws of physics by occupying the same space at the same time. Sarah held her foot on the brake pedal until the antilock system kicked in. The car slowed. A police officer held up his hand as they approached, then waved them around.

"How much farther?" she asked. While she'd never admit it to Goddard, the tension of driving in the snow was starting to get to her. She took one hand off the wheel long enough to rub the back of her neck.

Goddard checked the GPS. "Maybe half a mile. Tell me again why you're so sure this weekend house is where she's taken him."

"It was the photo, the one of Lance and Tiffany as a couple. For a long time, I didn't think much about where it was taken. It's an outdoor shot, and you can see a little water in the background, but other than that, there's nothing that would tie it to a particular spot. But then when I was trying to figure out where Tiffany would have taken Hugo, I remembered her coworker saying that Tiffany sometimes used a casino john's weekend house for parties, and it clicked. I'd bet any money that's where the photograph was taken. It's the perfect hideout. It's remote, she has a key, and there's no direct connection between her and the house.

And according to Jaycee, the old man it belongs to hardly ever visits. Even less chance in this weather. The only reason we even know where it is is because the owner filed a police report against her. The charges were dropped, but his name and this address are still on the record."

"You're a genius."

Sarah accepted the compliment with a tip of her head. Her I.Q. was on the high side of normal, but her real talent was seeing the details that others missed.

As they got closer, Goddard counted off the house numbers. "There," he said, pointing to a stone and brick mailbox at the end of a long driveway. Sarah turned in. The security gate was open. A single set of tire tracks marred the otherwise pristine, snow-covered drive. The tracks were close together, like they'd been made by a compact car. Tiffany's red Toyota?

"How do you want to play this?" she asked as she put the car into park. "Wait for backup, or storm the castle alone?"

"I doubt she's got the cannons loaded. If she *is* inside with the boy, she's been there for hours. Enough time to hunker down. I'll call for backup, but I say *we* move now."

Sarah passed him her radio, then turned off the engine and pocketed the car key. She checked her weapon in its holster. As a detective, she didn't have to draw her gun often, but she was an excellent shot when she needed to be—something that, if Tiffany made it necessary, Sarah had no compunctions about proving.

They started walking up the drive. It curved through thick woods and down a hill. Evergreens mixed with hardwoods, the kind of forest Sarah liked best. Snow weighed down the branches. The woods were silent except for their crunching footsteps. A shower of snow fell from the branches of a pine tree as their approach put an owl to flight. No doubt other creatures were watching. The woods outside the city were home to a variety of wildlife, and not just chipmunks and coyotes. Bears occasionally wandered up the rail lines along the south shoreline, and a few years ago, a cougar was captured and radio-collared in Discovery Park.

The drive emerged from the trees into a large white expanse Sarah assumed was the front yard. The house looked like a castle, built into the side of a hill and constructed of the same white limestone and red brick as the mailbox. A curved depression in the snow cover defined the front walkway. No footsteps led to the door, but Tiffany could have entered the house through the attached garage. It looked like the tire tracks they'd been following ended at one of the garage doors. Sarah counted four bays and a service door. This was practically a mansion. Tiffany had clearly been good at picking her marks. At least until Lance. But that had been Neil's idea, hadn't it?

"Ready?" Goddard asked.

"Let's do this."

They crossed the lawn and mounted the wide, wooden veranda. Sarah rang the bell. Waited. No sound came from inside the house. Goddard looked at her and shrugged. Time for a change of tactics. He pounded loudly on the door with his fist.

"Police!" he shouted. "Tiffany! We know you're inside. Open up!"

Silence. It was so quiet that Sarah could hear the soft shhing sound as the snow fell. From the woods, a crow called.

"Police! Tiffany! Open the door!" she called as Goddard pounded on the door again.

More silence.

"Wait here. I'll go around the back." Goddard drew his service piece and moved off.

The porch was broad, with a swing on one side and two Adirondack-style rocking chairs on the other. Like the veranda of a southern plantation. Sarah moved down its length, checking the house and peering in the windows she passed. A living room and a dining room on the right side of the door. On the left, a den. Floor-to-ceiling bookshelves on the three walls that she could see. A desk the size of a small continent in the middle of the room that might have been made of cherry or walnut wood. Everything, from the house to the furnishings, spoke of conspicuous wealth.

She checked her watch. Goddard should have been back by now. She pounded on the door and called again. Still no answer.

She walked down the steps and followed their tracks back up the long driveway to the car. Knocked the snow off her boots and got inside and turned the key. She dialed the heater to "high" and blew on her hands to warm them and shook the snow from her hair, then keyed the radio.

"This is Detective Linden. I'm at 32 Parkview. I need an updated ETA on backup."

"Closest unit is less than ten minutes out," the dispatcher replied. "Might be a little longer, depending on the roads."

"Copy." Sarah clicked off the transmit button.

Ten minutes. If Tiffany was inside with the boy, anything could happen during that time. Like Goddard, she didn't really think that Tiffany would hurt Hugo. But if there was one thing she'd learned over the course of their investigation, it was that she really didn't know Tiffany Crane at all.

She turned off the car and got out. Fingered the gun in her holster, flipped her hood over her head and retraced her path to the house, then diverted toward the garage and followed Goddard's footsteps around to the back.

"I was just coming to find you," he said as she turned the corner. "All's quiet. I don't think she's here."

"I just checked with dispatch. They're talking another ten minutes before we get backup. Did you check the garage?"

"Not yet."

Sarah signaled for him to follow and went around to the front of the house. She drew her gun and approached the garage's service door, then craned her neck as she looked through its window for a better angle.

"I think I see the Toyota. Can't be sure from here. But there's a red car parked in the same bay where the tracks end."

"Let's try another window." Goddard led her around the side of the garage. The window was above their heads where the ground sloped away. Goddard laced his fingers and Sarah stepped in.

"I see it!" she exclaimed after he'd boosted her up. "Tiffany's Toyota. And the floor beneath the car is wet. It's been on the road this morning."

"Great. Get down and let's get moving. We'll go in from the back. That front door could hold off an army."

She followed him around the end of the garage. The back yard sloped away from the house to an iced-over pond and a patch of woods. Sarah recognized the location where the photograph of Lance and Tiffany had been taken. She *had* called it right.

Goddard climbed a flight of steps to the back deck. Sarah checked the windows. A coffee cup on an end table. Newspaper sections scattered over a footstool.

"Wait a minute. I heard something." She cocked her head and held up her hand. The tinkle of a wind chime. Sleet against the glass.

"I don't—"

Sarah shook her head and shushed him again with her hand.

Then the sound came again. Goddard nodded to show he heard it too. Somewhere inside the house, a child was crying.

"Police!" he shouted. He banged his fist on the door. "Tiffany! We know you're in there! Open the door!"

No response. Sarah tried the knob. The door was locked.

"I got this," Goddard said. He motioned her to the side and raised his foot. Kicked, and kicked again.

The door flew open, and they were in.

# 40

They were in a wide hallway. Two doorways opened off the hallway on either side. Goddard signaled to Linden to take the left, while he moved to the right, his gun drawn.

A dayroom, or possibly a TV room. Easy chairs arranged in a semicircle facing a cabinet that likely housed a sound system or a television. The cabinet looked custom-made.

"Clear," he called to Linden.

"Clear," she called back from across the hall.

"Okay. Spread out." He raised his voice. "Tiffany! This is Detective John Goddard! We don't want anyone to get hurt. We need to talk!"

No response. The house was so huge, Goddard's shouts practically echoed. His stomach churned. This was exactly the sort of situation in which people *did* get hurt. He wished he and Linden had waited for backup. The house was too big for two people to search by themselves. But it was too late to turn back now.

The dayroom opened into a breakfast room set with small tables. It looked like a restaurant or a café. He cleared the room, then moved on to another expensively furnished room, and then another. As Goddard cleared each room in turn, he realized that not only did the house look like a palace from the outside, it was laid out like one, too. The rooms around the perimeter were connected to each other in a continuous chain. In the middle were the more utilitarian rooms, coat closets, and bathrooms.

The layout of the house unnerved him. There were just too many rooms. As they entered and cleared each room in turn, all Tiffany had to do to keep ahead of them was to keep moving. And she knew the house, while he and Linden did not. In theory, Linden coming from the other direction would eventually corner Tiffany and they could grab and cuff her, but the reality wasn't that simple. He and Linden could search the perimeter all day and never catch up to her.

He thought again about the layout. If he was Tiffany, where would he hide with the boy? Not the perimeter rooms; they were too open and exposed. If Tiffany was here with Hugo, they were in the middle of the house. Goddard was sure of it. He wished he had a way to let Linden know. Another reason they should have waited for backup.

"Tiffany!" he called again. "This is Detective Goddard! I need you to show yourself!"

Silence. The main entrance was directly in front of him. Should he continue clearing the perimeter rooms, or move to the ones in the middle? He made his decision and turned down a central hallway. He moved confidently, but cautiously, stopping every few feet to listen.

"Hugo," he called out gently, trying another tactic. Calm and reassuring. Like a father to his son. "I know you're scared. This is Detective Goddard. I'm here to help you. Where are you?"

Still nothing. He checked his watch. Backup should have been here by now. He continued down the hallway. The next door opened into a billiard room. He stepped inside with his gun drawn.

"Hugo? Are you in here?" He checked behind the leather chairs, beneath the pool table, anywhere a small boy could be hiding.

"Tiffany? Can you hear me? Show yourself. You know this is pointless. There are half a dozen patrol cars outside. You're surrounded. Give yourself up before someone gets hurt." He stopped, listened, moved on.

The hallway dead-ended at a library. Under other circumstances, Goddard might have whistled at the size and scale of the room, the sheer quantity of books lining the walls, the size of the antique library table, the artwork.

"There you are," Linden said from behind him. He started. "I've been looking all over for you. This place is enormous."

"Nothing?"

"Not a thing. I checked all the side rooms up to the front hallway, and then I cleared the upstairs. I don't get it. I was sure I heard a child crying."

"I did, too. I'll call it in again. Meanwhile, we should verify that really is Tiffany's car." Now that they were inside the house, it would be a simple matter to access the garage through the connecting door.

"Hold on." Linden put a finger to her lips. A child's cry, just at the edge of hearing, coming from behind a wall of bookcases. But there was a gap in the shelves, an area of blank paneling. No, not blank, a door, so well incorporated into the surrounding wood that it was hardly visible. She motioned to Goddard and took a step closer. Goddard did the same. Their footsteps were muffled by the heavy carpet. He held his breath and strained to listen, cupped a hand around his ear.

From behind the door, the faint crying sound came again.

# 41

A closet. *Hugo was in a closet*. Sarah flashed back to another little boy… hiding in a closet… peeking out through the crack beneath the door. Terrified. Traumatized. Alone. Seeing things no child should ever see. And the blood. His mother's blood. So much blood—

"*Linden*." Goddard's whisper brought her back. His gun was pointed at the closet door. He signaled her to step to the side. She shook her head. There was no way he was taking the lead on this one. Not this time. Not when there was a little boy inside.

She moved in front of him. Took a ready stance and drew her weapon. Held it steady with both hands in front of her and pointed it at the door.

"Tiffany," she said, keeping her voice firm yet neutral. Not scolding her. Not condemning her or judging her. Just telling her what she needed to do. "We know you and Hugo are in there. We don't want anyone to get hurt. I'm going to open the door now so you can come out."

"No!" Tiffany's voice was shrill, panicked. Claire said they'd gotten high together last night. She probably still was. "I have a gun! I'll shoot! I'll shoot Hugo! I'll shoot myself!"

"Don't shoot," Sarah told her evenly. "Nobody has to get hurt. We just want to talk."

She studied the closet. The door was so cleverly disguised, only the small wrought iron door knob gave it away. She caught Goddard's eye and tipped her head toward the knob. Signaling to him that she was going to open the door no matter what Tiffany wanted.

He shook his head fiercely. *Backup*, he mouthed and jerked his head in the direction of the front door. Telling her to wait.

She shook her head just as emphatically. *Trust me*, she mouthed back.

He pressed his lips together and shook his head again.

She turned back to face the closet, her gun aimed at the center of Tiffany's body mass, assuming the woman was standing. Above Hugo's head. Unless Tiffany was holding him in her arms, or crouching down with him in front of her, or otherwise using him as a shield. There was no way to know.

"Tiffany," she said again. "This isn't helping. You can't stay in there forever. Hugo's going to get hungry. And thirsty. And he's going to need to use the bathroom. I'm going to open the door now."

"Who else is with you? Who's out there?"

"Nobody. Just my partner and me."

"Prove it."

How could you prove a negative? Sarah looked helplessly at Goddard and shrugged.

"This is Detective Goddard," he said. "Detective Linden is telling you the truth. It's just us out here."

"Daddy?" a child's voice said at the sound of Goddard's voice. "Daddy?"

Sarah's heart broke. "Tiffany—don't do this," she pleaded. "Please."

"*Sarah*," Goddard hissed from his position behind her. She turned around. He touched his ear and nodded toward the front of the house. *Listen*, he mouthed.

She cocked her head. Sirens. Faint and in the distance, but growing louder by the second. The backup team would arrive at any minute, swarm the house, break down the door if they had to, enter the room… Tiffany would hear them, she might panic… shoot at them… shoot the boy… shoot herself… They had to resolve the situation now.

"Tiffany," she pleaded one last time. "I know you don't want to do this. I know you just want to take care of Hugo. To keep him safe. That's why you took him. I know you love him." Guessing at the motivation. Hoping she was right. "We'll make sure nothing happens to him, but we can't help until you open the door. Let him go. Then we can talk."

She waited. The sirens grew louder. She gripped her weapon tighter. Tiffany had to be able to hear them, even through the heavy paneling. She had to know they were coming. That the end was near. That if she didn't do as she was told, the confrontation could end badly. For her, for Hugo, for everybody.

"Okay," Tiffany said at last. She sounded resigned. Angry. "Okay, okay, okay, okay. I'll let Hugo go. Just don't shoot me."

"I won't shoot. I promise. Open the door."

The closet door opened a crack. Sarah moved out of Tiffany's line of sight and kept her gun aimed at her target. Behind her, she could feel the air in the room shift as Goddard did the same.

The door opened wider, and then suddenly, Hugo burst out. Sarah couldn't tell if he was running of his own volition or if Tiffany had pushed him out. Quickly, she holstered her weapon and dropped down on one knee. She opened her arms wide, ready to scoop him, desperate to make him safe.

But Hugo angled to the right and ran past her. Sarah whirled around in time to see Goddard shove his gun into its holster and snatch the boy up. Of course Hugo had run toward Goddard. Sarah should have anticipated that. The most important person in Hugo's life had been his father.

She whipped out her weapon again and resumed her stance as the closet door opened wider. Behind her, she could hear Goddard moving across the room with the boy. Carrying him out of the line of fire. She heard the library door open and close. She heard Goddard's footsteps returning.

"Hugo's in the hallway," Goddard told Tiffany as he resumed his position behind Sarah. "But he's all by himself. Put the gun down so we can all go there with him."

"I said *all right*! Stop yelling at me!" The door opened fully and Tiffany appeared in the doorway, holding a small-caliber pistol under her chin. The murder weapon? Possibly.

Sarah ignored the clear panic in Tiffany's eyes and smiled. "That's great. You're doing great, Tiffany. Now put the gun down. See? I'm putting down mine."

She bent her knees keeping her eyes locked on Tiffany's and laid her weapon on the carpet. Straightening, she held out her empty hands and smiled again. "Now it's your turn."

Tiffany shook her head. Her hand trembled.

"Okay," Sarah said. "That's all right. It's okay if you want to keep the gun for now. Nobody wants you to get hurt. We just want to talk to you."

Tiffany didn't move.

"I get that you're afraid," Sarah went on, keeping up the patter. "But it's okay. No one is going to hurt you."

"It's too late," Tiffany said. "I killed him." The gun pressed harder beneath her chin.

Him? Was she talking about the Marsee brothers? Had she killed just one of them? Rutz had said that Campbell killed the brothers and forced Tiffany to watch. Was she confessing to the truth, or was it another lie? Sarah decided to go with Rutz's version.

"Tiffany, we know that's not true. We know Campbell killed Lance and Guy. Dr. Rutz told us. He said you told him that Campbell made you watch."

"I loved him!" Tiffany cried. "I loved him! How could he do that to me!"

"Making you watch was a terrible thing to do. But shooting yourself would be terrible, too. What will happen to Hugo if you hurt yourself? He needs you. Put the gun down. You don't want to do this. We can help you."

"No one can help me." Her voice grew small. Crying. Shrinking in on herself. She looked and sounded like a little girl.

There was a loud banging from behind Sarah and Goddard, muffled by the thick wood paneling—the backup team breaking down the front door. Tiffany started, pressing the gun harder into the flesh of her chin. Running footsteps in the hallway. "Is everything all right in there?" someone called. "Linden! Goddard! Talk to us!"

"We're fine!" they answered in unison. "Stay out! Stay back!"

"Tiffany," Sarah said as decisively as she knew how. Putting all of the "I'm the mother and you have to do what I tell you" into her voice that she was capable of. "They're here. We have to go now. It's time. Put the gun down."

"I killed him," Tiffany said again. "I loved him and I killed him. I killed Neil."

Neil? Tiffany was confessing to murdering Neil Campbell, and not Lance and Guy? But Neil had died at his own hand, from the burns he suffered in the meth fire. Tiffany hadn't gone to the hospital, had she? Tampered with his meds or his IV line or whatever else would cause him to suddenly flatline? Was she clever enough or diabolical enough to do something like that? Sarah supposed it was possible. Anything was possible.

"How did you kill him?"

"Gasoline," she sobbed. "I killed Neil with gasoline. I filled a milk carton with gas and put it on top of the fridge. In the back, where he wouldn't see it, and Hugo couldn't climb up and get to it. I made a hole in the cap with a pin. Just a small one, small enough so the fumes could still come out, but Neil wouldn't smell them."

Sarah's mind was reeling. "How did you know how to do it?"

Tiffany wiped her streaming eyes with her free hand. They were raw with tears and bright with craving. She must be going into withdrawal. "I read about how to do it online. I knew what would happen the next time he cooked."

She cried harder. Whether for the death she had caused or for herself for having caused it, Sarah didn't know.

"Neil hurt you, so you hurt him." Trying to make Tiffany's actions sound reasonable.

"I had to! But it wasn't for me. I did it for Hugo."

"For Hugo?"

"Neil was a bad man. I knew that even before—before—before he did what he did. I couldn't risk Hugo being around that. I had to make sure it never happened again."

"You took good care of him. Now it's time to put the gun down so we can go out in the hallway and so he can see you. He needs you."

Tiffany's expression faltered. She lowered her hand.

"That's good. Now put the gun on the ground and come out with your hands in the air. You can do this. One step at a time. Put the gun down."

Tiffany took a step toward Sarah. The pistol dangled from her fingers. She let it fall to the floor and put her head in her hands. Her shoulders shook. She swayed, took another step, staggered and crumpled to her knees. Sarah ran over and grabbed her right wrist, snapped a cuff around it and moved behind her and pulled her arms back and fastened the other.

It was over. Sarah fought to control her breathing as she came down from the adrenaline high and walked Tiffany toward the door. That Tiffany was damaged goods was without doubt. A part of Sarah felt sorry for her. But what she'd done to Hugo was unforgiveable. No one should ever hurt a little boy. No one.

# 42

Goddard knocked on the wall beside the open doorway to Kath's hospital room, then stuck his head in. He carried an art magazine in one hand and a vase of flowers in the other. Daisies. Kath's favorite. The flowers she'd carried as her wedding bouquet.

Kath's bed was by the window. Except for the two small bumps her feet made beneath the hospital blanket, she was hidden by the dividing curtain. Sophie was sitting in a chair in the corner—a green vinyl number that could have been a contender for the ugliest chair in the world. Possibly also the most uncomfortable. Sophie didn't seem to mind.

"Daddy! Daddy! You're here!" she called and jumped up as he strode into the room. He set the flowers and the magazine on the window ledge and bent to give Sophie a hug. Arianna was sitting in a chair beside her mother's bed. He kissed her forehead, then moved to his wife. Kath opened her eyes and smiled at him. She looked utterly whipped. Goddard had honestly thought the birth would be easier than the last two because the baby had been so small, which only showed how little he knew. Kath's labor had been long and the birth itself was tough. Probably because of her age.

"You look wonderful," he said as he ducked beneath the IV line and moved to the head of the bed so he could smooth back her hair.

She smiled up at him. "I bet you say that to all the girls."

"Only the ones who've just given birth to my son."

*My son.* He didn't think he'd ever get tired of saying the words. He'd noticed Linden said them all the time: "He's my son. *My* son." Fierce. Tender and protective at the same time. Now he understood why.

His son was in the neonatal ICU down the hall. The nurses promised he was going to be fine. Goddard had peeked in on his way to see Kath. The ICU nurse had pointed out which baby was his as Goddard stood on the other side of the window in the hall and grinned as goofily as every other new dad. Nathan Christopher Goddard looked exactly like the others. Scrawny. Red. Wrinkled. Impossibly frail and tiny. Nathan. Nate. *His son.* Linden had had to practically kick him out the door with a promise that she'd get started on the paperwork as soon as Tiffany had been booked, but the moment he saw the baby, he couldn't imagine why he'd wanted to linger.

"Did you find him?" Kath asked. "The little boy?"

"Who? Our boy?"

She laughed. "The one who was missing in the storm. Hugo?" She pointed to a portable radio that was almost hidden in the clutter on her nightstand and blushed. "I heard about it on the police channel. I know it's silly of me, but I like to listen. I like to know what you do."

Her admission took him by surprise. Goddard had always assumed Kath didn't want to know the details of work. Maybe he'd been wrong. Maybe it wasn't that she was disinterested. Maybe he was the one who'd shut her out.

"Yes, we found him. He's fine."

"I'm so glad. I hated the idea of anything happening to

him. Or to you." She closed her eyes.

"Girls, your mom's tired. Why don't you go check up on your little brother?"

"Come on." Arianna took Sophie by the hand and led her away. Goddard watched them leave. He couldn't remember the last time Arianna had willingly done anything with her younger sister.

He sat down in the chair Arianna had vacated and took his wife's hand. Held it and thought about the changes the day had wrought, about what the future held for him and his family, as Kath drifted off into a well-deserved sleep.

# 43

Holder pulled up in front of Claire's mother's apartment building and honked. Two times. The signal that it was him. The front door opened and she hurried down the sidewalk. She was dressed all in black, which was appropriate seeing as they were going to a funeral, though Holder doubted the preacher was going to appreciate her miniskirt and fishnet stockings.

"Hey, baby," she said as she got in.

"Hey yourself."

He checked his watch and pulled away from the curb. They'd just make the service in time if he hit the lights right. It was hard to believe that a week ago, Seattle had been smothered in snow. Today the sky was blue and the sun was out. It didn't seem like the right kind of day for a funeral, but he supposed the dead didn't mind.

Tiffany wasn't coming. Thanks to the kidnapping charges and the obstruction of justice charges and the drug charges and the accessory to murder charges and whatever else the police thought to throw at her, she was going to be staying inside for a very long time. But Claire had gotten it into her head to go in her friend's place. No matter that, at least in

Holder's estimation, Tiffany had a big share of the guilt for these deaths. Holder had agreed to go along, partly to keep an eye on Claire, and partly because *someone* had to go. Better him and Claire than nobody. That just wouldn't have been right.

He pursed his lips. Funerals always made him feel uncomfortable. He supposed that was the point. *Don't think you're sitting pretty, wearin' a suit an' tie and with your hair combed driving around with your girl in your car*, the dead seemed to say. *Won't be long, and you'll end up like this.* He thought about Tiffany missing all the fun stuck in her jail cell. He couldn't imagine what it would be like to lose someone. Even less to have a hand in their death.

He realized Claire had been talking. "What you say, babe?"

She shot him a look. "Just that it's so sad. They were going to buy a house, you know? Get married. Her and Neil and Hugo, like a family." Holder didn't reply. Whatever Campbell had promised, he doubted Tiffany would have got her fairytale ending. Claire's tone worried him. Like it was time for her and Holder to do likewise. He pretended not to notice.

They got to the church five minutes late. Inside, it was almost empty. They slid into a pew at the back. Besides him and Claire, there was a large man with manic white hair sitting up front, and further back, a redheaded woman with a tight ponytail, a man sitting beside her.

He hoped when it was his turn, his life would've made more of an impact. The audience was almost outnumbered by the caskets.

Two boxes. One for Lance, one for Guy. A double funeral. The caskets were identical. Dark wood, white satin lining, the top half open so people could see the bodies while the bottom half was covered with flowers. Holder was surprised the caskets were open. He knew both brothers had been shot in the head. Undertaker must've done a hell of a job. Both men were blond and stocky, wearing matching suits and ties. No doubt they'd been different when they were alive. Different hopes and ambitions, different loves. Whatever. But in the end, everyone went out the same.

Beside him, Claire started to cry. He took her hand. He knew it was hard. He was a cop. He was used to seeing dead bodies. Or as used to it as a person could be. These might be her first, although she couldn't have known either man well. Might never have met Guy at all. She squeezed his hand, laid her head on his shoulder. Holder let her keep it there, though he wasn't quite sure how he felt about it.

Thing was, he knew she was high. He'd known it the minute she walked out her apartment building's front door. She had the look. Smiling, bouncing happily down the sidewalk, the neurons in her brain working overtime. He'd specifically asked her not to come to the funeral stoned, told her it was disrespectful, that Tiffany wouldn't like it, but she'd gotten high anyway. He worried she'd do something to embarrass him at the service, or worse, draw attention to him. When a person was high, there was no telling what they'd do. Look at poor Tiff.

Thankfully, the minister kept the service short. Maybe he figured it wasn't worth much effort because the crowd was small. He finished with a prayer and invited the audience to come to the front.

"You wanna go up?" he asked Claire.

She shook her head. "Let's just go."

"Come on. We should go up. Pay our respects. For Tiffany."

He took her by the hand, pulled her to her feet and started toward the altar. The other mourners must've viewed the bodies before the service because they all headed for the back. Holder turned his face to the side as he and Claire squeezed past the redheaded woman and her companion. The woman had "cop" written all over her. He was pretty sure he'd never seen her before, but after his recent fake arrest, he couldn't risk her recognizing him and blowing his cover.

When they reached the caskets Claire squeezed his hand tighter. In his head, Holder said a prayer. Not for the men who had been murdered, but for Claire. For all the junkies trying to get clean and the single moms raising up their kids and the people who were struggling to make a living without catching a break. There wasn't any shortage of people who needed help. Holder's buddies at County would've laughed if they found out he had a spiritual side, but whenever he had a good day at work, whenever things had gone especially right, he felt like he was partners with The Big Guy.

"Baby?" Claire asked. "You okay?"

He opened his eyes. "Never better. Come on—le's get outta here."

They walked back up the aisle through the empty church. The minister was waiting in the foyer. As he shook their hands and thanked them for coming, Holder spotted a stack of N.A. flyers behind him on a table. When the minister turned them loose, he walked over and grabbed one of the flyers for Claire and stuck it in his back pocket.

"Ready, baby?" she asked.

"Ready." He took her by the elbow and guided her out the door.

# 44

The snowstorm that had shut down the city was barely in evidence as Rick and Sarah enjoyed their long-postponed dinner date at last. Technically, it was a lunch date at a café a short walk from the church where the Marsee brothers' funeral had been held instead of the romantic dinner Rick had originally planned, but he was okay with that. Sarah was a hard person to pin down, and not just because of the erratic hours imposed on her by her job. He knew enough about her background to understand why she had commitment issues, just as he understood that if their relationship was going to go forward, he needed to cut her some slack. He didn't mind that her choice of restaurant had been determined by her work, either—or not enough to gripe about it, at any rate. He was just happy she was sitting on the other side of the table from him at last.

Sarah seemed to know what he was thinking because she reached across the checkered tablecloth to take his hand. "Thanks for coming to the funeral. Goddard couldn't—new baby and all—but I felt like someone had to represent the department." She sighed. "And thanks for understanding. These past couple of days have been intense."

Rick's first thought was that her entire life had been intense. Sarah was the kind of person who felt everything more strongly than most, she often took things too much to heart and wound up getting hurt. But he kept his opinions to himself. Sarah was a deeply private person. She didn't like to be made to feel as though he knew her better than she did herself. Even though he often did.

"It's my job to understand," he said lightly, and they both laughed. Rick was "Dr. Richard Felder" when he was on the job. A psychiatrist.

"I was thinking," he said as he continued to hold her hand. "Now that your case is resolved, maybe we could go away this weekend. I'm thinking Sonoma."

He didn't tell her that Sonoma was where he'd grown up. He didn't want her to get the wrong idea. He wasn't thinking of a get-to-know-the-family weekend, though he had so many relatives in the area and Sonoma was such a small city that avoiding running into one of them could present a challenge. More of a this-is-where-I-grew-up, hope-you-love-it-as-much-as-I-do weekend.

"I'd like that," she said, and smiled again. She pulled her hand away to check her watch. "Sorry. I'm going to have to cut this short. The funeral ran longer than I thought it would. I have to pick up Jack."

"Let's pick him up together." It was a risk. Sarah hadn't yet introduced him to her son. But it felt like the right time to make the next move. "The three of us could go to the park, shoot some hoops."

"Really? You'd do that?"

"Really." He smiled. Most people responded well to his smile—a slightly rakish, lopsided grin that complemented his outdoorsman looks that he'd taught himself when he first started working by practicing in front of a mirror. "I don't have anything scheduled for the afternoon."

He didn't say what he was really thinking: *I'll go anywhere as long as it's with you.* Too much, too soon. But that was okay. Dr. Felder was a patient man. Sarah could have all the time she needed.

## ACKNOWLEDGEMENTS

Thanks to my editors, Cath Trechman and Miranda Jewess, for your keen insights, and to the rest of the Titan team for their hard work in bringing out this book; to my agent, Jeff Kleinman, for his assistance with this and my other novels (*Freezing Point*, *Boiling Point*), and to Scott Anderman, Jim Doherty, Allison Leotta, Rich Peach, Kathleen Ryan, and Diane Vogt for your most valuable advice and assistance. Most off all, thanks to my husband, Roger. I couldn't have done it without you!

## ABOUT THE AUTHOR

**Karen Dionne** is the internationally published author of the science thrillers *Freezing Point* and *Boiling Point*. She is co-founder of the online writers community Backspace, and organizes the Salt Cay Writers Retreat held annually on a private island in the Bahamas. Karen is a member of the International Thriller Writers, where she served on the board of directors alongside thriller luminaries Douglas Preston, Lee Child, Steve Berry, Joseph Finder, Peter James, and R. L. Stine as Vice President, Technology. Karen has been honored by the Michigan Humanities Council as a Humanities Scholar for her body of work as an author, writer, and as Backspace co-founder.